DEATH AT VILLA DE LACEY

DE LACEY AND SQUIRES MYSTERIES
BOOK 1

AVIVA ORR

ARE YOU SIGNED UP FOR DRAGONBLADE'S BLOG?

You'll get the latest news and information on exclusive giveaways, exclusive excerpts, coming releases, sales, free books, cover reveals and more.

Check out our complete list of authors, too!

No spam, no junk. That's a promise!

Sign Up Here

www.dragonbladepublishing.com

Dearest Reader;

Thank you for your support of a small press. At Dragonblade Publishing, we strive to bring you the highest quality Historical Romance from some of the best authors in the business. Without your support, there is no 'us', so we sincerely hope you adore these stories and find some new favorite authors along the way.

Happy Reading!

CEO, Dragonblade Publishing

ADDITIONAL DRAGONBLADE BOOKS BY AUTHOR AVIVA ORR

De Lacey and Squires Mysteries
Death at Villa De Lacey (Book 1)

Love and Literature Series
Love and Literature (Book 1)
Love and Vengeance (Book 2)
Love and Liberty (Book 3)

The Lyon's Den Series
The Lyon and The Rose of Mayfair
The Imperfect Lyon

CHAPTER ONE

Windermere, Westmorland, 1820

BRIDGET DE LACEY strolled across the sprawling grounds of Villa De Lacey—a magnificent three-story, eighteen-room stone villa trimmed with pale-blue French shutters, a matching two-paneled double door, and a fleur-de-lis iron railing that framed the raised portico at its entrance.

It had been built from Lutetian limestone—the very same stone from which much of Paris had been built—on a sloping hill above Lake Windermere by Bridget's French grandfather who'd come to the wild, barren Lake District region of England and fallen in love with the area's sublime majesty.

And who could blame him? Bridget thought. Life was idyllic in this land of endless blue lakes, magnificent mountain peaks, and lush green fells. This was the land that inspired England's greatest poets—Southey, Coleridge, Shelley, Keats, and, of course, Wordsworth, who lived a few miles from Villa De Lacey in his home called Rydal Mount.

A floral scent wafted through the air as she passed the small rose garden centered around a rectangular fountain out of whose waters emerged a perfectly sculptured bronze statue of Venus, standing on a scalloped seashell, as depicted in Botticelli's famous painting.

"Come along, Bijou," Bridget called her little white terrier, who had darted from her side to chase a family of lapwings.

With Bijou scampering again at her heels, Bridget continued

to the edge of the garden, which culminated in a stone patio secured by an elaborate balustrade wall that surrounded the grounds of Villa De Lacey. Bridget leaned her forearms on the balustrade and gazed at Lake Windermere, two hundred feet from the entrance to Villa De Lacey. The spectacular lake, surrounded by majestic mountains and green fells, stretched for miles and had a calming effect on all who gazed upon it. But today, Windermere's waters had turned choppy, and a mist hovered over the horizon. What had started as a fine day with blue skies and calm waters had quickly turned stormy. But that was not unusual. The weather in the Lake District was changeable and unpredictable.

"A storm is brewing, Bijou." Bridget looked down at her terrier, who'd raised himself on his hind legs to rest his front paws on the skirt of her white empire dress. "We'd best go inside." She bent to lift the dog into her arms. "Oh, look how you've soiled my dress," she said upon seeing the muddy prints her pup had left on the white material. The little dog responded by licking her face. Bridget giggled and showered him with kisses before starting back up the hill toward her home.

As she approached the house, she turned to see that a dark cloud had settled over the lake. It seemed the storm had grown perilous. Bridget shivered. She hoped it wasn't an omen of things to come. It had been three weeks since her papa had departed for London to attend to some business, and she'd yet to hear a word from him. Now, she'd started to worry in earnest. He'd been distracted for months prior to his trip and seemed in low spirits when he'd left for London. It terrified her to think that all was not well with Papa. Her beautiful and spirited mama had died after she'd fallen ill when Bridget was four. Since then, she'd feared losing her papa too. After her mama's death, she'd become so clingy toward her father that his widowed sister left her home in Dorset and moved in with them to assist her brother and care for his child when he traveled. But despite her aunt's presence in the home, and even though she was now an adult of one-and-twenty,

Bridget continued to worry every time her father left Winder-mere.

Oh, Papa, why haven't you written? Bridget inspected the clouds and then dropped her gaze to the two giant stone gargoyles that flanked the entrance to Villa De Lacey, guarding it against evildoers while inviting friends and neighbors to venture up the long, winding carriageway that led to the villa. *Come on, Papa. Do send word soon.* And then, as if she'd conjured it with her thoughts, a black coach turned into the property, slipping past the gargoyles and snaking its way up the gravel path. Bridget's heart leapt.

At last!

Bijou struggled in her arms and barked at the approaching vehicle. "Shh!" she soothed the little dog while tightening her grip on him, fearing that he'd race toward the carriage and get caught under its wheels.

As the carriage drew closer, Bridget saw that it bore the mark of the local magistrate, and her heart stilled. Perhaps he'd come to check on her and her aunt, or mayhap he'd had word from Papa. That thought gave her pause. Why would Papa message the magistrate? He'd never done so before. In all likelihood, Magistrate Hunt's presence could only mean one thing—bad news.

She stood paralyzed as the coach stopped in front of her home and the magistrate stepped out. He was a portly man with round blue eyes and a bulbous nose. A few sparse gray hairs populated his mostly bald head, which was oddly accompanied by bushy sideburns and a full beard.

Bridget found her feet and stepped forward. "Magistrate Hunt. How do you do?" She greeted the gentleman and re-strained herself from rudely blurting out the questions that ran through her mind.

"Miss De Lacey." The magistrate bowed in greeting. And Bridget saw that he looked notably somber—an observation she found rather unsettling. A cheerful magistrate on a social call was less likely to be the bearer of bad news.

Bijou continued to yip and struggle to be put down. Bridget

stroked her pup's fur, calming him.

"Is your aunt also at home by chance?" the magistrate asked. "I should like to speak with both of you."

"Yes, of course, she's inside." Fear rose in Bridget's chest, and she could no longer restrain herself from interrogating the gentleman there and then. "But why do you wish to speak with us? Is something the matter, sir? Have you had word from my papa?"

"I will be happy to address all of your questions inside, if you don't mind, miss." The magistrate's grave expression did little to calm Bridget's nerves.

"Of course." Bridget felt the color rise to her cheeks even as her heart sank. She'd always had a hard time practicing patience. "Do come in."

"Thank you," the magistrate said, removing his top hat as he followed her inside, where they were greeted by the housekeeper Eliza Moon. She was a petite, middle-aged spinster with a small, pale face, thin lips, deep-set brown eyes, and stringy brown hair, which she kept partially tucked under a white bonnet. Eliza had served the family faithfully since before Bridget's birth and now filled both the roles of housekeeper and lady's maid. Papa had long ago done away with the butler and a host of other servants who were no longer needed after he'd shut eleven of the eighteen rooms in the house to save expenses.

"Is my aunt in the drawing room, by chance, Eliza?" Bridget asked.

"She is, miss." Eliza's dark eyes narrowed as she saw the magistrate follow Bridget inside.

"Take the magistrate's hat and coat, please, Eliza. And then bring some tea to the drawing room." Bridget smiled at her maid, who she suspected felt the same trepidation at the magistrate's presence as she did.

"That's not necessary," Magistrate Hunt said. "I shan't be here long."

Bridget quivered inside. The magistrate's refusal to leave his coat and hat was ominous, indeed. This was not a social visit. And as the bearer of bad news, the magistrate would want to make a quick escape. "Bring the tea anyway," she told her maid. "I am feeling quite thirsty. And you'd best take Bijou to the kitchen while I speak with the magistrate." She lifted the terrier and kissed his nose. "Cook is sure to have some meat scraps for you, my sweet," she said before handing the wriggling pup to Eliza.

Eliza took the dog and curtsied before departing.

"Follow me, sir," Bridget said, leading the magistrate to the drawing room. Before stepping inside, she called out to her aunt.

"Bridget?" Her aunt looked up from her embroidery. She wore a long-sleeved burgundy day dress with a ruffled white collar and bonnet.

"I have a guest with me, Aunt. It's Mr. Hunt, the magistrate. He would like to speak with you—us. He'd like to speak with us."

"What about?" Her aunt put her sewing down. "Did something happen?"

Bridget entered the drawing room with the magistrate in tow.

"Mrs. Brixton." The magistrate bowed in greeting to her aunt.

"Do come and sit down, sir," Bridget said, seating herself on the pale-blue velvet sofa next to her aunt.

The magistrate fiddled with the rim of his top hat and hesitated as though sitting down would commit him to staying longer than he wished. Bridget could see that something heavy weighed on his mind, and it caused her heart to drum against the wall of her chest.

"Please, magistrate. Sit." Aunt Marianne gestured toward an upholstered velvet chair. "You'll take some tea with us, won't you?" she asked as Eliza entered the drawing room with a tea tray.

Magistrate Hunt cleared his throat and nodded as if coming to his senses. "Of course. Yes, thank you." He relented and seated himself as Eliza set the tray on the table.

"You may leave it. Thank you, Eliza," Aunt Marianne said as

the maid started to pour the tea.

Eliza hesitated and glanced nervously at the magistrate.

"Thank you, Eliza," Aunt Marianne said again.

Eliza curtsied, and retreated with obvious reluctance.

Aunt Marianne then busied herself, pouring three cups of tea. "Cream and sugar, magistrate?"

"Oh yes, two lumps of sugar for me. I enjoy a sweet cup."

Aunt Marianne smiled and plopped two lumps of sugar into his cup.

Bridget noticed that the man's hand trembled slightly as he accepted the tea from her aunt. He took a small sip before placing the cup back in its saucer on the table.

Bridget's stomach twisted. Something was wrong. She could feel it. Something awful had happened.

As if he'd read her thoughts, Magistrate Hunt said, "I'm afraid that I have some bad news."

His words sounded like a death knoll in Bridget's ears. She placed her teacup on the table and folded her hands in her lap, steadying herself. "Is it Papa?" she asked, her voice quivering.

Magistrate Hunt nodded. "I'm afraid so," he said, and Bridget could see the pity in his blue eyes.

"Not Bernard!" her aunt squeaked. "Has something happened to my brother?"

Bridget reached for her aunt's hand. "Tell us, sir. Please."

Magistrate Hunt ran a hand over his full beard. "I received word early this morning, via letter, that Mr. De Lacey is"—he swallowed—"deceased."

"No!" The exclamation came from the hallway, and Bridget looked up to see Eliza standing in the doorway, her eyes wide, and her hand clapped over her mouth. But Bridget didn't have the time or the energy to reprimand the housekeeper for eavesdropping. She was too busy trying to absorb the magistrate's words, which seemed unreal.

Aunt Marianne's quiet sobs sounded beside her, but she could not make sense of them. She felt as though she was trapped in a nonsensical dream.

"Deceased, you say?" Bridget repeated the magistrate's words, not quite able to accept them. *That can't be right. Not Papa. I must be having a terrible dream. This can't be real.* She pinched her arm. *None of it is real.* She pinched herself again. *Wake up, Bridget! Wake up!*

"Miss De Lacey! Why are you pinching your skin? Stop, you'll hurt yourself." The magistrate was by her side, hovering over her.

Papa dead! How? It can't be true! The room seemed to swim before Bridget's eyes. She felt the nausea rise in her throat.

"Miss De Lacey?" The magistrate raised his voice. "Shall I call for Doctor Elias?"

She shook her head, determined to regain control of her senses. "No, thank you. I'm quite well. It's just the shock."

"Here, take a sip of tea." He picked up her cup and handed it to her. She took it with shaky hands and forced herself to sip the liquid if only to appease the magistrate. Her ploy must have worked because he returned to his seat.

Beside her, Aunt Marianne dabbed at her eyes with her handkerchief.

"Can you tell us what happened?" Bridget managed to say, although she still did not believe it to be true. She was sure there had been some terrible mix-up, and her papa would walk through the door any minute.

The magistrate pressed his lips together. "Do you have anyone whom I can call—a male relative—who can help—"

"No," Bridget said, anxious to know why the magistrate seemed to be stalling. "You know very well there is no one. It's only me, Aunt Marianne, and Papa..." Her voice faltered. She sucked in her breath. "Now, please tell us what accident has befallen Papa."

Magistrate Hunt tugged at his collar as if it choked him. He seemed to be avoiding eye contact.

"Magistrate Hunt, please! I need to know what has happened

to my father. How did he—how did it happen?" Bridget said, still convinced the magistrate had made a mistake. Once she knew the details, then she'd be able to point out that it was all a misunderstanding. Her papa wasn't dead. Whoever had sent over that message had made a terrible mistake.

Aunt Marianne gave another loud sob and buried her nose in her handkerchief.

"I'm afraid that Mr. De Lacey"—he paused—"took his own life."

"What?" Bridget's stomach plummeted. She felt as though she'd been pushed off the tallest peak in Westmorland and was falling unprotected and uncontrollably down to bottomless earth.

Her aunt lowered her handkerchief and stared at the magistrate, shaking her head. "What are you saying?"

"I'm saying he died of a self-inflicted gunshot wound."

A crushing weight slammed into Bridget's chest as she made her harsh landing back to reality. "That's impossible," she said. "You must have the wrong man. Papa would never do such a thing. What explanation could there be for him to take his own life?"

"It seems he lost his entire fortune in a series of card games"—he swallowed—"including this villa."

Bridget heard a loud gasp, but she wasn't sure if it came from her own throat or her aunt's.

"Villa De Lacey?" she asked, stunned. "He lost our home?"

"It was his last hope. He gambled the villa in the hope of winning back his money, but he lost it to the Earl of Westerly, whose family name is Squires."

The room swirled before Bridget's eyes. She was vaguely aware of her aunt sobbing beside her and of the magistrate talking, but his voice grew distant as the room continued to whirl.

"Papa dead. Villa De Lacey lost to an earl by the name of Squires," Bridget echoed in a whisper before everything went black.

CHAPTER TWO

Five Weeks Later...
Mayfair, London

NATE SQUIRES SAT across from his brother, the Earl of Westerly, and wondered how two people who shared both a mother and father could be so different. Only four years Nate's senior, Edward's blond hair was already thinning, which made him look years older. His tall, wiry frame, pallid complexion, ice-blue eyes, and almost transparent eyebrows and eyelashes were the opposite of Nate's thick, wavy black locks and midnight-blue eyes, which took shelter under long black lashes and dark eyebrows. Like Edward, Nate was tall, but, unlike his brother's shoulders, his shoulders were broad and his body muscular.

Edward was a stiff man. He had a stiff posture, a stiff expression, and he lived by stiff rules. The man had been born uptight. Nate would not have cared what rules his brother chose to live by, but it irked him that he expected Nate to follow his rigid ways of thinking and living too.

"This is the last straw, Nathaniel." His brother sat, back straight and hands intertwined, behind his mahogany study desk, upon which neat piles of books and papers were stacked. That was another difference between them—Edward liked things orderly and perfect, whereas Nate enjoyed a little chaos. It made him feel alive.

"I've warned you ample times before," Edward continued in the irritatingly authoritative voice he liked to use when talking to

Nate. "Your philandering and gambling have got to stop. It's time you contributed to this family's well-being."

Nate raised an eyebrow. "For someone who enjoys gambling as much as you do, I find that statement quite hypocritical."

"When I gamble, I win." Edward assumed a look of superiority. "Unlike you."

Nate nodded. He had to admit that Edward had a point. They both enjoyed gambling, but Nate lost more often than he won.

"As I said, it's time for you to grow up and do your part for this family."

Nate snorted. "Are you suggesting I get a job?"

"Don't be ridiculous!"

"Well, if you're thinking of sending me off to some rural estate that Father had hidden away, think again. I won't go."

"Actually, I've decided it's time for you to marry. It's been two years since your failed engagement to Miss Morley—two years filled with nothing but debauchery, I might add—and I've decided it's time for a change."

"You've decided!" Nate laughed, although inside, he was boiling. How dare his brother mention Miss Morley? He got up and went to pour himself a brandy.

"For God's sake, Nathaniel, it's only ten in the morning."

Nate downed his brandy, poured himself another, and returned to his seat, brandy in hand.

"I am not your younger sister, Edward. It's not your responsibility to ensure that I secure my future by making a good match—or any match, for that matter."

"Nonetheless," Edward said, his stony expression back in place, "I have arranged a fine match for you—one that will enhance our family's fortune and reputation."

Nate placed the glass of brandy on a small table next to his chair. His brother was an arrogant pillock. It amused and annoyed him to think that Edward believed he could command him to marry. But seeing an opportunity to ruffle Edward, he decided to play along.

"Is the young lady in question at least beautiful? You know how much I enjoy the company of beautiful women."

Edward's eyes narrowed a fraction. "She's the daughter of Viscount Eamont—the very *rich* Viscount Eamont," Edward added.

Nate laughed. His brother truly had gone mad. "You want me to marry Adelia and Lydia Eamont?"

"Not both of them. Only Adelia."

"There's no such thing as one Eamont sister. They come as a pair. They are identical twins in both their looks *and* their irritating personalities. Did you know they speak in unison? Have you asked yourself why they are in their third—or is it fourth—season and still unmarried, despite their large dowries?" Nate picked up his brandy glass and swallowed the contents before slamming the glass back down just to irritate his brother, which he sorely deserved. "Well, brother, this has been lovely. Thank you for considering my future, but if you don't mind, I quite enjoy the bachelor lifestyle, so I've decided not to marry at all." He started to get up from his chair.

"You will marry. Because until I am blessed with a son, you are my heir, and it's time you behaved accordingly."

Oh, bollocks. Nate settled back in his seat. "I'm not sacrificing my freedom lest you don't have a son. It's not my fault if you can't do your duty."

Edward's jaw tightened, and a vein pulsed in his neck. The sight brought a smile to Nate's lips. It pleased him whenever he could rouse any expression from his stony brother. "Don't be unreasonable," Edward said. "It's not as if you cannot continue whatever you enjoy doing after marriage. You merely need to be discreet about it."

Nate cocked his head. Sometimes, Edward disgusted him. "Is that what you do to your wife?"

Edward's face remained stony. "I've arranged for you and Miss Adelia Eamont to meet this Saturday. You'll take a ride in Hyde Park at ten. She'll be chaperoned, of course. Still, I expect you to treat her with the utmost courtesy."

"Until we're married, of course. That's what you mean, isn't it, Edward?"

"What happens between a man and his wife is no one else's business but theirs. Now, make sure you are on time for this meeting. I don't want Miss Eamont kept waiting."

"No, thank you, brother."

"What?" Edward said.

"I said, *no thank you.*" Nate raised his voice slightly.

"I heard what you said, but perhaps you don't understand that this isn't a request."

"You're ordering me to marry?" Nate smirked, more amused at his brother's cheek than angry.

"I'm telling you that I have arranged this marriage, which benefits the family, and since you live entirely off the substantial allowance I give you, it will behoove you to do as I say."

"So, you're threatening to cut me off, are you?" Nate leaned forward, confronting his brother.

Edward's long, thin fingers turned white as he squeezed his hands together. "The choice is yours," he said.

"Very well, then." Nate leaned back in his chair. "I shall have to get a job. I wonder what people will say when they hear that the Earl of Westerly's brother has had to resort to teaching French to schoolboys. What a stain on our family that will be. Papa would turn in his grave."

"You won't do that. We both know you are far too lazy and spoilt to work. You've never worked a day in your life."

Nate crossed his legs. "You're right, brother. I certainly wouldn't make a good role model for young boys. However, I'm an excellent lover, and the Dowager Reeves has been begging me to move in with her. She's already ostracized from society, so the gossip won't bother her."

"It might interest you to know that the Dowager Reeves moved to France two months ago—with her newest lover."

Nate felt chagrined. How had he not known about that?

"Well, I'm sure I can find another desperate widow who will take me in," he said coolly.

"It's time you stopped this foolish talk," Edward said. "I will not allow you to disgrace our family name. Now, I expect you and your horse to be at Rotten Row on Saturday morning at ten o'clock sharp, do you understand?"

"Sorry, Edward." Nate stood up. "But I really must go now. If you are to cut off my allowance, then I need to take the money I have left to the gambling tables and triple it."

"We both know that's a losing battle for you," Edward said dryly. "Now, why don't you sit down so we can finish our discussion."

Nate moved toward the door.

"Fine. If you refuse to marry, then I have one other proposition for you."

Nate turned. "What is it?"

"I recently acquired a property that needs managing. It's rather large to my understanding—a great deal of land. I haven't had time to see it."

"A recently acquired property you haven't even seen? How so?" Intrigued, Nate returned to his seat.

"I took possession of it from a gentleman who could not pay his debts."

Nate blinked. "Do you mean to say—was it that chap who put a bullet in his head with his own pistol?"

Edward shifted in his seat. "He chose to sit down at the card table and gamble his home. Then he lost. What do you think I should have done? Forgiven his debt? He played as a gentleman, and gentlemen pay their gambling debts."

"Well, you could have shown some mercy—worked out some sort of payment plan. It's not like you need the money."

"No, I don't. But the property is now making itself useful."

Edward's coldness was vile. "I won't manage it for you like some servant," Nate said.

"It's not for me; it's for you. I am prepared to sign over the deed to you."

"You want to unload your bloody acquisition onto me to rid yourself of the shame?"

"I have no shame over collecting what is owed to me, brother. Now, if you don't want the property, then you always have the option of marrying. But if you refuse both propositions, know that you will no longer have access to the Regent's Park townhouse."

"You can't throw me out of my home. It's scandalous. People will gossip."

"That is why I am partially gifting you a new home."

"Partially gifting? How do you partially gift something? Isn't that an oxymoron?"

"You will own ninety percent of the property, and I will retain ownership of a mere ten percent. That will ensure that I can go to the property whenever I wish. But more importantly, it means you will not be able to sell the property without my consent. Moreover, you must agree not to return to London without first asking my permission, which I will only grant for extenuating circumstances." Edward's face was a marble slate.

Did his brother possess any feelings at all?

"So, you intend to banish me for life?"

"Not at all. You decide your future. For instance, if you decide to marry Miss Eamont, you will be free to live in London, and you will have all the wealth you desire."

"And if I continue to refuse? How long do you think you can keep me prisoner for?"

"I'm not a monster, Brother. I only want what is in your best interest. That said, I'd be willing to revise the situation in five years."

"Five *years*! Did you simply pick an arbitrary number out of your top hat and decide, *that's the amount of time I'll banish my brother for?*"

"I believe that ought to be enough time for you to mature and come to your senses. And why do you keep saying 'banish' as if you mean 'abandon'? I am gifting you a valuable property and allowing you to keep your allowance. I would say that is quite generous of me."

Of course, he would see it that way. "Where is it?" Nate asked.

"Northwest England. Westmorland, to be exact. I understand it is quite beautiful there. More and more people are being attracted to the area."

Nate went cold. *The Lake District?* He'd imagined that he'd be sent to the countryside in Kent or Yorkshire, or even Cornwall, but the Lake District? What was there? A few scenic lakes and a handful of poets? "I told you before, I won't go to some remote estate."

"And I told you that you have a choice. Marry Miss Eamont or leave London."

Nate chortled. He knew what game Edward was playing. He was threatening to banish him from London in order to force him to submit. That was exactly the type of manipulative game Edward liked to play, but two could play the same game.

"Your little scheme isn't going to work." Nate folded his arms. "I have no intention of getting married, especially to a woman you have chosen for me."

Edward shrugged and pushed the deed and a quill pen toward Nate. "The choice is yours."

Nate forced a smile. "Very well, if you insist on gifting me a property, I'll take the house, but I want all of it. One hundred percent. If you only wish to retain ten percent to stop me from selling the property, put a stipulation in the deed that says I agree not to sell without your permission for five years."

"Seven," Edward said.

Nate looked into his brother's cold blue eyes, and then, making his decision, he stood. "Very well, have the papers drawn up, and I will sign them." Then he took a deep breath and strode out of his brother's study. He would go to the remotest ends of the earth before he let Edward control him.

CHAPTER THREE

W AKING WAS THE most painful part of the day. In her dreams, Bridget's papa came back to life. Sometimes, she was a little girl curled up on one of the big leather chairs in his study while he sat behind his mahogany desk with a furrowed brow, studying his account books or penning letters. And other times, she was her full-grown self, meandering down the cobbled streets of York, arm-in-arm with Papa on one of their shopping trips. And sometimes, they'd be back together in the drawing room at Villa De Lacey, playing cards, taking tea with Aunt Marianne, or strolling along the shores of Lake Windermere. In her dreams, Papa's blue eyes would twinkle with life again, and she'd feel the warmth of his embrace and smell his comforting, leathery scent. She'd wake up smiling until she remembered her new reality, and then a searing pain would hit her in the chest like a flame.

But most painful of all was the cruelty of his burial. She had not even had the comfort of burying her father's remains. His body had been taken from his place of death and buried at a random crossroad—the whereabouts of which, she didn't know— and, as was done to all those who committed self-murder, it was likely a stake had been driven through his heart. Her beloved Papa was a sinner in the eyes of the Church and the people, who would have insisted that his restless soul needed to be contained.

Fearing for her health, the magistrate had waited a week to break the news of her father's burial to her. And when she'd finally learned that her papa's body would not be coming home, a fit of anger so violent welled inside her that she risked damaging a great deal of crockery and other breakables. So, she'd run from the house and kept going until she'd reached a remote spot along the shores of Lake Windermere where she'd screamed her throat raw, battered the earth with her fists, and finally sobbed until she'd depleted her body of energy.

When she could cry and scream no more, she'd picked herself up and staggered back to the villa, her eyes swollen and her chest still heaving with pain. She was determined to do right by her papa. He would never rest in peace beside her mama in the churchyard. But she would give him a place close to home, so she took the only thing she had left of him—a lock of his golden hair—and placed it in a small chest with the letters her mama had written to him when they were courting. Then she searched for a peaceful spot amongst the trees behind the villa to bury it. The kind Sexton, Mr. Gould, who'd made her mother's gravestone, agreed to carve one for her Papa, and she, Aunt Marianne, and the servants held a small, private funeral for him two weeks after receiving the news of his tragic death. Now, a little part of Papa lay close by, and she and her aunt had a grave on which to lay flowers.

That had been six weeks ago. Her papa was now two months gone, and each day she anxiously awaited the arrival of the dreaded lord who now owned Villa De Lacey. What was she to do when he came for her home? She could not—would not—leave her papa. Was she to dig up his lock of hair and bury him elsewhere? Tear herself from the home she loved—the only home she'd ever known?

"Oh, Papa," she whispered as she lay a single rose on the small mound that was his makeshift grave. "What am I to do now?"

$\wp$

Seven years! Nate fumed as his coach rumbled through the rugged, muddy landscape. The journey from London to Westmorland had taken almost a fortnight, but Nate had no idea how close they were to their final destination. It was dark and a torrential downpour had begun. If they didn't find an inn soon, they were sure to get stuck in the mud for the night. Nate shivered, covered himself with a woolen blanket, and closed his eyes, willing the motion of the carriage to lull him to sleep. But it was to no avail.

He longed for his large, plush four-poster bed in his regency townhome, which now stood empty on his brother's orders. *Damn Edward!* He missed the comfort and opulence of his home, its proximity to all the best gentlemen's clubs in London, and the sweeping views of Regent's Park from the many mullioned windows that let in the sunlight. He cherished that townhome, and Edward knew as much. But, like everything else, it belonged to his brother. As the eldest son, Edward had been bequeathed every penny and piece of property in their father's estate, leaving Nate wholly at his brother's mercy. And Nate hated it. Being the second son of an earl was little better than being the daughter of an earl—someone was always going to tell you what you could or could not do with your life.

Irritated, Nate threw off the blanket and peered out the window once again, but the night was so black he couldn't see a thing. Rain pelted the carriage, which the exhausted horses seemed to be dragging rather than pulling up a hill. Nate wished he knew where they were. It seemed as if they'd been driving forever since their last stop, which he hoped was some twenty miles back, but with all the sludge and rain, it was impossible to tell for certain. He sighed and lay his head against the buttoned leather carriage seat. *One day, brother, I will make you pay for this!*

Edward had told him nothing about his new home but knowing his brother, it was a most undesirable property—after all, the goal was to force his hand into marriage. He only hoped it wasn't some sort of farm. He could bear something remote if he had to, but he was not one for pigs, cows, and sheep.

The carriage suddenly slowed and soon came to a halt. Nate sat up, alert now and curious as to why they'd stopped. Were they stuck in some country sludge? Or had his driver located an inn? His stomach rumbled, crying out for a tall glass of ale and a large portion of mutton and potatoes. He envisioned himself sitting by a warm fire with a hot plate of food, and his mouth began to water. Then, the carriage door swung open, and a blast of cold air brought him back to reality. Nate's valet, who'd been riding in his second carriage with his luggage, stood in the pouring rain, holding a large black umbrella and a lantern. "We've arrived, sir."

"Where?" Nate felt he had to shout over the wind and rain, even though his valet had kept the same monotone he'd always used, and Nate had heard him perfectly. "Have we located an inn?"

"We have arrived at your new residence, sir."

"Have we?" Nate's heart sank. He wasn't ready to spend the evening in a cold, remote estate that had no doubt been left to ruin by its bankrupted owner. All he wanted was a cozy inn that would provide him with a blazing fire and a hearty meal. Nate's stomach rumbled again as he stepped reluctantly from the carriage. Grateful for the shelter of the waiting umbrella, he turned to look at the house, but all he could see in the darkness was the silhouette of a rather large structure.

"I hope there's someone here to let us inside. I didn't ask my brother if he'd retained the staff from the previous owner," Nate said as he and his valet hurried up the short flight of stairs that led to a raised portico, leaving the two coachmen waiting with their carriages. They came to a double two-paneled door, pale blue in color, with a lion-faced knocker attached to the right panel. His valet lifted the knocker and rapped several times on the door.

After what seemed like an agonizingly long wait, his valet knocked again. Only then did the door creak open. A diminutive, middle-aged housekeeper dressed in black swung a lantern in front of their faces and peered at them from beneath her large black bonnet.

"The Honorable Mr. Nathaniel Squires," Nate's valet announced. "I assume you've been expecting him?"

"Expecting him? At this hour?" The housekeeper narrowed her dark eyes. "I shouldn't think so. The madam and the misses have already retired to their chambers."

"What are you talking about?" Nate said. "Would you please step aside? I don't fancy standing out here in the rain." He pushed past the housekeeper, his patience having reached its limit, and stepped into a dimly lit but vast hallway.

"Sir! What do you think you're doing?"

"I'll need a fire, some brandy, and a hearty meal. As will my valet and coachmen, waiting outside. Show them to the servants' quarters, will you? And have the stable boy take care of my horses."

The housekeeper blinked in confusion. Then her face hardened. "Get out, I tell you! The ladies of the house have already retired for the night and—"

"The ladies of the house? What ladies?" Nate frowned. Edward hadn't mentioned anything about ladies.

"Eliza?" A woman's voice sounded, and Nate looked up to see a petite young woman descending the stairway. Like the housemaid, she was dressed entirely in black and carried a lantern.

"I'm sorry for the racket, Miss Bridget. This here gentleman seems to be lost."

"Lost. I don't believe so. My driver was given a very detailed map of where to go." Nate spoke with confidence, but in truth, he knew they could well be at the wrong location.

"And where is it that you were wanting to go, sir?" The young lady stepped forward. Butter-blond ringlets framed her lovely face. She had the creamiest porcelain-like skin he'd ever seen, wide, almond-shaped blue eyes, a sweet button nose, and beautiful rosebud lips.

Nate found himself momentarily distracted. He cleared his throat, which had suddenly gone dry. "Villa De Lacey," he said.

"Then you have come to the right place." She nodded to her housekeeper, who then moved to close the front door, shutting out the wind and the rain. "What might your business be here at such a late hour?" she asked.

"My business is to move in. Villa De Lacey is my new home." He drew the deed out of his breast pocket and presented it to the young lady.

She hesitated before taking it with a slightly trembling hand. She held it next to her lantern and scanned the deed but seemed to do more for show than anything else. "I see," she said, returning the deed to Nate. "Well, then, you'd best make yourself at home. I hope you won't see fit to turn me and my aunt out tonight. We didn't realize you'd be coming quite so soon. We are still digesting the news of my father's death."

Nate swallowed. *Damn Edward.* He hadn't said anything about the house still being occupied, and by the deceased gentleman's daughter, no less.

"No, of course not, Miss…"

"De Lacey," she supplied.

"Of course." He nodded.

"Good. Then we can discuss the situation in the morning. In the meantime, Eliza will take care of all your needs."

She was trying to be strong, but Nate heard the tremble in her voice, and it made him feel like a criminal. Her father had taken his own life, for goodness' sake! And now she was to be thrown out of her home. *Damn Edward. Damn him to the devil!*

"Good evening, sir," Miss De Lacey said, and before Nate could respond, she'd turned and hurried back up the stairs.

BRIDGET DASHED TO her room, barely able to hold back her tears before she closed the door behind her. Once she was safely ensconced, the tears flowed freely down her cheeks. Sensing her distress, Bijou jumped off his bed cushion and ran to her. She set her lantern onto her writing desk and scooped the little dog up in her arms, pressing him to her chest for comfort. She had known that the new owner would be arriving one day, but she didn't think he would be coming so soon.

The notion enraged her. *How dare he?* Her dear papa was only two months gone! Still, she'd been foolish not to prepare. Or maybe she'd avoided doing so because the thought of leaving Villa De Lacey was unbearable. Where would she and Aunt Marianne go? They'd been too busy burying and mourning Papa to think about that awful Squires. She sat on her bed, setting Bijou down next to her, and wept until it felt as though she'd used up all her tears. The terrier jumped onto her lap and licked her, trying to comfort her. She held him, kissed his head, and whispered, "All is well, my love. I feel much better."

The gesture calmed him, and when she put him back down, he curled up next to her contentedly. Bridget smiled at the pup. *How wonderful to be a little dog with no worries in the world.* She shook her head and then inhaled deeply. *I mustn't fall apart now. There has to be a solution. All I need to do is calm down and think.*

Bridget bent to unlace and remove her boots. Then she stood and paced the length of her room in her stockinged feet, enjoying the feel of the plush cream carpet. Tomorrow, she'd have to speak with Squires—was he a Mr. or a lord? She frowned. It would be important to address him correctly. Didn't Magistrate Hunt say something about him being an earl? And if he was an earl, surely he wouldn't want to live at Villa De Lacey. Perhaps he would allow her and Aunt Marianne to take care of the place for him. She bit her lip.

But he likely had servants to do his bidding. *The servants! Oh dear! I haven't prepared them for this. They will lose their livelihood unless I do something. I must do something! Especially for Cook and dear Eliza. Villa De Lacey has been Eliza's home for one-and-twenty years and Cook's even longer than that!*

She walked to her dressing table and picked up a miniature portrait of her papa. His kind blue eyes looked back at her just as they had done in real life. *What's the matter, my princess? Don't cry. All will be well. There is no problem too big for you to solve. You are such a clever young lady. You'll think of something.* The words Papa had used so many times to comfort her echoed in her mind.

Oh, Papa. She kissed the portrait and pressed it to her heart. *Why did you leave us? Why didn't you talk to me? I would have helped you. We could have solved any problems we had together.* A fresh tear slid down her cheek.

Placing the portrait back on her desk, she caught sight of her brand-new copy of William Wordsworth's guide to the lakes. It had been a gift from her papa before he'd left for London—the last time she'd seen him. She caressed the leather volume, picked it up, and flipped through its pages.

"*Do you know, my dear, that Wordsworth has made our little part of the world quite famous? Rich Londoners cannot get enough of his book. I predict they're going to flock here by the dozens. The number of visitors we have now is surely going to quadruple. And our peaceful little slice of heaven will become quite overrun. It's a good thing we have so many rooms in which to hide.*"

"So many rooms in which to hide," Bridget repeated. Then a thought struck her, and she felt her heart lift. "I know just what to do, Papa!" she said aloud. "I know how to save our home!"

CHAPTER FOUR

THE NEXT MORNING, a gnawing hunger roused Nate from his sleep. He opened his eyes, thinking of mutton and potatoes and stormy skies, to find sunlight streaming into his room. Delighted, he threw back his covers, walked across the wood floor to the window, and pulled back the curtains. The view outside almost took his breath away. A crystal blue lake surrounded by rolling hills as green as emeralds filled the horizon. Nate inhaled deeply, stretching out his arms, wanting to embrace the beauty outside. A sense of calm washed over him. He'd never seen anything quite so serene and magnificent. It was a far cry from the tempest that had greeted him upon his arrival.

He put his hands on his hips and grinned to himself. Edward had been too busy trying to control his life to come here and see the property for himself—that much was obvious. Nate let his gaze fall to the garden. Once again, he was caught off guard by the beauty that met his eyes.

A sloping lawn, complete with a flower garden and fountain, was surrounded by acres of lush trees that formed a thicket around the property. *Wonderful!*

He inhaled deeply when suddenly, he spotted a black-clad figure on the lawn, peering up at him. He squinted, and recognizing her butter-blond ringlets, saw that it was Miss De Lacey, whom he'd met last night. A little white dog at her heels wagged his tail. He waved in greeting, but instead of waving back, the young lady turned abruptly and scurried down the lawn, her dog in tow. Nate frowned. He was doing his best to be friendly, but she was being downright impolite, ignoring him like that. *No matter.* He stretched again, enjoying the warmth of the sun on his body. That was when he suddenly realized the problem. He was stark naked.

🔍

NATE RANG FOR his valet, who appeared promptly with his morning tea. He swallowed the tea in two gulps, washed and dressed, and then exited his suite. He made his way along the rectangular landing on the first floor, pausing to look over the balcony and down onto the main hall as he made his way to breakfast.

Unlike the dining room, the breakfast chamber was on the first floor. It was a brightly decorated, sunny enclave that sported yellow wallpaper with a white floral pattern and a wall of windows, which allowed for breathtaking views of the garden. The carved rosewood table at its center held three silver dishes that smelled of eggs, bacon, and kippers.

The same strange housekeeper, all dressed in black, whom he'd seen upon his arrival came into the dining room carrying a fresh pot of tea, and Nate wondered why he hadn't seen a butler or any footmen. Clearly, Mr. De Lacey had cut his servants to the bare minimum to save on expenses. Yet, the garden was immaculate and keeping it that way would have been no small expense.

The housekeeper plunked the teapot down on the table in front of him without saying a word to Nate, but her dark eyes—too fierce and spirited for the rest of her mousy features—bore into him.

"Where are the ladies of the house? Am I to breakfast alone?"

"The ladies already breakfasted," she said abruptly. "They are *early* risers."

Nate smiled and nodded. He understood that the ladies of the house had likely purposely avoided him, and he could hardly blame them. Edward had sent him to do his dirty work. Now, he'd have to shoulder the guilt of having to turn two helpless women out of their home. But what choice did he have?

He poured himself a cup of tea. He'd have to deal with that later. All he wanted at the moment was to enjoy a hearty breakfast. His valet hadn't been able to rustle up anything more than a cheese sandwich after his arrival last night, and he was famished. He served himself a plateful of scrambled eggs, bacon, kippers, toast, and marmalade and ate until he finally felt satiated again.

After breakfast, he decided to look around his new property. He was more than impressed by what he'd seen so far. The house was beautiful, but much of the furniture needed repair or replacing. He even noticed some fraying on the yellow-and-white-striped-upholstered chairs in the breakfast chamber. The primrose-yellow rug covering the wood floor looked to be rather faded too.

He strolled out of the breakfast room into a large drawing room. It housed a pale-blue settee and several matching armchairs above which hung an exquisite glass chandelier that held eight candles. A fireplace sat tucked in an enclave near the seating, and Nate imagined it provided much warmth and light during the wintery months. Like all the rooms he'd seen so far, tall windows allowed for plenty of light and provided views of the magnificent lake and green hills outside. A few paintings in gilded frames decorated the walls, but Nate also noticed several areas where paintings had been removed, leaving a darkened imprint on the wallpaper. No doubt, De Lacey had been selling off his valuables.

Next door was the study, presumably Mr. De Lacey's, and then a rather impressive library with mahogany wall-to-wall shelves that reached the ceiling and housed numerous books of all sizes. Nate stepped into the room. He admired the burgundy, gold-tasseled curtains that matched the burgundy-and-gold-patterned carpet and paired well with the tufted leather sofa and chairs in the center of the room. Bronze busts of Shakespeare, Dante, and various Greek gods and goddesses decorated the room, along with several landscape paintings in ornate gold-painted frames. It appeared that the upkeep of this room, like the garden, had been well maintained, while other rooms had been somewhat neglected.

Nate inspected the rows of leather-bound books on the bookshelves. There were books about British history, British birds, and other natural wonders in one section of the shelves. A second section had been reserved for literature and contained sets of the complete works of Chaucer and Shakespeare as well as Dante and other great writers. Then there were volumes of poetry by Byron, Keats, Coleridge, Shelley, and Wordsworth. A smaller section housed a string of popular novels like *Rob Roy, Ivanhoe, Emma, Pride and Prejudice, Northanger Abbey,* and *Frankenstein,* amongst others. Someone in this house liked to read.

He was about to pick up a copy of Wordsworth's poems when the excited yapping of a small dog sounded in his ears. He turned to see Miss De Lacey enter the library, a book clutched to her chest.

"Oh, excuse me," she said, "I didn't know anyone was in here."

"Miss De Lacey." He shoved the book back in place and gave a slight bow in greeting. "I was just having a look around. Getting to know the place."

She nodded. "I'm sorry to have disturbed you. Please, carry on." She turned to leave.

"I saw you in the garden earlier," he said quickly. "I'd love a tour."

Her lovely, pale cheeks turned bright pink, and he realized his error. She had seen him naked, and he'd just reminded her of that embarrassment. *Oh, well.*

"Your library is very impressive," he said.

"Don't you mean, *your* library?" she said. There was no malice or spite in her tone, which both pleased and surprised Nate.

"Well, yes. I suppose it is mine." It was the truth, but it felt somehow wrong to articulate it.

"Tell me"—she strode toward him—"what was my father's demeanor before he…" She bit her lip. "When you played cards with him that fateful night? I keep going over the scenario in my mind. He seemed distracted before he left home for London—did he seem that way to you?"

"I'm sorry, but I couldn't tell you. I've never met your father."

"Oh?" She cocked her head, and Nate thought she seemed disappointed. No doubt, she'd been desperate to speak with the person who'd last seen her father alive. Nate wished he could provide her with that solace—some words of comfort. On the other hand, he felt pleased that he could reassure her that he was not the monster who'd taken everything from her papa.

"It was my brother who played cards with him—on several occasions, I believe."

"And each time they played, Papa lost more of his fortune until it was all gone—even our home."

"Yes," Nate said. "That has been the misfortune of more than one gambling gentleman, I'm afraid. But I knew nothing about your father or this house until my brother handed it over to me— well, that sounds a bit too generous. The truth is that my brother banished me from London because I refused to do his bidding."

Miss De Lacey raised her eyebrows. "What did he want you to do?"

"He wanted me to give up my bachelor lifestyle and live by his rules. I refused. So, he banished me to this remote corner of the country."

"I see." Miss De Lacey pursed her lips and walked to the window. "How sad for you." Her voice dripped with sarcasm. "Do you know that I've lived in this house all my life? It was built by my grandfather, who loved this part of England with all his heart, as did my father, and as do I. What you look upon as a place of exile, I look upon as home."

Nate swallowed. Why is it that he felt like a criminal when he'd done nothing wrong? "I suppose we should discuss your future plans. I had no idea this house was still occupied. Of course, I am happy to let you and your aunt take as much time as you need before I sell it."

"Sell?" She turned to him, and the alarm on her face told him that his plans came as a surprise.

"Yes. My brother forced me to sign a contract that said I could not sell the house for seven years, but I intend to find a loophole and get myself back to London, where I belong. I have no idea how long that will take, but until then, you and your aunt are welcome to stay."

"I don't want your charity, Mr. Squires," she said. "In fact, I wish to help you."

"Help me?" He laughed. "And how do you propose to do that?"

"With this." She strode toward him and handed him the book she'd held since entering the library.

He read the title. *A Guide through the District of the Lakes in the North of England,* by William Wordsworth. He smiled. "It's funny you should give this to me. A friend tried to force a copy upon me before I departed from London. He thought it would cheer me up and make me 'fall in love' with my new home." He scoffed. "I didn't bother bringing it with me because as I said, I don't plan on staying here long. So, thank you"—he held the book out to her—"but neither Wordsworth nor any other poet can turn me from a city to a country dweller."

"I promise it never crossed my mind. That's not why I gave you the book, Mr. Squires. But believe me when I tell you that this book is the answer to all your problems."

Nate sighed. "I doubt that."

She smiled and two tiny dimples appeared at the corners of her mouth. "Why don't we take that tour of the garden, and I will explain exactly what I mean."

"Certainly," Nate said. He felt confident there was nothing anyone could say to him that would convince him to stay and make this his home, but he could think of no better way to while away his time than strolling in the garden with a charming young lady.

$$\rho$$

THE GARDEN WAS even more magnificent than Nate had first thought. As they strolled across the manicured lawn, he wondered how the bankrupted Mr. De Lacey had managed to pay for its upkeep.

"It must take a lot of work to keep the garden so spectacularly manicured," he said casually.

"You're wondering how my father managed its upkeep," she said, perceptively. "I've been wondering the same thing since—I mean, he kept his troubles quite well-hidden from me. Although, I now realize that it was partly my fault. Of course, I'd noticed that our furniture had grown a little shabby and that most of Mother's jewelry had started disappearing, along with paintings from the walls, but I turned a blind eye. Sometimes it's easier to stay in denial than to face one's harsh reality."

Nate nodded. "I can understand that."

"As to the garden, most of that is down to our faithful gardener, Mr. Thomas, who has served Villa De Lacey since before I was born. He is a magician with plants and flowers and lives in the cottage behind the house. But the work has been getting more difficult for him, so Papa had been urging him to take on an apprentice. Still, he has yet to do so." She smiled sadly. "Papa would have done whatever was necessary to keep the garden maintained—whether it be selling our valuables or borrowing money and getting himself deeper into debt. The garden was his pride and joy because it lies open to the world. It's easy to hide areas of neglect indoors but there's no hiding one's shame out in the open. Papa always said that how a gentleman kept his garden could tell one a lot about how he lived his life."

"Well, judging from this garden, your father's life would have been very orderly." Nate could not help but point out the irony.

"And it was for most of his life, I think. But it seems he got into the bad habit of gambling these past few years, and I suppose his life spiraled into a continuous cycle of chaos. Gambling, winning, and then losing, over and over again, until things got completely out of control. That's why I think he was so obsessive about his garden. If he could maintain that façade, then he could believe all was well. I certainly did."

Nate wondered how much responsibility Edward harbored for Mr. De Lacey's downfall. He knew his brother's strategy of loaning money to drowning men—men like Mr. De Lacey who owned valuable properties but couldn't stop themselves from gambling. De Lacey would have become increasingly mired in debt, at which time, Edward would have artfully suggested that he gamble his home, shrewdly convincing the drowning man that he could expunge his debts with one lucky hand. And to a man in the throes of despair, that would have sounded like a lifeline.

They strolled down to the viewing point secured by a magnificent balustrade at the garden's edge. There, the lake, a glassy sheet of blue that stretched on for miles, surrounded by mountain peaks and emerald-green fells dotted with a sea of oaks, yews, and brambles, worked its magic on Nate, who after a few minutes became quite mesmerized by Windermere's sublime beauty.

"It's majestic, isn't it?" Bridget said.

"It certainly is powerful," Nate replied. He'd known about the Lake District's reputation for its natural beauty, but he'd had no idea how awe-inspiring it would be.

"I find it quite interesting that your friend gave you a copy of Wordsworth's guidebook before you left London. I don't think he did so merely to make you feel better about the move."

"What do you mean?" Nate asked.

"When Papa gave me this book, he said that all the ladies and gentlemen in London were buying copies, and he believed it would make our little part of the world quite famous."

"I hadn't noticed," Nate said. In truth, he'd dismissed his friend's gesture as a bit of a joke, and then he'd forgotten all about it and ended up leaving the book in London. Come to think of it, Edward too had made some remark about the Lake District becoming increasingly popular, but he'd made it a rule several years ago to ignore most of what Edward had to say.

"Think about it. Imagine if you owned an exclusive inn right on Lake Windermere for wealthy patrons who wanted to escape the stressors of London. You could make a lot of money."

"Own an inn? What are you talking about?"

"I'm talking about this house." She turned and gestured to the magnificent French-styled villa. "Ladies and gentlemen of the ton would feel like royalty coming here. It would be like a trip to Versailles," she said.

"Versailles?" Nate raised his eyebrows. "I think that's a little far-fetched."

"Perhaps," she said, "but with a little sprucing Villa De Lacey could again become the luxurious French villa it once was. And in that respect, it would be quite different from the other inns in this area. The ton love anything that is exclusive—or so Papa always used to say."

Nate shook his head. "Gentlemen of the ton don't run inns. My brother would explode if I did something like that." He paused, as he realized the brilliance of his last statement.

A mischievous grin appeared on Bridget's face. "Isn't that the perfect revenge?"

Nate looked at her, and a swell of admiration and attraction rose within him. He smiled, put his hands in his pockets, and ambled forward, analyzing the villa. It truly *was* magnificent. He envisioned ladies and gentlemen of the ton arriving in their carriages for an exclusive stay at Villa De Lacey on the shores of Lake Windermere.

"There are eleven rooms in this house that are currently not being used. Those could be turned into bedrooms for the guests. That's in addition to the rooms you have already seen. There's also a large space on the ground floor that can be used as a ballroom or for other forms of entertainment. That's not counting the kitchen and servants' quarters below the stairs along with the stables and carriage houses behind the main villa. They are certainly big enough to accommodate the horses for a substantial number of guests."

"That is impressive," Nate said. "But I don't know." He shook his head. "The idea seems rather far-fetched. I don't know anything about running an inn—exclusive or not."

"That's why you need me to act as your hostess and manager. My cook, housekeeper, scullery maid, gardener, and stable boy, combined with your staff should be enough to get us started. All you would need to do is invest a little money to repair the furniture."

"My staff?" Nate laughed. "I have a valet, that's all. The rest of the staff remained in London on my brother's payroll."

"Well, we could make do until we—you—start seeing a prof-it, and then you can hire more people. We have but a few servants. Nevertheless, they are fine, hardworking people. You would need to retain them anyway to run the household. A home like this cannot keep itself. And I would be happy to take on the role of hostess to your guests, in exchange for my and my aunt's board and lodging."

Nate could not help but smile at Bridget's enthusiasm. And he certainly liked the idea of outwitting Edward, though the scheme seemed a bit outlandish. Still, he couldn't deny his interest. At the very least, it would detract from the boredom he'd otherwise face.

Of course, he'd have to consider the cost and the conse-quences. His allowance was substantial and would be enough to cover the initial repair costs, but if Edward got wind of what he was doing and became displeased with him, he'd cut off his allowance for good.

On the other hand, turning Villa De Lacey into an inn would mortify Edward, and if Nate stood his ground, Edward would likely beg him to sell. His brother would be forced to scrap the seven-year clause, faster than he could blink.

"I'd have to think about it. And investigate what expenses would be involved," Nate said.

"The chairs in the dining room would need to be reupholstered," Bridget said, "as would the sofa and chairs in the drawing room. But I know a wonderful seamstress in the village, whose labor would be much cheaper than you could find anywhere in London or Yorkshire. We'd also need to replace the missing paintings or simply rearrange the ones we have in place. And—"

"Why don't you make a comprehensive list for me?" Nate said.

"Yes, that's exactly what I need to do. Does this mean you are agreeing to my plan?"

"It means I'm willing to consider it."

"You won't regret it," Bridget said. "Just think, a few months from now this house will be filled with your friends from London. You can start by writing to the gentleman who gave you the copy of Wordsworth's guidebook. Tell him to spread the word about your exclusive inn, accessible by invitation only, and then you will see the people vying for an invitation to visit us. Papa always said the ton were like a bunch of sheep—always following the latest fashions and coveting what others have."

Nate cocked his head. She wasn't wrong. Perhaps, there was more to this idea than fantasy. The thought of Edward's reaction when he learned that Nate had turned Villa De Lacey into an inn was too thrilling to ignore. Earning his own money was something he'd never really considered outside of the gambling tables, but the idea of it filled him with pleasure. To be independent from his pompous brother—it was enticing indeed. If Edward intended to banish him from society, then he'd bring society to the Lake District. Oh, how that would irk Edward. He grinned.

"You're smiling," Bridget said. "I can tell you like the idea."

"It's growing more appealing," Nate said.

"Oh, please say yes, Mr. Squires. I know this will work. It simply has to work."

Bridget's blue eyes twinkled and the enthusiasm in her voice was hard to ignore. She seemed to be an intelligent and capable young lady. With her help, he might be able to make the scheme work—at least to the point where Edward would start taking him seriously and he would have some leverage against his brother.

"All right, then. Let's get that list of repairs drawn up and see what it will take to bring the ton to the Lake District. What do I have to lose?"

🔍

BRIDGET FELT AS though she was floating on a cloud. It had worked. She'd managed to persuade Mr. Squires to let her and her aunt stay at Villa De Lacey—now all she had to do was convince Aunt Marianne that it was a good idea to turn her brother's villa into an inn.

Bridget was quite pleased that the handsome Mr. Squires wasn't the villain in the story of her life—as it turned out, that title belonged to his brother. Life would have been much harder had she been made to share a home with the man who'd contributed to her father's misery and death. But Nathaniel Squires was, in fact, innocent of that crime and quite a pleasant gentleman too. He didn't seem to care for his older brother, who had treated him badly. It hadn't been Nate's choice to move to Villa De Lacey. His brother had forced him to leave London, and Bridget was going to use their feud to keep herself and her aunt in their home.

She smiled to herself. It didn't hurt that Nate was pleasing to look at either. She liked the combination of his dark hair and midnight-blue eyes. As for his physique—well—the thought of him standing unclothed in the window set her cheeks aflame. She'd been quite mortified when he'd waved at her—ashamed that she'd been staring—but she'd been mesmerized by his muscular torso and those lower bits that had been half-obscured by the window ledge. It had been impossible to turn away.

Bridget slid onto the settee in the drawing room, where her aunt sat with her embroidery. Bijou, exhausted from his romp in the garden, jumped onto the settee and curled into a ball beside her.

"My dear," her aunt said, looking up from her work and pushing her spectacles from the bridge of her nose close to her forehead, "who was that man I saw you conversing with in the garden? He was too finely dressed to be a servant. Are you trying to cause a scandal?"

"That's what I'm here to talk to you about, Aunt. The gentleman you saw is Mr. Nathaniel Squires—the new owner of Villa De Lacey."

Aunt Marianne paled. "He's come to claim our home already." She lowered her embroidery to her lap as if she no longer had the strength to continue with it. "Oh, my dear Bridget, what are we going to do?"

Bridget put a comforting hand on her aunt's forearm. "You mustn't worry yourself. Mr. Squires has no intention of forcing us out of our home. He's letting us stay."

"Letting us stay!" The suggestion seemed to ignite a fire within her aunt. "The cheek of it! This home was built by my father. I was born here, as was my brother, and I will die here."

Bridget clasped her aunt's hand. "I know how important Villa De Lacey is to you, Aunt. It's equally as important to me. But, like it or not, the house belongs to Mr. Squires now, and the only way we can stay here is with his permission."

Her aunt's forehead creased into a frown, and she blinked several times. She looked defeated, and Bridget's heart went out to her. "Why would he do that? Are we to pay rent? How much does he want?"

Bridget shifted in her seat. "Actually, I've made a business deal with him."

"A business deal? Ridiculous! Young ladies don't make business deals."

"Well, I did. I've convinced him to turn Villa De Lacey into an exclusive inn for wealthy tourists." Bridget spoke quickly and then held her breath, waiting for her aunt's response.

Aunt Marianne turned whiter than winter frost.

"Did you hear what I said, Aunt?" Bridget prompted.

Her aunt blinked. "You want to fill our home with strangers? Have you gone mad?"

"Paying strangers, Aunt—wealthy ladies and gentlemen— who wish to come and see the magnificent Lake District Mr. Wordsworth describes in his new guidebook." She handed the book to her aunt.

Her aunt took the book and stared at it blankly. "Bosh! Mr. Wordsworth published one of these years ago. He does it for the money, that's all."

"This time it's different. This edition has attracted a lot of attention. People want to come to the Lake District, and we have the space for them."

"This is all too much for me." Aunt Marianne rubbed her forehead. "Strangers in our home. I can't imagine such a thing."

"You won't have to do anything. Mr. Squires and I will handle all the details. He will fund the repair of our furniture and make the house as beautiful again as it once was. Think of it—our home will be filled with guests—full of life again. Think how wonderful that will be."

Aunt Marianne narrowed her eyes at Bridget. "Your father is a mere two months in his grave. We are still in mourning."

Bridget swallowed, pushing down the guilt that had risen in her chest. "I know that, and I feel his loss deep in my heart every single day." She squeezed her aunt's hand. "But we are alone now, and we must fend for ourselves. If Mr. Squires turns us out, we will have nowhere to go. Papa wouldn't want that. He wouldn't want us to lose our home. If filling it with strangers is the only way for us to keep it, then so be it. I couldn't bear to leave Villa De Lacey, and neither could you."

Aunt Marianne nodded stiffly, but she shifted her body so that it was angled away from Bridget.

All will be well, Bridget told herself. *She will grow accustomed to the idea, and then she will see that filling Villa De Lacey with strangers is better than losing it forever.*

CHAPTER FIVE

THE FOLLOWING TWO months were a whirlwind of activity. Bridget inspected every room in the villa, noting chairs, sofas, and cushions that needed reupholstering, curtains that wanted mending, and carpets and wallpaper that required cleaning or replacing. A few of the dressers and wardrobes were in desperate need of a carpenter's skilled hands. Moreover, she would need to order extra beds, linen sheets, blankets, and pillows from Yorkshire, amongst other necessities. Finally, every room in the house would have to be scrubbed. They certainly did not have enough staff at Villa De Lacey for such an enormous task, so a few new housemaids would need to be employed.

Once Nate approved the list of necessary repairs and purchases, it was time to get started. From the beginning, Bridget involved her aunt, who'd been quite reluctant about the plan to transform Villa De Lacey. But a trip to Yorkshire to buy fabric for the reupholstery of the furniture cheered her and seemed to change her attitude. Next, Bridget put her aunt in charge of hiring the new housemaids, as despite Eliza's many years of experience at Villa De Lacey, she was far too reserved to manage a large staff. The arrangement worked well, as it gave Aunt Marianne a purpose, and very soon, she'd become the lady of the house again, administering orders and taking pride in her family home. Soon, the villa teemed with seamstresses, maids, carpenters, and chimney sweeps, who worked for weeks to ensure that Villa De Lacey sparkled as bright as Versailles.

Then it was time for Nate to write to his friends in London. The end of the London Season was approaching when most of the ton would be preparing to retreat to their estates in the country. It was Nate's job to convince them to spend part of their off-season in the Lake District.

This was the most anxiety-inducing period for Bridget. The Lake District was a good 270 miles from London—an arduous journey by carriage that took at least a fortnight—sometimes longer, depending on the weather. But for those who had estates in Yorkshire and other parts of northern and central England, it would certainly be worthwhile.

Still, Bridget knew the length of the journey wouldn't be a deterrent to the ton if the idea of the Lake District as the most fashionable place to holiday had indeed caught on. Reportedly, the latest edition of Mr. Wordsworth's guidebook was selling like hot meat pies on a cold rainy day, and if that were indeed the case, it would do half the work for them.

Waiting for replies to Nate's letters was agony, and had induced Bridget to handwringing. Then, one morning, as Bridget stood admiring the newly upholstered pale-blue sofa and chairs in the drawing room that had been paired with a blue-and-gold floral rug and matching curtains, Nate strode inside and announced, "Our first visitors will be arriving in a fortnight!"

Bridget's heart leapt as she spun around to face Nate. "Who is it? Who will our first guest be?"

"Our first *guests* will be my dear friends, Lord Frederick, Lord Dodsworth, and Mr. Jefferson. They have all accepted their invitations."

"Your *friends?*" Bridget's heart sank at the way Nate had said "friends." He sounded like an excited schoolboy. "They are not paying guests, then?" she asked, feeling a little deflated. She didn't like the idea of Villa De Lacey becoming Nate's playground for his friends. She wanted it to be a proper, respectable establishment for high society.

"Well, no, they're not paying guests. But they are working

hard on our behalf. They are spreading the word about our exclusive inn around London as we speak. Frederick and Dodsworth are both peers, so their word will travel far."

"How exciting," Bridget said, feeling somewhat more optimistic and silently pleased that Nate had referred to Villa De Lacey as "our inn." They'd grown closer during the past few months while they'd worked tirelessly to get Villa De Lacey ready for guests. And although Bridget missed her father dearly, Nate had proved to be good company. Both he and the work had eased her pain considerably.

Nate grinned. "My brother tried to banish me from London, so I brought London to the Lake District. And it's all because of you." He strode toward Bridget, picked her up around the waist, and twirled her about the room. "You're a genius! An absolute genius!"

"Put me down!" Bridget gasped, both shocked and elated by Nate's forwardness. The thrill that passed through her upon feeling his hands on her body took her by surprise. She recalled seeing him standing fully unclothed in the window that first day after his arrival, and the memory set her cheeks aflame with—not shame—but an excitement she'd never felt before.

"What is going on here?" Aunt Marianne's voice sobered Bridget and caused Nate to set her down and step back.

"We were celebrating, Aunt. Did you hear? We have our first guests coming in a fortnight."

Aunt Marianne, who'd been glaring at Nate, turned wide-eyed to Bridget. "A fortnight, did you say?"

"Yes, Aunt. And there will be many more coming, I am sure."

"Well then"—Aunt Marianne squared her shoulders like a soldier ordered to report to duty—"there is much to plan— breakfast, dinner, and tea menus. Oh my, I'd best get started," she said and bustled out of the room.

Bridget let out a sigh of relief. *What had Nate been thinking twirling me around like that?*

NATE DID HIS best to keep himself busy and avoid being alone with Bridget in the following weeks. When they did interact, he kept a polite distance. But it had been tricky. She was attractive and clever, and he enjoyed her company. Yet knew it wouldn't do to engage in a dalliance. He didn't want to insult or injure her reputation, and furthermore, a dalliance would make for a very uncomfortable partnership. In truth, he certainly could not make the inn work without her. She was going to be a charming and knowledgeable hostess. However, he would have to warn his friends—especially that rake Frederick—to keep their distance. He didn't want them pestering her with unwanted attention.

Nate stopped in the foyer, where Aunt Marianne had the three housemaids, and the footman lined up like army recruits. She was enjoying herself, taking on the role of an officer as she strode up and down her line of "soldiers" and inspected every-thing from their clothing to their nails.

Abigail, a young lass from Yorkshire and the newest addition to the staff, smiled at Nate as he came up behind Aunt Marianne. She was a lovely creature with red curls, green eyes, and a sprinkling of freckles across her nose. He returned the smile.

"Mr. Squires," Aunt Marianne turned and greeted him coldly. She'd never warmed to him the way Bridget had done. "Is there something we can do for you?"

"Merely checking all is in order. Our first guests should be arriving any minute now."

Suddenly, Bijou came racing down the stairs, yapping madly. He was followed by Bridget.

"Why is that dog making such a racket?" Aunt Marianne cried, putting her hands over her ears.

"I think he hears the carriage," Nate said, peering out the glass that paneled the pale-blue front door and seeing a yellow chaise snake up the curved pathway.

"Maids, take your places in the kitchen until you are called," Aunt Marianne said. "And James, stand at the ready to help our guests with their luggage when I direct them to their rooms."

"Oh, you needn't bother with all the formalities," Nate said, yanking open the door. "It's only Frederick."

"Bridget, pick up that dog! We can't have him yapping at our guests' heels." Aunt Marianne's sharp voice sounded behind Nate as he strode outside to meet his friend. Despite the order, Bijou dashed after Nate and ran circles around the parked carriage, barking as though he'd explode from excitement. Nate thought he might burst from happiness himself as his friend stepped out of his chaise.

"Squires, old boy, how we've missed you in London."

"Believe me, I have missed London and all of you too." He opened his arms to embrace his friend but took a step back when he saw a woman climbing out of Frederick's carriage. She wore a peacock-blue dress, high-waisted and low cut in the neckline to reveal her ample bosom, and had a noticeable amount of makeup on her face—a pretty face to be sure—but not one that exuded innocence. She'd arranged her light-brown curls in a sort of hive atop her head, and faux diamond earrings dangled from her ears.

"May I introduce Miss Bouffant?" Frederick said.

Nate bowed in greeting. "What a pleasant surprise," he said through gritted teeth. Miss Bouffant was no guest. He knew a courtesan when he saw one.

"Mr. Squires." Aunt Marianne strode forward, holding her list of guests. "May we show our guests to their rooms? They must be tired after their journey. Let's see"—she consulted her list—"who do we have here?"

"Lord John Frederick, madam." He removed his hat and bowed, which seemed to please Aunt Marianne. She gave him a tight smile and nodded.

"Ah, yes. Your room is ready, sir." Then she looked expectantly at his companion. "Is this Lady Frederick?" she asked coldly.

"This is Miss Bouffant," Frederick said.

"How do you do, madam." The courtesan nodded in greeting.

Aunt Marianne frowned as she studied her list. "No, I don't see her as being invited to stay."

"That's because *I* invited her," Frederick said.

Aunt Marianne blinked. "Well, I…" She turned, stony-faced, to Nate.

"You don't mind, do you, Squires, old chap?" Frederick slapped Nate on the back.

He wanted to wring Frederick's neck, but he forced a smile and turned to Aunt Marianne. "Surely, we have an extra room for a last-minute guest," he said, even though he knew full well they were nowhere near full capacity and had plenty of extra space.

"That's not possible. We don't have—"

"She can stay with me if there's a lack of rooms," Frederick suggested.

Aunt Marianne stiffened. "This way, Miss Bouffant," she said. "I'm sure we can find something suitable for you."

Miss Bouffant grinned at Frederick and followed Aunt Marianne.

"What on earth do you think you're doing bringing a courtesan with you?" Nate hissed when the women were out of earshot.

"She's not a courtesan. She's an actress."

Nate folded his arms. "Do you take me for an idiot?"

"Oh, don't be such a stick in the mud. I only came here to cheer you up and inject some life into your country exile."

"Is that so? I daresay I'm flattered."

"To be honest, it was Dodsworth who badgered me into coming—he kept carrying on about how peaceful and lovely it would be—waving his copy of Wordsworth's latest guidebook in my face. I only agreed because I wanted to shut him up and see you, of course. But you can't begrudge me an actress or two for company. I wouldn't have come if I'd known two months in the land of the poets would turn you into a sap."

"It's not a sap to want one's home to be respected," Nate said.

"You wouldn't bring a courtesan to someone's country estate, would you?" He shook his head. "Never mind. Of course, you would."

"But this isn't a country estate," Frederick objected. "It's an inn, and people pay to stay here."

"An *exclusive* inn," Nate said, "for peers, gentry, and their families."

"What's gotten into you?" Frederick frowned.

Nate folded his arms and looked at his friend, refusing to relent. In truth, he was worried that the courtesan would upset Bridget, which he loathed to do. But he wouldn't admit as much to Frederick.

"Maybe you have a point." Frederick sighed, patting Nate on the back. "Perhaps it was a bad idea to bring her along. But she's here now, so let's not argue about it any longer." His friend lifted his gaze and said, "I say, who might that exquisite creature be?"

Nate turned to see Bridget walking toward them. "She's the inn's hostess, so don't even consider it," he warned.

"Why? Are the two of you lovers?"

"Heavens, no! She's a respectable lady."

"Betrothed, then?"

"No! For goodness' sake."

"Are you telling me that you live platonically in this secluded villa with that gorgeous creature?"

"We don't live alone. She has an aunt. Besides that, I've only known her a few months, and she's in mourning for her father."

"Aah, hence the black. So, her father was the *felo de se*? The man who took his own life after your brother ruined him?"

"Be quiet," Nate snapped, "here she comes." The idea that Edward was partially responsible for Mr. De Lacey's death filled him with shame. He hated to think that his brother was the cause of Bridget's pain.

"Do you know, Squires—" Frederick folded his arms and looked at his friend—"I think you have a soft spot for that young lady."

"Don't be ridiculous. I'm the same man who left London two months ago."

"You never fooled anyone with your rakish act." Frederick patted his friend on the back again. "We all know you're a romantic at heart. Don't you think it's time you put Miss Morley behind you, and find someone new? It's been two years."

Nate stiffened at the mention of the woman who'd once been his betrothed. "You're wrong, Frederick. I'm not the marrying kind. Helen Morley did me the favor of a lifetime." Nate said the words, but they didn't sound convincing, even to himself.

CHAPTER SIX

NATE'S FRIEND, LORD John Frederick, was tall and slim, with a pale complexion. He had a bushy head of brown hair connected to long sideburns, thick eyebrows that sheltered a pair of lovely chocolate-brown eyes, a Roman nose, and a rather charming cleft in his chin.

He gave Bridget a dazzling smile as she approached.

Nate made the introduction. "Miss De Lacey, allow me to introduce my dear friend, Lord Frederick."

Lord Frederick gave a slight bow. He wore a white shirt and cravat with a light-brown waistcoat and trousers, an olive-green fitted tailcoat, and black knee-high boots. "I'm charmed to meet you, Miss De Lacey. I do hope we'll be seeing a lot of each other during my stay here."

"Pleased to meet you, Lord Frederick. My aunt has shown your companion to her room. Would you like to get settled in your quarters?"

"If you'd be so kind as to show me the way, certainly."

Just then, a second coach entered the open gates of Villa De Lacey, passing by its two watchful gargoyles, and started its assent up the winding path to the house.

"That's Doddy's coach," Frederick said. "He and Jefferson traveled together."

As the carriage drew nearer, Bijou started yapping while spinning in a circle as he often did when excited, his short tail wagging madly.

"Bijou!" Bridget called. "Come here, boy."

But the terrier was too excited and could not contain his frenzied barking. Bridget would have liked to stay and meet Nate's friends, as she was curious to learn more about him and his set, but Bijou's needs came first. "Please excuse me," she said as she stepped forward to scoop Bijou up in her arms. "I need to take him inside where he'll be safe. There's far too much excitement here for him today."

"Yes, take him. And don't worry, I'll show Frederick to his room," Nate said.

"It's been a pleasure, Miss De Lacey." Frederick gave her a lingering look and then bowed.

Nate only scowled, making Bridget wonder what Lord Frederick had done to annoy him. She bid the men good day and took Bijou inside, almost colliding with Sarah and Abigail, two of the newest maidservants, who scurried out from behind the curtain, startling her like two mice underfoot. Bijou, who'd also been startled, broke out in a fresh symphony of yapping.

"What is going on?" Bridget demanded.

"It's Lord Frederick, miss," Sarah said. She was a local lass, who had a round face, springy light-brown curls, and droopy blue eyes. "He's arrived."

"I know that. I just came from outside. But what are you two doing here?"

"We thought to come and help with the guests, miss," Abigail said.

"Is that why you were hiding behind the curtain, spying on the arriving guests from the window?"

Sarah bit her lip and Abigail hung her head in mock penance.

"We wanted to see what he looked like," Sarah said. "To see if he were as handsome and charming as Mr. Squires."

Bridget pursed her lips to stop her smile from spreading. They really should have done a better job of hiring maidservants, but with such short notice, they'd only been able to find a few inexperienced young ladies from nearby towns, so they'd chosen the best they could. It would take some time to train them properly.

"Well, then, you are lucky Aunt Marianne wasn't the one who caught you spying on the guests instead of tending to your work," she said, not wanting to sound too harsh. "But I'll forget all about it if you take good care of Bijou for me." Bridget handed the terrier to Abigail. "Take him down to Cook and tell her to give him some scraps. That ought to keep him out of the way while the guests are arriving."

"But"—Abigail started to say as she strained to look behind Bridget—"more guests have arrived. Won't Mr. Squires require our help?"

"No, those are his friends, and he wants to tend to them himself. All you need to do is make sure Bijou gets what he needs downstairs."

Both maidservants frowned, and Abigail opened her mouth as if to protest again.

"Now, please," Bridget said.

The maidservants nodded in unison, looking slightly sulky.

Bridget sighed. It was clear that these young women still had a lot to learn. She could only hope they wouldn't cause any trouble in the meantime.

BRIDGET MADE FOR the stairs, intending to find her aunt, who had been gone longer than expected. But as she approached the staircase, she spotted Eliza motioning to her a few feet away. She turned and walked to her.

"What's the matter?"

"It's Lord Frederick's lady friend," Eliza hissed. "She's none too happy about bein' placed in a room so far from the other guests. She wants to be closer to Lord Frederick, I expect." Eliza's eyes darkened a shade. "But your aunt is having none of it, an' rightfully so."

"Where did Aunt Marianne place her?"

"In one of the shuttered rooms toward the rear of the main floor, above the servant's quarters. She's asked me to fetch bedding to make up the old bed."

"Heavens! That room is not fit for guests. It will be uncomfortable, not to mention out of the way."

"But Mrs. Marianne is right to put her there. The woman's a disgrace. She and Lord Frederick traveled together like man and wife when they are not wed. And Mrs. Marianne says she's a—"

"Nonetheless, she's still a guest here," Bridget interjected, hastily cutting off Eliza's words.

Eliza's face hardened, indicating her deep disapproval.

This was the type of issue Bridget had not anticipated when proposing they turn Villa De Lacey into an inn. It wasn't anything she had experienced before. But that didn't mean she wouldn't encounter similar guests in the future. She needed to establish a decorum—now—for the servants, and her aunt, and herself, for the future. "Why don't you go and watch the front door in case more guests arrive while I sort out Miss Bouffant?"

Eliza nodded stiffly and walked away without saying another word. Bridget sighed and hurried to the rear of the house, passing the steps that led to the kitchen and servant's quarters. Then she turned and moved even farther to the left of the main floor. As expected, she heard a commotion coming from one of the nearby rooms. Bridget turned in the direction of the raised voices. Miss Bouffant stood in her appointed room with her hands on her hips, scowling at Aunt Marianne, who glared back at her with equal ferocity.

"I know what you are trying to do, putting me here so close to the servants. You're hoping the other guests will take me for one of them. But I am a guest of Lord Frederick's, so I demand to be—"

"I can assure you that is not the reason," Bridget heard Aunt Marianne say. "This is simply the only room we have left. You were not on our guest list."

Bridget inhaled and squared her shoulders before making her way to the room. "Miss Bouffant, you seem upset. May I help with anything?"

"Your housekeeper has had the cheek to put me in this back room like a servant. She's ashamed I'll embarrass your finer guests, but I came here with Lord Frederick, and I demand to be put upstairs with the other guests."

Bridget silently cursed Nate. How could he be so stupid as to allow his friend to bring a courtesan to Villa De Lacey? This was to be a respectable inn—a place for the wealthy to come and relax and unwind—not a bawdy house. She needed Villa De Lacey to work. It was her only chance to remain in her home—it was *her* home—and she wouldn't let this woman or anyone else take it from her.

Bridget forced a smile. "This is my aunt, Mrs. Marianne Brixton, *nee* De Lacey, not my housekeeper."

"Aah, I see then why she is so bossy. A relation to the previous owner, now reduced to a living off charity." The woman's tone was sharp and condescending, though Bridget supposed she didn't blame her. No doubt her aunt had spoken to her in a similar way.

Even now, her aunt declared, "My brother would turn in his grave if he knew his house was being populated by the likes of—"

"If I may interject," Bridget said, silencing the two women. "Miss Bouffant, there is no need to be rude to my aunt. She was quite right in thinking there are no open rooms and so did the best she could by you. However, I received notice by messenger of a cancellation," Bridget lied, "so fortunately we now have a much larger room available for you. I shall be happy to move you in there. But you cannot share Lord Frederick's room. This is a respectable inn, and only married couples can share a room. If you don't like that arrangement or continue to make a fuss, I'm afraid you will have to leave."

The mention of a larger room seemed to calm Miss Bouffant,

who surprised Bridget when she nodded in agreement. "Very well, I'll be on my best behavior as long as you move me out of this dungeon immediately."

"Exactly what room are we talking about?" Aunt Marianne asked.

"Number thirteen," Bridget said. It was a suite her father had made up for himself on the ground floor two years prior after he'd injured his leg in a riding accident and found it difficult to walk up the stairs.

"Bridget, you cannot be thinking of—"

"It's for the best, Aunt." Bridget put a loving hand on her aunt's arm. "Trust me." She turned back to Miss Bouffant. "The room is still on the ground floor, but it is spacious and well-furnished. I think you will find it to your liking," Bridget said, glancing at her aunt, whose jaw was set in a hard line.

Miss Bouffant seemed pleased with that explanation and willingly followed Bridget to her new room.

"Oh yes, much better," she said as Bridget opened the door to the large room with its canopy bed, an elegant, carved dresser, and a seating area consisting of two plush blue-velvet chairs and a tea table.

"I must ask that you pretend not to know Lord Frederick or to have met him before. You were the first to arrive, so no one will be the wiser that you came together. You can pretend to strike up a friendship while you are here, but I will ask you to remain discreet as to the true nature of your relationship. We have other ladies and gentlemen coming to stay, and I should like to avoid any behavior they might view as scandalous taking place directly under their noses."

Miss Bouffant shrugged. "I can play any part you wish. If you wish me to be a respectable lady and blend in with your other guests, then that's what I shall do."

Bridget frowned. She doubted that anyone from London society would be fooled by this woman.

"I'm not uneducated. I'm an actress, and as a result, I know

Shakespeare. I can even speak French."

"Can you?" Bridget said, surprised.

"*Oui, bien sûr, mademoiselle. J'ai grandi à Paris.*"

"You grew up in Paris?"

"I left when I was nine—adopted by my English aunt after I became orphaned. But she was a cruel woman, so after three years in her care, I turned to the theater to earn my way."

"That's wonderful!" Bridget said, an idea forming in her brain. "How about I introduce you to the others as a widowed lady from France..." Bridget hesitated. "Do you still remember how to speak with a French accent?"

"But of course," the lady said in a convincing French accent.

"Very good. Now, here's the plan. You will tell people that you have traveled to the Lake District from Paris for a holiday." Bridget tapped her chin as she thought. The lie wasn't convincing enough just yet.

The answer came to her in a flash. "Wait here. I'll be back in a minute." Bridget hurried down the hallway and bounded up the stairs to her room. There she retrieved her copy of Wordsworth's *Guide to the Lakes*, two Parisian shawls, a feathered hat, and a pair of gloves, all of which her papa had brought her from France over the years. *That ought to do the trick!*

She raced back down the stairs and almost collided with Nate, who was ascending with Lord Frederick and two other gentlemen.

"Miss De Lacey!" Nate said. "Where are you off to in such a rush?"

"Oh, just getting our lovely French lady, Madam Bouffant, settled into her room downstairs."

"Madam Bouffant?" Frederick raised his eyebrows in question.

"Yes, she's a *widow* from Paris, who traveled all the way here after reading about the tranquility and beauty of the lakes in Wordsworth's guidebook."

"Nonsense!" Frederick said. "She left France when she was nine years—"

Lord Frederick's words were cut short when Nate's elbow hit his ribs.

"I dare say! What are you about?" Frederick exclaimed when he regained his breath.

"What are you about bringing a courtesan to my *home?*" Nate lowered his voice to a hiss. "Let's hope Miss De Lacey's ingenuity saves the day. Now, the least you can do is play along."

"I say, Frederick, that was a rather bold move." A sandy-haired, bearded gentleman with deep-set gray eyes and a gentle face remarked.

"Shh, it's a secret, apparently." Frederick grinned.

Nate glared at his friend.

Frederick shrugged. "It was an error in judgment."

"I'll say as much," the fourth gentleman said. He had dark curls, round black eyes, and plump lips.

"Miss De Lacey, may I introduce Lord Dodsworth and Mr. Jefferson."

The two gentlemen gave a slight bow and then exchanged a look that plainly said *she's the daughter of the* felo de se. Bridget lifted her chin, determined not to let their opinion of her papa affect her.

"We're off to the smoking room," Nate said, with a look that clearly said, *I'm sorry.* Bridget nodded, somewhat relieved that he had turned one of the unused rooms into a smoking room for the gentlemen to enjoy their cigars.

"That sounds lovely. Gentlemen. I hope you enjoy your stay at Villa De Lacey. Dinner will be served at six o'clock." She bid them goodbye and continued down the stairs. Upon returning to Madam Bouffant's room, she placed the clothing and the book on the canopy bed.

"What's all this?" The actress picked up the copy of Words-worth's guidebook and frowned at the cover.

"You said that you can read, correct?"

"Of course! I am an actress, so I have had to learn."

"Excellent," Bridget said. "Then, I'd like you to read as much of that guidebook as you can. Carry it with you, so you can gush about what you've read and how it inspired you to cross the Channel for a visit. Bear in mind, I will want it back, so I intend to retrieve it from you sometime later."

"*Ooh la la*, this is fancy." Madam Bouffant dropped the book onto the bed and picked up the soft green shawl. She wrapped it around her shoulders and smiled. "Very elegant."

"It's from Paris, so it might help your disguise."

"My disguise? I am Parisian, so it's not a disguise," she said, now speaking in an impressive French accent.

"I think you know what I mean." Bridget lowered her voice. "You are playing the part of a widowed, upper-class French lady, so you will need to dress more conservatively. The shawl will help you with that."

Madam Bouffant glanced down at her ample bosom peeking out of her low-cut neckline and threw back her head, laughing. "I see what you mean, yes. And I have just the thing to pin this lovely shawl together and keep my bosoms hidden from the fair ladies." She opened her reticule and pulled out an elegant floral brooch encrusted with emeralds and diamonds.

Bridget gasped. "How exquisite!" She wondered if it was real. If it were, it must have cost a fortune. Then to her shame, a fleeting thought that Madam Bouffant could have stolen it passed through her mind.

"I know what you're thinking. I didn't steal it."

Bridget felt her cheeks pink. "Not at all."

"Of course, you did." The actress chuckled. "Anyone would think as much. That's why I rarely wear it. Either I'll be accused of stealing it, or a real thief will have it off me in seconds."

"Where did you get it, if you don't mind my asking?"

"I'll tell you, but you won't like the answer." She smiled, seemingly enjoying Bridget's discomfort.

"Oh, well, never mind. You don't have to—I mean, it's none of my business."

"I have recently acquired a generous patron who is quite

besotted with me." She lifted her chin with pride.

"Do you mean Lord Frederick?"

The corners of her lips curved upwards in a sly smile. "A lady never kisses and tells," she said, "but, no, not Frederick. The young ones are too cheap and not as easily flattered as the older, married gents."

Bridget's forehead creased as she wondered how many "patrons" Madam Bouffant favored at the same time, and whether or not she was capable of discretion.

"Don't look so worried, *mon cheri*, as I have already told you, I am an accomplished actress and have played many parts in my time. No one will discover the truth," she said as if she'd read Bridget's thoughts. "This will be a wonderful adventure."

Bridget left Madam Bouffant's suite with mixed feelings. She'd taken control of the situation, but she wasn't quite sure she'd be able to keep things from blowing up in her face. Lord Frederick's thoughtlessness could have—and might still— jeopardize Villa De Lacey's reputation before it had even begun to establish one.

※————————————————————————※

CHAPTER SEVEN

B RIDGET ARRIVED OUTSIDE in time to see an elaborate burgundy coach followed by a second smaller carriage ascending the pathway toward Villa De Lacey.

"I am sorry to have taken so long, Aunt."

"Oh, never mind me. What have you done about that awful woman?"

"We've come to an understanding." Bridget glanced at her aunt. "She has agreed to go by the name Madam Bouffant and tell the other guests that she is a widow who traveled from Paris to visit the Lake District after being inspired by Mr. Wordsworth's guidebook. She speaks fluent French, and she's an actress. No one will discover the truth."

"No one will believe that story," Aunt Marianne snorted. "A lady would never travel from France on her own. At the very least, she'd come with a lady's maid."

Bridget sighed. She hadn't thought of that. "I suppose we shall have to say that her lady's maid became ill and had to return home, so Eliza is acting as her lady's maid while she is here."

"Eliza is our lady's maid."

Bridget shrugged. "I shall make do on my own, if necessary. The most important thing is that our guests are not made to feel uncomfortable by Lord Frederick's thoughtlessness. This is a family inn, after all."

"I cannot believe you put that woman in your father's room. It's a disgrace to his memory."

"I had no choice. I'm simply doing the best I can to help us survive."

Aunt Marianne pursed her lips as though she'd held something distasteful in her mouth. Bridget sighed. Her aunt looked tired. While all this activity was helping Bridget cope with her loss, she worried that it was too much for her aunt. "Why don't you give me that list and go upstairs and take a rest? I can stay here and greet the guests."

"I cannot leave you alone." Aunt Marianne shook her head. "Mr. Squires should be here, helping us greet our guests. But I suppose he is upstairs enjoying your father's brandy while we are relegated to servants in our own home," she said bitterly.

"Don't say such things and upset yourself so, Aunt. You know that Mr. Squires cannot play the role of innkeeper. His reputation would be ruined, and his brother would withdraw his allowance, which he will need until the inn is able to support itself. I am the hostess; therefore, I am the one who should be greeting the guests. I enjoy doing it, truly. Now, please go and get some rest. There are plenty of servants available to help me if I'm in need."

"Those silly little village fools we hired? They are not capable of much."

"They will learn, and in the meantime, you can send Eliza outside to help me."

"Very well." Aunt Marianne handed the list to Bridget. "I suppose a little rest before dinner will do me good."

Bridget smiled and kissed her aunt. "I do miss Papa so much, Aunt. You mustn't think all this hullaballoo changes that. It's only a distraction, that's all. And I know he would have wanted us to remain in the house."

"I'm sure you're right, my dear." Aunt Marianne patted Bridget reassuringly on the arm and then went back inside.

Guilt niggled at Bridget as she watched her aunt depart. Not only had her aunt lost the brother she'd adored, but she'd lost the peacefulness of her home. And although Bridget's heart ached for want of her papa, the rebirth of Villa De Lacey excited her.

Despite her agonizing loss, she'd never felt more alive.

ρ

"LADY DARBY," THE driver of the crested black coach announced before opening the carriage door.

Bridget was even more grateful that she'd convinced Aunt Marianne to make her escape the minute the scowling Lady Darby stepped out of her carriage, leaning on her walking stick and followed by her lady's maid.

"Lady Darby," Bridget said. "Welcome to Villa De Lacey. I'm Bridget De Lacey."

Lady Darby was a cantankerous woman with a head of faded red curls, streaked white with age, blue eyes under which loose skin gathered in folds and thin lips. She scowled in response to Bridget's greeting.

"Where is that blasted nephew of mine?" Lady Darby said, peering down the carriageway. "He was supposed to be following directly behind me with the luggage."

"I'm here, Aunt." A man with bright copper curls poked his head out of the much smaller carriage parked directly behind Lady Darby's coach. "Right behind you, as promised."

"What's taking you so long to exit your carriage? I want to go inside. It's been a hellish journey, and I'm tired."

"Mrs. Harley is feeling a little unwell," he said as he pushed open the carriage door.

"Unwell?" Lady Darby appeared almost gleeful. "In what way? Is she experiencing nausea?"

"I am a little nauseous, yes," Mrs. Harley said as her husband helped her from the carriage. She was an exceedingly pale and thin woman with light-brown curls, a snub nose, and downturned blue eyes.

"That is something. Mayhap, you might finally provide my nephew with an heir. Heaven knows you've taken long enough."

Bridget stepped back, alarmed by Lady Darby's aggressive tone and rude manner.

"Perhaps." Mrs. Harley offered a weak smile.

"Don't just stand there. Go and lie down immediately. If such a miracle has occurred and your inadequate womb has managed to produce something, we cannot take any risks."

"Let's not jump to conclusions," Mr. Harley said, "but I agree that resting is a good idea."

"Conclusions are all I have!" Lady Darby snapped. Then she turned to Bridget. "Show us to our rooms, girl."

Bridget bit back a retort to the woman's rudeness and summoned Eliza and James, the footman.

"I say, why is everyone dressed in mourning clothes? Is it for Mad King George? He's been dead for months already," Lady Darby said as Eliza approached, wearing her black crepe dress. She'd insisted on wearing full mourning attire since Mr. De Lacey's death, which, although odd, Bridget found enduring.

"It's for my father, Mr. De Lacey," Bridget said.

"Oh, yes. The *felo de se* who gambled away his fortune." She looked Bridget up and down. "You are an unfortunate creature, aren't you?"

Bridget gave the woman a tight smile. But she would have liked to shake her. How dare she speak about her papa in that callous way? Had her circumstances been different, she would not have held her tongue. But how could she bear such insults for a whole month? These guests had traveled many miles to reach Villa De Lacey, and all had planned a long and relaxing stay.

Lady Darby then turned her eyes to Eliza. "What is her reason for wearing full mourning? Is she also a relation?"

"Eliza has been working at Villa De Lacey for years, since before I was born. She feels Mr. De Lacey's loss very deeply."

Lady Darby pulled her mouth down at the corners. "Nonetheless, a servant is not family. A black ribbon would suffice, but full mourning attire like a widow—it's unnatural."

Bridget responded to Lady Darby with another tight smile

but made a mental note to ask Eliza to change her dress. Much as she disliked Lady Darby, she had to admit that the lady had a point. With so many people dressed in black, Villa De Lacey looked more like a morgue than an exclusive inn near the shores of England's most beautiful and serene lake.

A flicker of anger flashed in Eliza's dark eyes, but to her credit, she kept quiet, squaring her shoulders and responding with silent dignity to Lady Darby's rudeness. Bridget did the same but found it maddeningly difficult. She'd desperately wanted to give that nasty curmudgeon a piece of her mind. Bridget exhaled her relief as she watched Eliza lead Lady Darby's party and their servants to their respective rooms. *I hope the remaining guests are not as difficult as her.*

"Are you out here all on your lonesome?" Nate's voice sounded behind Bridget, bringing a smile to her face. It never failed to surprise her how his presence lifted her spirits.

"I am. My aunt has gone upstairs to get some much-needed rest, and Eliza is showing Lady Darby and Mr. and Mrs. Harley to their rooms."

"Lady Darby, indeed. She's a charmer, isn't she?"

Bridget giggled. "I do feel sorry for her nephew and his wife."

"Yes, poor old Harley lives at her mercy, and I know a bit what that's like. Having to constantly please a wealthy relative is a painful existence." Nate's jaw tightened.

"Dear me! He puts up with all that nastiness toward himself and his wife because of money?"

"You'd be surprised what people will do for money." Nate put his hands in his pockets and gazed at the horizon. "It's easy to forget when submerged in this beautiful landscape, but it's a cruel world out there for the destitute."

An agonizing image of her broken papa holding his pistol to his temple flashed in Bridget's mind, and she gasped out loud, shocked by the pain it engendered within her chest.

"I'm sorry." Nate put a comforting hand on her shoulder. "That was insensitive of me. I wasn't thinking."

Bridget nodded. "I know. It's not your fault—it's only that your words ring so true. I've been sheltered my whole life, living in this wonderful little bubble while poor Papa struggled all on his own."

"What could you have done?"

"I've heard it said that some young women marry wealthy men to save their family fortune, but Papa never pressed me to marry. He talked of my having a Season in London, but I kept putting it off because the thought of leaving him and Villa De Lacey distressed me so. This year, I turned one-and-twenty and hinted that I might finally be ready for a Season in London, but he seemed less enthusiastic. He was distracted. I didn't understand it at the time, but now I realize that he didn't have the money to fund a Season for me. And I'm afraid that his frequent trips to London were made in order to raise money to do so." She swallowed the rising lump in her throat. "Instead, he ended up losing everything."

"It's not your fault. If anyone is to blame, it's my brother. He is merciless."

"At least you don't have to worry about him anymore." Bridget pointed at two more carriages coming up the long pathway that snaked from Villa De Lacey's gated entrance toward the house.

"We shall see, but let's hope so." Nate narrowed his eyes as he peered at the approaching vehicles. "Who remains on the guest list?" he asked.

Bridget consulted her list. "Only the Eamont family. It's Lord and Lady Eamont, and Miss Adelia—" she stopped. Nate was no longer by her side.

She turned to see him walking backward toward the house, his face pale.

"Where are you going?" she called out to him.

But he only shook his head at the arriving carriages while muttering something she couldn't hear. Then he turned and disappeared into the villa.

"LORD AND LADY Eamont," the driver of the coach announced as he opened the carriage door. A short and somewhat stocky gentleman with a generous head of salt-and-pepper hair and long, bushy sideburns stepped out of the coach. He wore a smart navy-blue tailcoat over a cream waistcoat, which had been paired with cream trousers and black boots. He was followed by his much taller, sharp-faced wife, who wore an emerald-green traveling dress.

After she stepped out, two young ladies, the image of Lady Eamont, both with their tight brown curls secured in a top-knot bun, emerged from the carriage. They wore identical travel dresses. One in sapphire blue and the other in burgundy.

"The Honorable Miss Adelia Eamont and the Honorable Miss Lydia Eamont," the driver announced.

Out of the second carriage, the Eamont's lady's maid and valet emerged.

Bridget stepped forward to greet the family.

"Lord and Lady Eamont, welcome to Villa De Lacey. I'm Miss De Lacey, your hostess."

"Our *hostess*?" Lady Eamont gave Bridget a cold stare. "I thought Mr. Squires, the Earl of Westerly's brother, owns this place."

"Yes," the two young ladies spoke in unison, "we thought the same. It's the reason we agreed to this arduous journey."

Bridget forced a smile. "You are correct. Mr. Squires does indeed"—she cleared her throat, finding that she had to force the words out—"own Villa De Lacey, and he is currently upstairs entertaining some of his guests. He has appointed me as hostess of the inn to see to the comfort of his guests. So please do not hesitate to ask me if there is anything you need during your stay with us."

Lord Eamont merely frowned in response, as if Bridget's

presence continued to confuse him.

"We will relay any concerns we have to our servants as always," Lady Eamon said haughtily. "They will be the ones to address any problems or requests with you."

"Oh, but I'm not a servant," Bridget tried to explain, but Lady Eamont and her two daughters turned up their noses as if breathing the same air as Bridget offended them.

Bridget's chest flamed. She may not be part of the ton, but she was as much a lady as they were. Could they not see the size of the house in which she'd been raised?

As though reading her thoughts, Lady Eamont turned to look at the sprawling garden and the magnificent view of Lake Windermere nestled amongst the green hills of Westmorland.

"Do you know, girls, now that Mr. Squires has his own, rather magnificent, estate, I imagine it won't be long before he takes a wife."

"Not long at all, Mama. We are practically betrothed, as it is," Adelia said.

Bridget frowned. *Practically betrothed? Was Nate somehow involved with this woman? Had he made promises to her that he no longer wished to keep? Is that why he ran away when he saw their carriage approaching?*

"Well, my dear, you have the Earl of Westerly's blessing, so I should think that in a short while you could be mistress of this magnificent villa. How wonderful it will be to spend our summers out here."

Bridget blinked back her shock. Had they been sent here by the earl? Were any of their visitors actual paying guests?

"Oh, the first thing I shall do is remove these hideous blue shutters for something more modern like white sash windows. Not to mention that ghastly *fleur-de-lis* railing. It will have to go."

"Excuse me?" Bridget could not stop the words from escaping her lips.

"In fact," Adelia continued, ignoring Bridget altogether, "the entire house is rather too French for my liking. When I am the lady of the villa, I shall redo everything."

A fire ignited in Bridget's chest, but she forced herself to remain calm and said, "This is a French villa, built from Lutetian limestone by my French grandfather—the very same stone used to build much of Paris itself."

Miss Eamont glared at Bridget as though she were an annoying buzzard that had flown into her line of sight. Then she turned to face the garden and said, "How lovely this garden is, Mama. I do so adore flowers."

"Oh, yes," Mrs. Eamont said, turning to the garden, "you must ask Mr. Squires to give you a tour of the grounds tomorrow. I am sure he doesn't realize that you are quite the botanist."

"I adore flowers too, Mama!" Lydia Eamont said, and her sister turned to give her a scathing look.

"Perhaps, all of you would like a tour of the garden tomorrow." Bridget swallowed her fury, wanting to be a polite hostess. "I too am quite the botanist, so there is much I can explain."

The two Miss Eamonts looked to their mother in horror. Lady Eamont stiffened. "I'm sure we'd prefer for Mr. Squires to show us the garden," she said, "he is the owner after all."

"And I'm sure you will not want to come, Mama," Adelia said. "You know how flowers make you sneeze. And dear Papa cannot tolerate grass."

"Ey?" Lord Eamont seemed surprised to hear his name being spoken. He'd been distracted as if he had other priorities on his mind.

"Perhaps your sister and I will follow behind, if only as chaperones," Lady Eamont said, making Lydia scowl. Then she turned back to Bridget and snapped, "Are you going to show us to our rooms, or are we to stand here all day?"

Bridget's cheeks flushed, but she straightened her shoulders and beckoned Eliza and James, who'd just returned to their stations.

"Show Lord and Lady Eamont and the Miss Eamonts to their rooms, please, Eliza. Then take their servants to their quarters."

"Of course, Miss," Eliza said, a flash of distaste passing over her features as she looked at the party of four. Bridget couldn't blame her. She'd thought it would be delightful to host the ton at Villa De Lacey, but that was before she realized they'd view her as nothing more than a servant and her home as something to criticize.

ℒ

ONCE AGAIN, BRIDGET sighed her relief when the guests left and disappeared into the villa behind Eliza. Who knew that life as an innkeeper could be so exhausting? She rubbed the back of her aching neck and wondered if turning Villa De Lacey into an inn had indeed been a good idea. Instead of welcoming gracious guests, it felt as if her home had been invaded.

Then again, Villa De Lacey no longer belonged to her, and perhaps the sooner she accepted that, the better. But, no, she decided, looking toward Lake Windermere. She couldn't let it go. She'd do what she had to, put up with whomever she had to, in order to stay in her home.

"I see the Eamont clan left you feeling a little overworked." Nate's voice sounded behind Bridget, and she turned to face him.

"Coward," she scolded playfully.

"You're right. I was being a coward."

"Adelia Eamont seems to think she is about to be betrothed to you—with your brother's blessing. Is that true?"

"Good Lord, no. Lady Eamont has been trying to unload her daughters for years. Adelia is older by two minutes, and so her mama insists she must marry first. She made Lydia debut a year after his sister. Absurd woman."

That didn't exactly answer her question. "And how did you become entangled in their plans for marriage?"

"My pompous brother took it upon himself to try and force me into a marriage with Adelia Eamont. I refused, but it seems neither he, nor she, has given up."

"Aah, so *she's* the reason you were banished to this nether region of England. You poor soul."

He took a deep breath and gazed out at the horizon. "As it turns out, not so poor after all."

A warmth flowed through Bridget, and she smiled. She liked that Nate was starting to appreciate the Lake District and all it had to offer.

"You may have temporarily escaped Adelia Eamont, but she expects you to take her for a tour of the garden tomorrow. And I think her sister is a little jealous and might want her own tour, too."

"Surely, you're far better equipped to give guests a tour of the garden."

"I am, but it seems that they don't want me. They want you."

Nate groaned. "I shall have to spend the next month in hiding."

"Oh, it won't be all that bad. If I can be gracious to our guests, then so can you." She smiled at the pained look on his face. At least she didn't have to worry about Adelia Eamont becoming the lady of the house at Villa De Lacey.

CHAPTER EIGHT

D INNER WAS A rather elaborate affair. Aunt Marianne had done an excellent job with the menu, ordering Cook to deliver dishes of soup, carved meat, roasted chicken, and fish pies. Several silver-tiered trays held an array of vegetable dishes, accompanied by bowls of puddings and fruit. It all looked quite delicious. The guests arrived and took their seats with murmurs of approval. Bridget was relieved to see that Madam Bouffant had taken her advice and worn the green shawl, which she had pinned together using her floral, emerald and diamond brooch. It did a decent job of covering the actress's cleavage, and Bridget hoped it was enough to fool the other guests into thinking she was a lady—albeit an eccentric one—from France. After all, a foreigner could get away with oddities in her dress and mannerisms that an English lady could not.

Bridget smiled at Madam Bouffant and nodded her thanks but froze when she caught Lady Eamont staring at the actress. Lady Eamont twisted the large ring on her finger and narrowed her eyes as if she sensed something suspicious about Madam Bouffant. Bridget's stomach knotted as she took her seat at the table next to her aunt. *Why had she thought she could fool ladies of the ton?*

James stepped forward and began to pour wine and port for each of the guests.

"This is a splendid house, Mr. Squires," Lady Darby said, and Bridget was relieved to see Lady Eamont turn her attention away from Madam Bouffant. "I must say I am quite pleased with the view from my suite. The lake—what's it called—"

"Lake Windermere," Nate said.

"I concur. It is magnificent." Lord Dodsworth, having finished his soup, dished some asparagus onto his plate, already heaped with carved meat and potatoes. "Exactly as Mr. Wordsworth describes in his guide."

"I find it reminiscent of Montreux in Switzerland. Sir Allen, may he rest in peace, and I holidayed there shortly after our marriage."

Nate lifted his glass of wine in a mock toast. "To Windermere. England's Lake Geneva," he said.

The guests raised their glasses. "To Windermere," they parroted.

"And to the magnificent Villa De Lacey. I hope you all enjoy your stay here."

The smiling guests sipped their wine, and Bridget's heart almost exploded with pride. Until reality came knocking.

"Your brother did well taking this property off the original owner. It's shameful that he could not pay his debts. But to gamble his home? Imagine being so negligent with money that you lose a treasure like this one," Lady Darby said.

Bridget suddenly found that she could not swallow the sip of port she'd just taken. The lump in her throat was too large. *Has Lady Darby no shame? How dare she continue to insult Papa!*

She finally managed to swallow and was about to say something in her father's defense when Lady Eamont chimed into the conversation. "I couldn't agree more, Lady Darby. And how very charitable of Mr. Squires to have taken on De Lacey's dependents—not to mention allow them to dine with us. Most unusual." She turned to Nate, her soup spoon poised in midair. "I can't imagine what a burden it must be to a young man like yourself. Don't they have any family to provide for them?"

Bridget's blood bubbled hot in her veins. The woman had the gall to continue to talk about them as if they were not present in the room. She opened her mouth to speak, though so many responses hurtled through her mind she wasn't sure where to start.

"Yes, in fact, we do, Lady Eamont." Aunt Marianne put down her spoon. "I have another brother who lives in New York. He sailed there two-and-twenty years ago before Bridget was born. But he is in India now. We will be going to America when he returns in approximately six months."

Bridget turned in surprise to look at her aunt. Everything she had said was a complete fabrication.

"What? Why didn't you tell me of this plan—" Nate began but stopped when Bridget gave him a quelling look.

"Well, that must be a relief for you, Mr. Squires!" Lady Darby said.

"I agree," Lady Eamont concurred. "It's bad enough being a poor relation but having to depend on a stranger for charity is simply appalling."

"Charity has nothing to do with it," Nate said. "I couldn't even begin to manage this house without the help of Miss De Lacey and her aunt, so I can assure you that I will do my utmost to persuade them to stay here. And as for them dining with us, they do so because this is, and always has been, their home. There is nothing unorthodox about it."

"Don't be so modest, Mr. Squires. You've taken on both the man's aged sister and his daughter. Of course, it's an act of charity to take on another man's responsibilities," Lady Eamont said.

Bridget felt her aunt tense beside her, and her chest flamed. How humiliating to be spoken about as if they were a pair of stray dogs! These people were positively horrible!

"You must realize that you cannot keep them on once you get married," Lady Eamont continued. "Surely, your wife will want to run her own household."

Bridget bit her lip. She wanted desperately to speak up in her own defense, but what could she say? Everything Lady Eamont was saying was true. She was only living a fantasy. How long would it be before Mr. Squires grew tired of her and her aunt?

"Well, I certainly wouldn't want two strangers living in my home when I am married," Adelia Eamont said. "Nor should I want to be a charity case." She looked pointedly at Bridget, whose chest blazed anew.

She could no longer hold her tongue. "Married?" Bridget blurted before she could stop herself. "Are you to be married soon, Miss Eamont?"

Her sister, Lydia, giggled. "Definitely not. She's had her fourth season without any prospects."

"And you are not far behind me with three seasons completed!" Adelia said icily. Then she peeked at Nate and fluttered her eyelashes "I've been saving myself for a love match. I won't settle for anything less."

"So, you have rejected many suitors, then?" Bridget asked.

Nate put a gentle hand on Bridget's arm under the table, letting her know that she needed to stop and let well enough alone, but her temper had gotten the better of her.

A blue vein jutted out from under the pale skin on Adelia's neck.

"Let me give you a piece of advice." Lady Darby turned to Adelia. "You'd best not be too fussy. You're not pretty enough to wait for a love match, and if you wait too long, your womb will dry up, like my nephew's wife's."

Bridget shrank back, no longer wishing to partake in the conversation. These people were awful, and she'd let them rope her into their cruelty. She felt ashamed of herself.

"We don't know that, Aunt," Mr. Harley said. "Mrs. Harley is resting in bed as we speak, unable to eat due to nausea. There is hope yet."

Lady Darby snorted. "Another month of false hope, I suspect. But we shall see."

"I am a widow," Madam Bouffant said, "and I am deliciously happy. It is wonderful to be an independent woman, free to come and go as you wish and with whom you please."

Bridget glared at the actress. Had she been sitting beside her, she would have given her a good kick under the table.

"It is one thing to be a widow and quite another to be a spinster," Lady Darby said as she eyed Miss Eamont.

"And just where do you come from, Madam?" Lady Eamont asked.

"Paris." Madam Bouffant drained her glass of port and then held it out to the footman who hovered beside her with the decanter. "Fill it to the top," she instructed the servant, who did as she bid and then moved quickly to the next guest.

"Indeed," Lady Eamont said, giving Madam Bouffant a disapproving look. "And when were you last in Paris? That shawl you are wearing is at least four seasons old."

Bridget bit her lip. She hadn't thought of that.

"And I do wonder about your dress," Lady Eamont continued. "You are not one for the latest fashions, I take it?"

"Yet that brooch of yours is quite remarkable," Lady Darby said. "Where did you get it, I wonder?"

"It was Wordsworth's *Guide to the Lakes* that brought Madam Bouffant here all the way from Paris," Bridget said, trying to steer the conversation in a different direction. "Isn't that right, Madam?"

"Yes." Madam Bouffant held up the guidebook, and Bridget sighed. She hadn't meant for her to bring the book to the table.

"So many beautiful descriptions of the lakes." Madam Bouffant waved the guidebook at Lady Darby. "I could not resist coming to see it for myself."

"If the weather permits tomorrow, might I suggest everyone take a rowboat onto Lake Windermere?" Bridget said, trying to take the focus off Madam Bouffant. "We have several boats for guests to use."

"I wouldn't dare go out on my own," Adelia said. "But, perhaps, Mr. Squires and his friends will be kind enough to accompany us and our mama, of course."

"He'd love to," Bridget answered for Nate. "Wouldn't you,

Mr. Squires? You can go after you give Miss Eamont a tour of the garden."

Nate gave Bridget a hardened stare.

Bridget suppressed a smile. If Nate thought she was the only one who had to work hard to please their guests, he had another think coming.

"I am sure Lord Eamont would like to accompany his wife and daughters in the rowboat. It would be a lovely family outing. Am I right, sir?"

"Eh?" Lord Eamont, who'd been decidedly quiet, said. "Well, I—what did you say?" He appeared flustered.

"I think they are talking about rowing on the lake," Madam Bouffant said, smiling at him.

Lord Eamont's cheeks pinked. "Oh, well, if you like."

"With your family," Lady Eamont asserted.

"I'm not one for water and boats," Lord Eamont said, and Lady Eamont's eyebrows came together in a frown.

"I agree," Madam Bouffant concurred. "Sailing makes me feel—how you say—queasy. A walk alongside the lake would be so much nicer."

"Oh, yes, that does sound nice." Lord Eamont smiled at the actress.

An agitated Lady Eamont turned the ring on her finger and glowered at Madam Bouffant.

Bridget's stomach tightened. She sensed trouble brewing.

🔍

AFTER DINNER, NATE and his friends retired to the smoking room, which was purposely situated far from the drawing room where the women congregated. Here, the men could gamble, drink, and smoke cigars to their hearts' content without disturbing the ladies.

"Oh, come on, Squires, it will be most entertaining. The

moon is beautiful outside." Frederick sat, cigar in hand, on the dark-brown buttoned-leather sofa next to Dodsworth and Jefferson. All three men wore matching burgundy smoking robes.

Nate pushed aside the burgundy curtain, coordinated to match the robes, and peered out the window. The night was indeed clear, and the moon was out, shining over the lake. But after two months in the Lake District, he knew the weather could turn on a moment's notice. Clear skies could become covered by fog in seconds, and calm could be replaced by sudden storms.

Besides that, he was exhausted after the stressful day of receiving guests. And although it was early by London standards, he desperately wanted sleep.

"Do let's go for a row on the lake now, old chap," Frederick said. "Why wait for tomorrow?"

"Have you gone mad?" Nate replied. "You lot are far too drunk for that. One of you will end up falling in and drowning. Don't be fools."

"He has a point," Dodsworth said. "I'm a strong swimmer, but throw me in the lake right now, and I'll sink like a leaking ship."

At that, all three of his friends burst out laughing.

"I have a better idea," Jefferson said.

"Do tell." Frederick leaned forward and filled his brandy glass.

Jefferson fished in his pocket, extracted a copy of Wordsworth's *Guide to the Lakes*, and proceeded to fumble through it.

"Good Lord!" Frederick snickered. "You don't plan to read poetry under the moonlight, do you?"

"No, it's much better than poetry." He took a folded piece of paper from between the pages. "I came across this in a book on wildflowers and fungi before we left London." Jefferson unfolded the paper. "It's a type of wild mushroom found in this region that can give you the most delicious hallucinations. I say we go out and hunt for it and then see how it changes the way we view the sunrise."

"Splendid idea!" Frederick said. "What's it called?"

"Who knows? Plants don't grow out of the ground with labels. Here. I drew a picture of it." Jefferson handed over the drawing.

Frederick reached for the paper, but Nate swiped it away first. "Let me see that." He inspected the sketch. Jefferson had drawn a small, long-stemmed mushroom with what looked like a domed cap on top. Nate frowned. "Do you realize how much wild fungi grows in these parts? And some of them poison? You can't risk eating a mushroom based on a crude drawing."

"Good heavens, Squires, you sound like someone's mama—or worse—wife! I came out here to cheer you up, but it seems you like being stuck in the doldrums," Frederick grumbled.

Nate shrugged. The truth was, he liked his life at Villa De Lacey more than he was willing to admit. "I only want you to be safe," he said. "You're not used to these parts."

"Oh, bosh! You fuss too much, Squires." Frederick downed his brandy. "What can happen to us here in this little plot of quiet countryside? Do you forget what London becomes at night? The worst thing that can happen to one of us here is that a moth might land on our coats."

All three of his friends began laughing again.

"Very well, do as you wish. But please, stay far away from the wild mushrooms. I don't need one—or all three of you—dying because you were stupid enough to ingest poison fungi. And be quiet if you venture out. The ladies are sleeping."

"Don't worry, we will creep outside like little field mice." Frederick grinned. "And, if it pleases you, we will ask your gardener's assistance in finding the edible gems tomorrow. That is, if he can make sense of Jefferson's drawing."

"Good idea." Nate silently thanked the Lord that he'd been able to talk some sense into his friends. "And do be careful on the lake. The weather can change at the drop of a hat here."

"It's you who should be careful when you row out on the lake with Miss Eamont tomorrow," Dodsworth said. "That Adelia looked like she wanted to eat you with a spoon."

"He's right," Frederick drawled. "If you are not heedful, she and her mama will connive to trick you into being alone with her, at which point she will accuse you of compromising her reputation, and you will be forced to marry her. Then you will be as miserable as poor Harley here."

Nate had almost forgotten about Harley, who sat apart from the others, quietly nursing a bottle of brandy.

"It's true. I am miserable," Harley said, looking up. "My aunt forced me into marriage by threatening my inheritance, and now she continues to threaten it because my wife is yet to produce an heir."

"You've been married four years, have you not?" Nate said.

Harley nodded.

"And she's never been with child?"

"Never," he said miserably.

"But earlier you implied that your wife might be *enceinte*."

Harley shook his head. "She isn't. Her nervous stomach is down to fear. She is terrified every month when she has to give my aunt the disappointing news that she is not with child."

"How awful," Nate said.

"Especially since it's my aunt's fault—forcing me to marry a barren woman."

"How do you know the fault lies with your wife?" Dodsworth asked.

"Pardon? What do you mean? Of course, the problem lies with her."

"I have heard that the fault can lie with the man," Dodsworth said.

"How dare you!" Harley said.

"Well, if you wish to know for certain, it shouldn't be difficult to find out." Frederick waved his hand casually.

"What are you talking about?"

"There are plenty of young, and might I say, fine-looking maidservants about. See if you can get one with child. If you do, then you will know that the problem lies with your wife and not with you."

"Are you suggesting I father a bastard child?"

Frederick shrugged. "It's not uncommon. I'm certain I have a few myself."

"You mean you don't know?" Nate asked with disgust. He'd always found Frederick's rakish ways amusing. Perhaps he'd been blind to reality.

"No, do you?"

"Of course. I don't have any children. There are ways to protect yourself." Nate spoke with conviction, but something inside him shrank. How could any man be certain?

"I protect myself if I engage the services of a bawd. I don't want a disease, but a maid is usually innocent—"

Nate shook his head. "Stay away from the maidservants at Villa De Lacey. I'm warning you."

"I'm afraid, I can't do that. There's a little redhead whose—"

"For goodness' sake, Frederick, don't you have enough on your hands already?"

Frederick shrugged. "I suppose. But one gets so easily bored."

"Well, you'll have to find another way of entertaining yourself. Eat hallucinogenic fungi and go for a midnight swim in the lake if you must but leave my servants alone." Nate glanced around the room. "All of you. I mean it."

The four men looked at him with bleary eyes and nodded obediently. But as he watched them exchange their smoking robes for their jackets, he wasn't convinced they'd keep their promise.

CHAPTER NINE

T HE FOLLOWING DAY, Nate was obliged to take Adelia Eamont for a turn around the grounds. Rather than joining them on the walk, Lady Eamont and a sour-faced Lydia insisted on trailing behind them to give the impression that they were chaperones, even though he had not asked Adelia to step out with him alone.

"You would have done better with Miss De Lacey. Her knowledge of these grounds is far superior to mine."

"But it's your garden, so it's time you became more familiar with it, is it not?"

He shrugged. "We have a gardener for that purpose." He nodded in the direction of the elderly man, clipping a hedge with enormous shears. "Since you are so interested in botany, perhaps I should ask *him* to show you around the garden. He has extensive knowledge of all the plants, trees, and flowers."

"How very thoughtful of you." Miss Eamont twirled the white parasol she carried to shield her from the morning sun. "I'm sure I will want to become well-acquainted with the gardener eventually. But I'm really only interested in how pretty everything looks and how wonderful the flowers smell. I don't care to know much else. If the garden looks lovely, the gardener shall have my praise."

Nate frowned at this rather odd response to his attempt at rebuffing her. He hoped she wasn't still harboring thoughts of becoming his wife.

"Lord Westerly told Papa that you were so eager to start

tending to your new estate that you abandoned London immediately for Westmorland." Miss Eamont peeked sideways at Nate.

He cleared his throat, uncomfortable with her obvious attempt at flirtation. "Is that so?"

"Yes, I must say, I was surprised to hear it, but that is the explanation he gave Mama and Papa for your putting off our meeting in Hyde Park."

"What meeting?" Nate asked, deliberately playing ignorant.

"The one Lord Westerly arranged with my papa. You must know your brother wants us to be married."

Nate stopped, silently cursing Edward. "I am sorry if Lord Westerly misled you, Miss Eamont, but I long ago informed my brother that I have decided to remain a bachelor. Therefore, I will not be marrying anyone."

To his surprise, she looked at him with sympathy rather than anger. "Is it because of what happened with Miss Morley—her abandoning you at the altar?"

Nate stiffened.

"Because—" she glanced at her mama and sister, who'd also stopped and appeared to be straining their ears to hear what was being said—"Mama says that it is only natural for you to be hesitant about marriage after suffering such treatment, but I can assure you that—"

"I can assure you that my reluctance has nothing to do with Miss Morley," he said through gritted teeth. He could not believe that Lady Eamont, and perhaps many others in the ton, were still discussing his private affairs after two years!

"Good, because although I may not be as beautiful as she, I want to assure you that I would be quite willing and dutiful as a wife." She locked her eyes on his. "Quite dutiful," she repeated, "and very willing."

Nate stepped back, hoping to break the awkward moment, but Adelia stayed steady and kept her eyes on his.

He turned to face the villa and said loudly enough for Lady

Eamont and Lydia to hear, "I think it is time we returned to our rooms. I shall need to change for the boating excursion." Then he bowed to the ladies and strode back to the villa.

LATER THAT AFTERNOON, James made several trips to carry six rowboats from the storage hut at the back of the house down to the shores of Lake Windermere, and two of the maids packed and delivered a picnic tea for the guests.

"Wouldn't it be wonderful if we had a boat race?" Lady Eamont said. "We can have a man to row and a woman as a passenger in each boat."

"That sounds wonderful, Mama," Adelia and Lydia exclaimed in unison.

Nate forced a smile. Was there no end to this woman's scheming?

"A race sounds like a good idea," Bridget said. "We will row to that rock at the edge of the lake, and whoever returns first will be the winner."

"Very well," Nate agreed. "Miss De Lacey and I will stay ashore to monitor the race." He sneaked a look at Bridget, hoping she'd agree, but she was too busy watching Bijou through her spyglass as the terrier raced up and down the shoreline.

"Can she not monitor it on her own?" Adelia asked. "There won't be enough participants."

"Let's consider that," Nate said. "You two can pair up with Lord Dodsworth and Mr. Jefferson respectively." He glanced at the sisters, bracing himself for some objection from Adelia, but their faces only brightened at his suggestion. It seemed that it didn't matter to them who they were paired with as long as it was to eligible bachelors.

"What about me?" Harley said. "My wife is still feeling rather poorly and stayed behind, so perhaps I can invite one of the servants to row with me." He smiled at Abigail, who stood with Sarah by the picnic baskets.

"You will take your aunt, and you will win!" Lady Darby said. And the smile on Harley's face faded.

"Then *I* shall take Abigail," Frederick said, completely ignoring the warning Nate had given him the night before.

Nate frowned. "Where's Madam Bouffant? Isn't she with you?"

"No, I haven't seen her since breakfast."

"And Lord Eamont seems to be missing too." Nate scanned the lakeshore. "It looks like you'll be taking Lady Eamont, Frederick." He smirked at his friend, but Frederick was no longer looking at him. He was staring at something behind Nate.

Nate was about to turn around when a familiar voice sounded behind him, making him freeze.

"Hello, everyone! Am I in time for the boat race?" He knew that voice. Even though it had been years since he'd heard it, he'd know it anywhere. But, no, it couldn't be her. He had to be imagining things.

⚲

SHE LOOKED AS she had the last time he'd seen her—luxuriant, dark curls framing her heart-shaped face, and large dark eyes sheltered under long lashes. But it was her mouth he'd longed for the most—plump, red, and sweet like a ripe berry.

Enough! Nate scolded himself. *That mouth may have tasted sweet once upon a time, but now the memory of it is nothing but bitter. What is she doing here? And why didn't I see her name on the guest list?* He turned to Bridget and frowned his question, but she seemed equally surprised to see their new guest.

"Lady Luxton." Frederick broke the awkward silence. "What a pleasant surprise it is to see you here. What brings you to the Lake District?"

"Spontaneity! I heard such wonderful chatter about Mr. Squires's new inn that I had to come see it for myself."

I'll wager you did.

"I hope you don't mind my impulsive visit to your lovely home, Nate. It's always wonderful to see old friends, is it not?"

He bristled at the use of her term "friend" and at her calling him by his Christian name. She'd lost both those privileges when she'd left him standing at the altar. "It's an inn. It's meant for guests," he said bluntly.

"Of course, it is. But I can't tell you my shock and delight when I heard you'd moved to an estate in Windermere. Why, it's less than a full day's carriage ride from our castle in Lochmaben." She laughed. "Imagine that. We are practically neighbors."

Good Lord, she was right. He hadn't realized how close his new living arrangement put him to his once-betrothed.

"Have you come on your own, Lady Luxton?" Frederick inquired.

"I've come with my husband. He's on his way down to the lake now."

Of course. Her husband—the Earl of Luxton—the man she'd chosen over him. *Why choose the spare when you can have an heir?*

"Lady Luxton." Bridget strode past Nate and introduced herself. "I am Bridget De Lacey, Mr. Squires's hostess. You'll need to get settled in your chambers, I presume."

"Yes, we will need three. One for myself, and my husband requires an adjacent room to his for his manservant."

Just then, a manservant, wheeling a frail man in a wooden chair, started down the hill toward them. Everyone watched as they made their way to the lake until the chair came to rest next to Lady Luxton.

"May I introduce my husband, Lord Luxton?"

Nate blinked. He'd known Lord Luxton was elderly, but this man looked to be ninety years old, and Helen was no more than three-and-twenty. Had Helen abandoned him for a man old enough to be her great-grandfather? And if so, why? Certainly not for love. So, it had to be for money. A bitter taste rose in his throat.

"Bring his lordship to the water." She bent to kiss her husband on the forehead and then strolled down the bank toward them.

"Now," she said, looking around at the other guests. "Whom am I to row with?"

"Well, I—" Nate frowned, finding he was at a loss for words.

"You shall go with Mr. Squires," Bridget said. "I have my spyglass." She waved the gadget in her hand. "I will monitor the race from the shore."

Nate's body tensed. Bridget was not to blame—she did not know his history with Helen—but he certainly would not be climbing into a rowboat with her.

"Excellent idea," Lady Luxton said. "Shall we begin?"

"Not so fast," Nate said. "Hand me the spyglass, Miss De Lacey. You will need to return to the villa and sort out Lord and Lady Luxton's rooms. I will monitor the race."

Bridget's smile faded, and Nate silently cursed himself. His discomfort with the situation had caused him to speak to her like an underling.

"Yes, of course, sir," she said tightly and handed him the spyglass. "Will Lord Luxton require a room downstairs?"

"No, that's quite all right," Lady Luxton said. "His manservant will carry him up and down the stairs as needed."

Bridget nodded and then, without so much as a glance at Nate, walked away. Nate's heart sank as he watched her go.

"Well then," Frederick rubbed his hands together, "it appears that Lady Luxton will be accompanying me today." He stepped away from Abigail, whose smile faded.

"Are you certain Madam Bouffant won't be coming?" Nate said.

Frederick shrugged. "I don't see her anywhere."

"And where is Papa?" Adelia said. "Who is to row Mama today?"

"I say. Isn't that Lord Eamont and Madam Bouffant over there?" Dodsworth pointed at two figures strolling together in the distance.

A momentary silence fell over the group. There was something about how the two walked together—a closeness that suggested a familiarity of some sort.

Frederick clapped his hands together, breaking the silence. "Well then, Lady Eamont, it looks like you are the odd lady out. Perhaps you'd like to row with one of your daughters?" Frederick looked from Lady Eamont to Lady Luxton. "Allow me to escort you both to the boats. He held out his arms, indicating that each should take one. Shall we go then, ladies?"

Lady Eamont ignored him and focused her attention on the disappearing figures of Lord Eamont and Madam Bouffant, her eyes narrow and her lips curled downward into an angry frown.

Nate squinted against the sun as he tried to keep track of the two. What on earth was Frederick's mistress doing with Lord Eamont? And why didn't Frederick seem to care?

CHAPTER TEN

THE NEXT MORNING, Bridget had just finished coiling her hair and pinning it into a loose bun when Eliza entered her room.

"Have you finished with Aunt Marianne and Madam Bouffant already?"

"Your aunt will take breakfast in her room."

"Is she ill?"

"She's tired of the guests and wants the privacy of her room, where she can mourn her poor brother in peace."

Bridget sighed. Poor Aunt Marianne had had a trying few days. Lady Darby and Lady Eamont had been exceedingly rude the first day they'd met her. Despite Nate's reassurances that he did not consider them a burden, the ladies of the ton kept treating them as such, and she worried that their behavior had left her aunt deflated. It angered Bridget. Aunt Marianne had been so keen and reenergized upon taking charge of the new household staff, but she, like Bridget, hadn't imagined that the guests would look down on them and treat them like servants as well. This new life was going to take some getting used to.

"And what of Madam Bouffant?" Bridget glanced at Eliza in the mirror.

"Why do you call her that? You don't need to pretend with me. We both know who an' what she is."

"As long as she is a guest at Villa De Lacey, she is 'Madam Bouffant,' a widow from Paris. And she must look presentable, or the others will get suspicious."

"You can change her hair all you want, miss, but that will do naught to save her soul."

"Eliza." Bridget made eye contact with her lady's maid in the mirror. "This is important. You haven't told the other servants the truth, have you?"

"Of course not. I have nothing to say to those cod's heads you hired."

"Good, so you'll see to her hair, then? Make her look like a lady of Paris?"

"If she'll permit me entrance to her room, I will."

"What do you mean?"

"She wouldn't let me into her room this morning. I tried the door, but it were locked. So I knocked, and she shouted for me to leave." Eliza inspected Bridget's hair and started to rearrange the pins.

"How strange. Perhaps it was too early for her."

Eliza pressed her lips together in a disapproving line as she continued to fix Bridget's hair.

"What is it?" Bridget asked. "Do you know something?"

Eliza shrugged. "Only that there were strange noises about the house last night. Lots of comings and goings during the wee hours, there were."

"Really? I heard nothing at all. Perhaps you were dreaming." Bridget had been so tired that she'd fallen asleep the moment her head had touched her pillow. She had no reason to doubt Eliza. Still, she thought it best to downplay the maid's comment. If Madam Bouffant's lover had snuck into her room last night, it was best for the servants not to be gossiping about it.

"Lots of comings and goings," Eliza muttered again as she went to the wardrobe to fetch Bridget's clean mourning dress.

As Eliza helped her into the black dress, Bridget glimpsed herself and her lady's maid in the mirror. Eliza's pale face and grim expression were accentuated by her heavy bombazine gown and oversized black bonnet. Lady Darby's words came back to

Bridget. She was a cruel woman, but she had a point. Their mourning attire did make Villa De Lacey appear rather drab and depressing.

"I was thinking," Bridget said carefully as the lady's maid buttoned her dress, "it might be better if you wore a black ribbon to commemorate my papa instead of full mourning dress. It's only that with Aunt Marianne and I dressed in full mourning as well, the household is starting to look a bit too melancholic."

Eliza's fingers froze on the button she was fastening.

"The master has only been dead mere months, miss. This is still a house in mourning."

"I know. But we shall have to keep that in our hearts because our very survival depends upon making sure the guests at Villa De Lacey have an enjoyable experience so that they will tell their friends to come and maybe even return themselves."

Eliza pursed her thin lips and stepped away from Bridget.

Bridget reached for Eliza's hand. "You mustn't think I don't appreciate your loyalty. I don't know what I'd do without you, honestly. It's a difficult time for us all."

Eliza nodded again and pulled her hand out of Bridget's grasp. Clearly, Bridget's suggestion had wounded the maid. Bridget was about to say something more when an ear-piercing shriek—so loud and bloodcurdling that Bridget's heart almost stopped beating from fright—sounded in the hallway outside. Both she and Eliza momentarily froze before Bridget jumped to her feet and the two of them raced out of the room.

Several guests, still dressed in their nightshirts, peeked out of their bedroom doors, and some had filtered into the hallway where they stood clustered around Lady Eamont.

"What has happened?" Bridget asked.

"My ring!" Lady Eamont emerged from the cluster of people wearing a robe as if she were the star of a Greek tragedy. She held out her hand and cried dramatically, "It's gone! My ring is gone!"

"Gone? What do you mean?" Bridget asked.

"My emerald-and-diamond ring. The one Lord Eamont gave

me for our anniversary. It's been stolen, I tell you! Taken right off my finger."

The audience of onlookers gasped.

Lady Eamont turned to her husband and clutched his arm as if she would faint. "Oh, my lord, who would be so cruel as to snatch that precious ring from my finger as I slept?"

"Taken off your finger?" Bridget frowned. "That makes no sense. You must have removed it and then forgotten where you put it. I am certain it is still in your room."

"Yes." Lord Eamont patted his wife awkwardly on the hand. "I'm certain that's what happened, my dear."

"I never remove it from my finger when I am holidaying. It's too precious, and I don't want to risk losing it."

"It's true," Adelia and Lydia Eamont said in tandem. "She never takes it off."

"Well, we should still search your room, if only to make certain."

"I've had my lady's maid turn my room upside down! It's nowhere to be seen. Someone has stolen it! I demand you call the magistrate."

"My goodness!" Lady Darby clutched her chest. "Are you saying that there's a thief at this house?"

"Or thieves!" Lady Eamont said.

"Let's not jump to conclusions, now." Nate stepped calmly into the fray, much to Bridget's relief. "You don't know that it has been stolen."

"I'd say you start by checking the servants' rooms," Lady Darby said. "I once caught a maidservant stealing food from my pantry."

Bridget frowned. "I am confident that the servants at Villa De Lacey are honest. They don't steal," she said, despite being unsure that her words were true. She hardly knew the servants. They were mostly inexperienced young girls, newly hired. And then there were the guests' servants. Lady Darby and Lady Eamont had brought ladies maids to serve the women in their families. And all of the men had brought their valets.

"I demand that you search every room in this house." Lady Eamont stamped her slippered foot. "Someone here has my ring!"

"I dare say!" Lady Darby said. "No one is searching my room or my nephew's. To do so would be to insinuate that we are thieves."

"Hear, hear!" Frederick bellowed but fell silent at the sight of Nate's hard glare.

"Miss De Lacey and her aunt will search the servants' quarters while everyone is breakfasting," Nate said, "if only to prove their innocence." He turned to the maids and footman, who had congregated upstairs after being drawn there by Lady Eamont's screams. "While I am certain that each of you is innocent, I'm afraid all of you will need to gather in the kitchen while we perform a thorough search of your rooms."

The staff murmured amongst themselves and were slow to move, as if shocked by the implied accusation.

Bridget lowered her gaze. That ghastly woman had probably taken her ring off and forgotten where she'd put it. Yet, she saw fit to humiliate the servants with her accusations.

"You heard Mr. Squires." Aunt Marianne, who'd been silently watching the events unfold, stepped forward. Sounding much like her old self again, she herded the servants back down the stairs, saying, "Gather in the kitchen, go on."

Bridget felt almost grateful to Lady Eamont for having caused this commotion. It seemed to have restored Aunt Marianne's sense of purpose.

"I do hope she misplaced it," Bridget said to her aunt as they watched the servants retreat. "We've only been open a few days. This could ruin us."

"I'm certain that silly woman *did* misplace her ring; nonetheless, we'll do our duty and thoroughly search the rooms. I won't have people accusing us of being thieves. We have no choice but to conduct a search and prove her wrong."

"Let's hope we do." Bridget exhaled. "Or we may be searching for a new home soon."

BRIDGET AND HER aunt spent the next hour opening drawers and wardrobes and searching under beds and mattresses, to no avail. The ring was nowhere to be found.

"That's all the rooms." Aunt Marianne wiped her brow with the back of her hand. "If one of the servants *did* take it, they didn't hide it in their room."

Bridget sank onto the bed she'd just remade after pulling it apart. They had to solve this theft, or it could mean the end of Villa De Lacey. She envisioned Lady Eamont at a London ball, holding out her shaking hand and telling the horror story of how her precious jewels had been stolen right off her finger as she slept at Villa De Lacey, which was teeming with pilferers and lowlifes. Bridget shook the awful image from her mind. "Perhaps we made a mistake rushing to hire so many inexperienced young ladies from the village."

"Every seasoned housekeeper started as a young, inexperienced maid," Aunt Marianne said. "Although, you might be right when it comes to Abigail and Sarah. Those two appear to be up to no good sometimes."

"What can we do?" Bridget asked.

"I should question them. If they took the ring, I'll scare them into telling me where they've hidden it."

Bridget frowned. Something about this whole situation didn't seem right. Blaming the young housemaids was too convenient. Also, Lady Eamont's hysteria had appeared overblown and unnatural. The dramatic way in which she clung to her husband, as though the missing ring somehow represented their love, cruelly ripped from her body, was almost comical.

Suddenly, the image of an agitated Lady Eamont twisting the ring on her finger while glaring across the table at Madam Bouffant flashed in Bridget's mind. She stood up. "I think I know where the ring is. Can you finish up here and then tell the servants to go about their duties?"

"Why?" Aunt Marianne objected. "I want to know who is responsible. We can't have thieves in our midst."

"If I am right, no one stole the ring," Bridget said. She hurried out of the servants' quarters and back up the stairs to the ground floor. Then she crossed the landing and made her way to Madam Bouffant's room.

"Madam." She knocked softly on the door.

"That didn't take long," Madam Bouffant said upon opening her door. "I knew you would suspect me of stealing, but I promise you, I didn't take the lady's ring."

"I believe you," Bridget said. "Now, may I enter?"

She held open the door and let Bridget inside.

"If you wanted to frame someone for stealing a piece of jewelry, you'd want it easily found," Bridget said, more to herself than Madam Bouffant.

"*Eh?*" the actress said.

"Under the mattress." Bridget strode forward. "Help me lift this mattress."

"I will do, but I can promise you the ring isn't under there—" Madam Bouffant stopped when she saw the emerald ring twinkling on the frame under her mattress.

"I didn't put that there," she said.

"I know you didn't. Keep the mattress elevated," Bridget said, reaching for the ring. She snatched it, and then Madam Bouffant dropped the mattress back into place.

Bridget held up the ring and sighed.

"I told you," Madam Bouffant backed away from Bridget, "I didn't take it—someone must have put it under my mattress."

"Your second patron is Lord Eamont, isn't it?" Bridget said.

The actress couldn't hide her surprise. "How did you know?"

"Does this remind you of anything?" Bridget extended the ring to Madam Bouffant. "Take a closer look."

Madam Bouffant stepped forward and peered at the ring. "It looks a lot like my brooch."

"Exactly," Bridget said as the actress turned to retrieve a box from a drawer in her dresser, then opened it to pluck out the emerald and diamond floral brooch.

Bridget took the brooch from her and held it next to the ring. The floral design of each, and the placement of the stones—not to mention the stones themselves—were strikingly similar.

"They look to be part of a set," Madam Bouffant said with wonder in her voice.

"I suspect they are. Lord Eamont must have ordered the set as a gift for his wife on their anniversary—but by the time it was ready, he'd met you and become your newest patron. He wanted to favor you with something special, so he split the set, giving the ring to his wife and the brooch to you."

"A very clever man," Madam Bouffant said.

"Not really, particularly if you are going to arrange for your mistress to be brought on holiday with you and your family." The details and the obvious signs seemed to paint themselves in Bridget's mind's eye. She wondered if anyone else would be able to put them together.

"Who told you that?"

"No one told me. It was plain to see. Frederick has shown no interest in you since the two of you arrived. And your interest in him was only a pretense. You both knew that you would not be put in the same room, and you pretended to be upset that you weren't upstairs with him simply because you didn't like the room my aunt first gave you. It was only fit for a servant in your eyes. How could you entertain your lover—a viscount, no less— in a tiny room with only a single bed?" She shook her head. "What I don't understand is how Lord Eamont managed to convince Lord Frederick to escort you to Westmorland and pretend that you were his mistress when he knew full well it would upset his dear friend, Mr. Squires."

"It was a because of some debt that Lord Frederick owed Lord Eamont. George said he'd forgive the debt if Frederick did him a favor."

"And the favor was to bring you to Villa De Lacey under the pretense of being his mistress."

Madam Bouffant nodded.

"Well, I dare say, bringing you on holiday with his family was a bold move on Lord Eamont's part. But I suspect his judgment is clouded because he is besotted with you, and you know as much. That knowledge has given you ideas and has made him easy to manipulate."

"What ideas?" Madam Bouffant frowned.

"Ideas of being a lady. You convinced him to let you come, didn't you?"

Madam Bouffant shrugged and gave a sly smile.

"I thought so," Bridget said. "You wanted Lady Eamont to know about your liaison. It's why you were so blatantly flirtatious in front of her."

"It's not that I wanted her to know." Madam Bouffant flopped onto the canopy bed. "It's that I am tired of hiding all the time. George isn't the first patron I've had, but he is the first one who truly loves me, and she should get used to that. She should accept my presence in his life. I will be discreet, but I won't hide anymore."

"Anymore? You said Lord Eamont was a new patron."

"Yes, but I intend to keep him. He's good to me, and he loves me."

"Lady Eamont isn't a timid woman, and she won't accept your presence in her husband's life—at least not if you flaunt it in her face. She will try to get rid of you by any means necessary. Why else do you think she planted this ring under your mattress?"

"Are you saying that Lady Eamont put it there?"

"Yes. That much is obvious. She very plainly stated that she never takes the ring off her finger. I doubt a thief would be so bold as to creep into her chamber in the middle of the night and remove the ring from her finger as she slept."

"She must have put it there when I took a late-night stroll

with George to see the stars. Afterward, we returned to my chambers and…" She trailed off.

"That wasn't very wise. I daresay she is keeping a sharp eye on her husband. She must have waited up until she heard him creep out of his chamber. It's adjacent to hers, after all. Be warned. This was her attempt to get you out of her life. And it won't be the last time she tries."

"Let her. I shall keep my wits about me. But in the meantime, what about the ring? I won't hang for something I didn't do." Madam Bouffant touched her neck.

"Yes. Stealing something as valuable as this ring is certainly a hanging offense. Let that be a lesson to you about Lady Eamont's character. Now, if you want my help, you must do what I say. I simply cannot have you and Lord Eamont ruining the reputation of Villa De Lacey."

"I won't give George up. He's my best patron," Madam Bouffant said firmly.

"I'm not telling you to—at least not forever—but you must give him up as long as you are staying here. That means no more secret smiles between you and Lord Eamont at the table and no more walks together. He's here with his family and humiliating his wife in public is going to end badly. You will have to separate yourself from the other guests, I'm afraid."

Madam Bouffant pulled her mouth into a pout.

Bridget held up the ring. "Or I can call the magistrate and have him arrest you for theft."

"You would see an innocent woman hang?"

Of course not! How could you think such a thing? Bridget's mind screamed. But she forced herself to remain expressionless and said coolly, "I'd rather not."

"I don't believe you." Madam Bouffant folded her arms.

"Then believe this. I want to keep Villa De Lacey more than Lady Eamont wants to keep her husband, and she has already proven that she is prepared to sacrifice your neck to do so."

The scowl on Madam Bouffant's face deepened.

Bridget sighed. She needed to make this woman understand. Threats weren't likely to help. "I'm sorry if I sound harsh, but recently, I lost almost everything. Now, this inn is all my aunt and I have. It's my home. Our survival depends on its success, so I will do whatever I must to ensure that."

The actress contemplated Bridget. Then she nodded. "I can understand that. But what am I to tell George?"

"The truth. His wife isn't stupid, but I imagine he's worked that out already and realized he has made a big mistake."

Madam Bouffant let out a defeated sigh and nodded.

"Good," Bridget said, "then all shall be well again." She smiled. "I'll have one of the maids bring a breakfast tray to your suite. You might want to stay in here while I sort out this mess with Lady Eamont's ring." She turned and exited the room, pleased to have gained the actress's cooperation but uncertain whether this was the end of the matter.

BRIDGET STOOD IN the hall with her back pressed against Madam Bouffant's door and her eyes closed. She looked exhausted and Nate felt a pang of pity for her. The guests had only arrived a few days ago, but they'd already caused her a mountain of problems. He wondered if this inn had been a good idea after all. He hadn't realized how difficult it would be trying to please ladies and gentlemen of the ton all day. It gave him a new appreciation for his valet, and he vowed to be less particular and demanding from here on in.

"Did you make any progress?" he asked, stopping in front of Bridget.

She opened her eyes, and for a moment he was taken aback by their pale-blue loveliness.

"Nate, where did you come from? I thought you were at breakfast."

"I was, but Lady Eamont wouldn't let me rest. She insisted that I search Madam Bouffant's room. Poor Lord Eamont grew so tired of her complaining that he broke into a sweat and looked positively ill."

"I am sure he did." Bridget held up the ring.

"Good Lord! Lady Eamont was right."

"Not exactly," Bridget said. "Walk with me and I will explain what happened."

"Heavens, I had no idea Frederick had gotten himself into a financial pickle," Nate said after Bridget explained what had taken place that morning. "So, she's not his mistress after all." He shook his head. "I suppose he did what he thought he had to do."

"I think you're far too kind. What he did was bring his problems from London here to us. I do hope Lord Eamont and Madam Bouffant will be wise enough to keep their distance from each other to avoid future trouble. I had a word with Madam Bouffant about it, and she seems to understand what needs to be done. Perhaps you can do the same with Lord Eamont."

"That won't be possible. A gentleman won't take kindly to another gentleman telling him how to conduct his affairs."

"What I don't understand is why Lord Eamont would risk having his mistress in the same location as his family. It doesn't make sense," Bridget said.

"I agree that it doesn't make logical sense, but for men like Lord Eamont, logic isn't always part of their world."

"What do you mean?"

"Well, he is entitled and used to everything going his way. He either doesn't care about shaming his family, or he thinks no one will be the wiser. But I'd say it's the latter. Men like Lord Eamont think they are too clever to get caught and become careless. Many women turn a blind eye to mistresses, but not too many will tolerate having their husband's mistress paraded in front of them. It's no wonder Lady Eamont took matters into her own hands. The question is, what do we do now that we have the ring? It won't do us any good to oust Lady Eamont as having framed Madam Bouffant."

"I thought about that. We'll take this ring back to Lady Eamont's room and leave it partially concealed somewhere—maybe, on the floor half-covered by the curtain or, even better, the duvet—so it looks like it slipped from her finger. Then, you'll ask Lord Eamont to come and help you search the room one more time. He'll find the ring, and all will be well again—as long as Madam Bouffant does as I asked and keeps her distance from Lady Eamont's husband."

As expected, Lady Eamont was none too pleased when Lord Eamont discovered her ring safe and sound in their room.

"Do be more careful next time, my dear."

"Yes, of course. How silly I am." She batted her eyelashes at her husband, but Nate noticed that they morphed into daggers as she turned to glare at Bridget. And he feared that the lady's thirst for vengeance had not been quenched.

CHAPTER ELEVEN

THEY'D HAD SEVERAL days of calm at Villa De Lacey following the "theft" of Lady Eamont's ring, and it unsettled Nate. The guests had spent their time playing croquet, rowing boats, and enjoying all Westmorland had to offer. They appeared cheerful and seemed to be entertained, yet tension lingered in the air.

Nate swallowed his brandy and moved to his window. It was close to midnight, and the moon shone above the lake. But even more impressive were the stars that dotted the sky. Such a breathtaking wonder, he'd never seen in London. He suddenly had the urge to go outside. Stargazing on such a night was not to be missed.

Lantern in hand, Nate made his way downstairs and outside into the garden. Inhaling the fresh, cool night air, he marveled at the star-filled sky. He was certain that he'd never once looked up at the night sky when he'd lived in London.

"Nate." Someone touched his arm, making him jump.

He turned to see Helen. Her pink evening dress was covered by a black hooded cloak. "What are you doing here?" he asked.

"Aren't you happy to see me?" She held up her lantern and gave him a coy smile. "Don't say no. I won't believe you."

"Go away, Helen. I don't know why you came here."

"I think you do know, Nate." She touched his arm tenderly, and for a second, the old feelings returned. Then he shook her off.

"Go!" he repeated.

Nate thought he saw a look of shock on her face, but it quickly passed. Then her eyes narrowed, and she whipped her hood up over her head, turned, and strode back to the villa.

Nate frowned as he watched her go. What right did she have to be upset with him? What did she want from him? She was a married woman, for goodness' sake. Why couldn't she leave him be?

$$\rho$$

BRIDGET AWOKE TO a barrage of thunder. Despite it still being dark, she threw back her covers and padded barefoot across her room to watch the war raging in the heavens. She had always been fascinated by storms. As a little girl, she'd loved to watch the drama unfold in the sky from the safety of her room, knowing that her papa was next door, ready to protect her.

Tonight, menacing clouds barreled across the sky, roaring like Titans in battle, hurling bolts of lightning at each other and striking the earth below. Windermere's mercurial weather was on full display for their guests. Yesterday evening had been calm and balmy, with a full moon shining over the lake.

What had the humans done to displease the gods? As if in answer to her thoughts, Bridget heard what sounded like a chilling wail from the hallway.

She paused, trying to blink her exhaustion away as she listened over the storm. Had she imagined it? Or was there going to be a repeat performance of last week's drama? Lightning struck again, and the wind shrieked, rattling the glass panes on her windows. An icy draft seeped through into the room, chilling Bridget to the bone.

She stumbled back to her bed, deciding that the wail must have come from the wind, which sometimes sounded like an Irish Banshee. She sank back into her bed and pulled the covers up to her chin, grateful for their warmth and comfort as the rain came down in full force, pounding the panes. She snuggled under the blankets and drifted back to sleep, forgetting all about the faraway cry.

When it came again—a terrifying shriek, competing for attention with the tempest outside—it woke Bridget from her slumber. She sat up with a start. It was different from Lady Eamont's overly dramatic cry for attention. This scream came from a place of fear, and it sent a quiver down Bridget's spine. Heart pounding, she jumped out of bed. And Bijou, who had been a shivering mound under the blankets at the foot of Bridget's bed as he always was during a storm, started wrangling his way from under the covers. Bridget grabbed her dressing gown and raced out of her room, taking care to close the door behind her, leaving Bijou safely inside.

She hurried across the hallway to the staircase and, passing the walnut grandfather clock on the landing, saw it was half-five. What an ungodly hour to be howling. This had better not be one of Lady Eamont's antics again, Bridget thought as she peered over the railing down into the main hall.

What she saw made her blood run cold.

A woman's twisted body lay at the foot of the stairs, her right leg bent at an unnatural angle and her head resting on a pool of blood.

CHAPTER TWELVE

*I*T'S *M*ADAM *B*OUFFANT! Bridget realized, a shock wave zipping through her. The actress wore the same cherry-red evening dress she'd worn at dinner, and for a second, the absurd thought that blood had ruined the gown passed through Bridget's mind.

"Good Lord!" Bridget cried, snapping out of her motionless state. She raced down the stairs but slowed midway, not wanting to approach the body. She'd never seen a dead person before—let alone a person she knew and had spoken with just hours earlier. She covered her mouth with her hand to stifle the scream that sat in her throat and was about to turn her face away when she felt an arm encircle her. She jumped back in fright, not knowing anyone else was there.

"It's only me, Bridget." Nate reached for her again. "Come here. Don't look."

She folded into Nate's arms and pressed her face against his chest, grateful for the shield his warm, masculine body provided against the cold horror at the foot of the stairs. The heat of his skin through his thin nightshirt and the power of his muscular arms around her—holding her tightly—made her feel safe.

"What is going on?" Lady Darby's shrill voice sounded above. "I heard shouting. And why is that dog making such a racket at this ungodly hour? Has someone's jewelry been stolen again?"

The guests, in various states of undress and in dressing gowns, began to gather at the railing, peering over to the horrific scene below.

"Good heavens!" Adelia and Lydia shrieked simultaneously. "She's dead!"

"My God! Clarissa! No!" Lord Eamont came barreling down the stairs in his nightshirt, his feet bare and his salt-and-pepper hair disheveled from sleep. "No!"

Nate let go of Bridget and stopped Lord Eamont as he made to pass them on the stairs. "Don't look at her. Turn around and go back upstairs. Comfort your wife and daughters," he said in a low voice.

Lord Eamont blinked at Nate like a confused child, and Bridget's heart broke for him, despite his treachery. She'd seen the same pain in her father's eyes countless times after her mama had died. Lord Eamont had truly loved Madam Bouffant.

"Clarissa," he said weakly. "Why? Oh, why?"

"Look away," Nate said again, somewhat sternly. "Turn around and go upstairs to your *wife* and daughters."

But Lord Eamont could not look away. He flicked his eyes back to Madam Bouffant's lifeless body, breaking whatever spell Nate had cast over him. He even attempted to push Nate aside but could not compete with Nate's youth and strength. He sagged against the younger man then, limp and visibly trembling as a sob escaped him.

To Bridget's surprise, Frederick came down the stairs and took Lord Eamont gently by the arm.

"Come with me," he said softly. "Don't look. You don't want to remember her this way."

Lord Eamont clutched onto Frederick's arm like a lost little boy and allowed himself to be led back up the stairs.

Bridget couldn't take her eyes off them. Lord Eamont, a powerful viscount, was like a broken man, clinging to one who'd not long ago been at his mercy.

But not everyone was as sympathetic as Frederick. As they reached the top of the stairs, Lady Eamont approached her husband, and even from where Bridget was standing, she could see the anger in the woman's expression.

As Lord Eamont turned his tearful face to his wife, she raised her hand and slapped him. The sound reverberated through the hall amidst the gasps from the onlooking guests.

"Mama!" Adelia and Lydia shrieked simultaneously.

"Good heavens!" Lady Darby said.

But Lady Eamont did not attempt to explain herself or apologize. She simply turned and walked away.

Lord Eamont didn't flinch. He stood staring at nothing as if numb to the world as his wife's anger spread across his cheek.

"Come along." Frederick put his arm around Lord Eamont's shoulders. "Let's get you a brandy."

"Someone bring me a sheet," Nate shouted to no one in particular. "We need to cover her."

"Yes." Bridget nodded, relieved that Nate was able to think of all the practicalities when the sight of Madam Bouffant's body had rendered her paralyzed.

"We also need to send for someone," Nate said. "Is there a constable in the area?"

"No constable, but we have Magistrate Hunt, and perhaps we should send for Doctor Elias, too. Although, he can't do anything to help poor Madam Bouffant now," Bridget said as the cold reality set in. One of their guests was dead! How had this happened? Was it an accident, or was it foul play? She shivered, fearing the latter and wishing for the warmth and comfort of Nate's embrace again. But that moment had now passed.

"Agreed. I think it is wise to fetch both men," Nate said, his tone brisk. "The doctor will determine the cause of death."

Bridget shuddered.

"What do you mean, 'the cause of death'?" Aunt Marianne appeared on the landing. "The foolish woman fell down the stairs. It's plain for all to see."

"It's true, miss." Eliza, still dressed in black mourning attire and carrying a white sheet folded under her arm, appeared next to Aunt Marianne. The two stood at the top of the stairway like reapers of death, dressed in crepe, looking down upon Madam

Bouffant with passionless white faces.

For a moment, everyone fell silent, looking at the pair as if mesmerized by the scene. Then Bijou's barking broke through the silence.

"You need to tend to that dog of yours, Bridget," Aunt Marianne scolded.

Bridget had forgotten about Bijou locked in her room, and after a stretch of silence, the poor little lad had taken to barking furiously again.

"Not to worry, miss. I can take Bijou to the kitchen." Eliza moved down the stairs with the sheet.

"Thank you, Eliza, but I'd like to tend to him myself. You go and help with the breakfast room." Bridget wanted nothing more than to bury her face in Bijou's soft fur and bask in the comfort of his innocent love.

Nate took the sheet and went to cover Madam Bouffant's body, while Eliza and Bridget went back up the stairs.

"I think we've all had a terrible shock." Bridget paused at the top of the steps and addressed the guests. "There's nothing more to see. It's early yet, so perhaps it's best if everyone returns to their rooms and tries to get some more rest. The magistrate will be here soon, and I expect he will want space to do his work."

"I should jolly well think so," Lady Darby said. "All this nonsense has disrupted my sleep. I do hope you are still intending to serve us breakfast. My nephew's wife must keep up her strength if she is to deliver him a healthy son. She's already a waif. If that child survives, it will be a miracle."

She looked to her nephew, who stood beside his pale, thin wife. The woman appeared to cringe in fear at Lady Darby's remark. Her husband put his arm around her shoulders and led her back to her room.

"You needn't worry," Aunt Marianne said coldly to Lady Darby. "Breakfast will be served at nine o'clock as usual."

The lady harrumphed and bustled back to her room.

"Well, I, for one, don't see what all the commotion is about.

If that woman fell down the stairs, the fault was all hers. She was a drunk."

Bridget looked at the speaker in shock. It was the beautiful Lady Luxton. How could someone so angelic looking speak so coldly and cruelly of the dead?

"She's broken her neck. Of course, there's a ruckus," snapped Mr. Jefferson, who was standing next to Dodsworth with his hands in the pockets of his silk robe. "Unless the breaking of necks is an everyday occurrence in *your* house, Lady Luxton?" He raised his eyebrows at the beauty.

Lady Luxton's plump, cherry lips curved into a smile. "We all die," she said, "some sooner than others. It's as simple as that. No need to be a bleeding heart about it. You didn't know her that well—or *did* you?" Her tone was accusatory.

Jefferson's face blanched.

"Come now, Jefferson," Dodsworth said. "Don't waste your time on that"—he pressed his lips together—"unfeeling creature."

As Dodsworth led his friend away, Jefferson shook his head and Bridget heard him mumble, "It's Andrew all over again."

She turned to look at the now-covered body on the floor. Was Madam Bouffant's neck broken? If so, how did Mr. Jefferson know? And who was Andrew? Moreover, what had Lady Luxton been insinuating? Had Jefferson been another one of Madam Bouffant's patrons?

STILL SHAKEN FROM the ordeal, Bridget returned to her room with her aunt. Bijou accosted her the minute she opened the door, and she scooped him up in her arms and pressed him close. The image of Madam Bouffant's corpse was still imprinted on her brain, and Bijou's warm, lively little body gave her a measure of comfort. Bridget shut her eyes, trying to erase the image of death, but she could not. Instead of Madam Bouffant's lifeless body at the bottom of the stairs, she envisioned her papa lying there—blood pooling from his head the way it had from Madam Bouffant's.

Bijou squealed, shaking Bridget out of her terrible reverie. She loosened her grip on the little dog, whom she'd squeezed too tightly in her distress.

"I'm sorry," she whispered to her pup, stroking his soft fur as he squirmed to lick her face.

"What did you say?" Aunt Marianne stood by the window, gazing at the rain.

"Nothing," Bridget said. "I was merely trying to calm Bijou."

Aunt Marianne sighed and turned to face her niece. "Good Lord, Bridget, what have we done? This used to be a respectable house. We used to be respectable people."

"And we still are, Aunt." Bridget walked to her bed with Bijou and sank onto her soft mattress. Exhaustion suddenly took hold, overwhelming every part of her body. "There is nothing disrespectful about trying to keep a roof over your head."

Her aunt turned back to the window, and for a few minutes they both stayed silent, listening to the pattering rain. Then her aunt spoke again. "What was that woman doing creeping about the house while everyone else was asleep?"

What indeed? Bridget thought, as she caressed Bijou. Surely, Lord Eamont wasn't foolish enough to invite his mistress to his chamber, which was on the doorstep of his wife's room. Then again, maybe he didn't ask her. Maybe Madam Bouffant went of her own accord. She'd enjoyed flaunting her liaison with Lord Eamont in front of his wife, and Bridget doubted she'd heeded her warning to stop. In that case, maybe she didn't fall after all.

"The woman's room was downstairs," Aunt Marianne continued. "There's only one reason she would have come upstairs, and it's utterly disgraceful."

"Let's not jump to conclusions," Bridget said more as a warning to herself than her aunt.

Aunt Marianne fell silent again, and Bridget lay back on her bed with Bijou snuggled in the crook of her arm. How she wished she could go to sleep and wake up to find that all of this had been a bad dream.

"I've had difficulty sleeping of late," Aunt Marianne continued to gaze out of the window as she spoke. "And I see a lot from my room. Things come alive here after dark. Unmarried men and women mingling together unchaperoned in the middle of the night. It's shameful."

Bridget propped herself up on her forearm. "How can you see anything after dark? It's pitch-black outside."

"Not when the full moon is out." Aunt Marianne turned briefly from the window to face Bridget. "And they carry lanterns. I see them moving about."

"Well, that's not a surprise. There's no mischief in wanting to see the lake under the full moon. It's lovely."

"Oh, there's mischief about, don't be fooled. That actress was always roaming around in the company of men. It doesn't surprise me she ended up at the bottom of the stairs."

"Aunt!" Bridget sat up. "How could you say such a thing?"

"She was a sinner." Aunt Marianne turned sharply on her words. "And your Mr. Squires—well, he's not as innocent as you think." She folded her arms and turned back to the window.

"What do you mean?" Bridget frowned, concern filling her chest.

"I've seen him in the garden with her. He's no different from his friends."

Bridget sighed. Who knew what her aunt thought she'd seen in the darkness? Her imagination could have been playing tricks on her. Bridget sank back onto her bed, resting her head against her soft pillow and snuggling close to Bijou, but she could not find peace. Her mind wandered back to her aunt's comment. How many lovers had Madam Bouffant had? Could Nate have become one of them?

Just then, the door to her bedroom chamber opened, and Eliza stepped into the room. "I've come to help you ready yourself before the magistrate and doctor arrive."

Bridget sat up. "Goodness, yes. I must hurry." She slid off the bed and went to sit on the ottoman in front of her dresser. She smiled as Eliza approached her, pleased that her lady's maid had disregarded her request to forgo her mourning attire. Eliza shared her loss and sorrow, and that was a great comfort to her. *Lady Darby be damned!*

Bridget handed her silver hairbrush to Eliza. "It's a bad business this, isn't it, miss?" Eliza said as she ran the brush through Bridget's hair.

"It certainly is." Bridget sighed, feeling the weight of the tragedy bear on her.

"I expect the guests will all want to go home now, won't they?" Eliza said.

"Oh, I do hope not." Bridget bit her lip. She hadn't thought about the effect the death would have on the other guests. *Especially, if the magistrate suspects foul play...*

"I dare say it will depend on what the magistrate and the doctor determine," Aunt Marianne said as if she'd read Bridget's thoughts. "If they determine it was an accident, the guests have nothing to fear."

"Of course, it was an accident!" Bridget exclaimed. "What else could it have been? Surely, we don't have a murderer in the house." Although the idea had crossed Bridget's mind, saying it out loud filled her with dread.

✦ ——————————— ✦

CHAPTER THIRTEEN

N ATE AND BRIDGET were seated in the parlor, nursing cups of tea, when Magistrate Hunt and Doctor Elias arrived. The rest of the guests had been asked to remain in their rooms. As it was still very early in the morning, they did not object. Aside from Lord Eamont and Frederick, most of the guests seemed annoyed to have had their sleep disrupted by Madam Bouffant's untimely death.

Magistrate Hunt peeled back the sheet Nate had placed over Madam Bouffant and inspected the corpse. He studied the angle of her body, looking up at the stairs and then back down at her several times. *"Hmm."* He ran a hand over his bushy beard and frowned. "What do you think happened here, doctor?"

Doctor Elias, a short man of about five-and-sixty years, had a shiny bald head, small brown eyes, and rather large ears. He knelt, peered at the body, and lifted Madam Bouffant's head slightly off the ground. The blood coming from her wound had congealed, causing a large patch of her hair to stick to the floor as the doctor lifted her head, and Nate saw Bridget flinch at the sight. He itched to comfort her but restrained himself from doing so.

"A terrible accident. It looks like she tumbled down the stairs and hit her head on the marble floor. Her neck is broken, and her body badly battered from the fall."

Bridget gasped. "A broken neck, did you say?"

"Would she have died instantly, doctor? No suffering?" Nate

emphasized the latter, hoping the doctor would catch his hint and provide some relief to Bridget.

"It's likely, but it's hard to say for certain," the doctor replied, much to Nate's irritation.

"Could-could someone have pushed her?" Bridget's voice trembled slightly.

Nate tensed. He knew what she was thinking—that Lady Eamont may have pushed the woman. And it was possible, but not very probable. Still, if Madam Bouffant had been foolish enough to visit Lord Eamont in his chambers with his wife in the very next room, it could have sent Lady Eamont to the brink. Despite Bridget's request that Madam Bouffant keep her distance from the viscount, Nate thought it more than likely that the courtesan had ignored Bridget's warning. Men like Lord Eamont who'd been entitled all their lives did not take kindly to being rejected, and their mistresses aimed to please them.

"I suppose someone could have pushed her." Dr. Elias took a handkerchief out of his pocket and wiped the blood off his hands. "But why would you think such a thing?"

"Is there anyone in this house that would have reason to hurt this woman?" Magistrate Hunt straightened his shoulders and directed his question at Bridget.

Bridget glanced at Nate. He shook his head slightly to indicate she shouldn't say what she was thinking—after all, one didn't go around accusing a viscountess of murder without first obtaining solid proof.

She wavered as if deciding whether or not to open Pandora's box. Finally, she shrugged and said, "One never knows. Shouldn't you do an investigation of some sort?"

The magistrate frowned. "Doctor Elias has determined that the woman fell, broke her neck, and cracked her head. He sees no evidence of foul play. Unless you are privy to some incriminating information that I don't yet know about, I see no reason for any further investigation." He paused, looking expectantly at Bridget, but she said nothing. "I will need to gather a few details about the deceased from you at any rate, so why don't we go somewhere to talk? And then perhaps the two of you can give me more insight into the situation." His gaze moved from Bridget to Nate.

"Certainly," Nate said. "There's a study upstairs."

"Very good." The magistrate nodded.

Nate led the way to the study. Once inside, he invited the magistrate to sit.

"I think I'll take the chair behind the desk if you don't mind. I'm going to need to make use of that quill pen and some paper." Magistrate Hunt nodded toward the writing instruments.

"Of course." Nate sat next to Bridget across from the magistrate, feeling much like a schoolboy at the headmaster's study. "There's paper in the drawer. Use as much as you need."

The magistrate extracted a piece of paper and dipped the feathered quill into the inkwell. "Now, shall we begin with the deceased's full name."

"Clarissa Bouffant," Nate and Bridget said simultaneously. They'd both heard Lord Eamont cry out Madam Bouffant's Christian name after he'd seen her lying at the bottom of the stairs.

Magistrate Hunt wrote her name on the paper and then looked up, quill in hand. "Her age?"

Both Nate and Bridget shook their heads. "I'm afraid I don't know. One isn't required to give one's age when visiting an inn," Nate said.

"Do you have any idea where she was from?"

"I believe she was born in Paris but currently lives in London," Bridget said.

"Did she travel to Windermere with her family?"

Bridget glanced at Nate, who hoped that his slight frown was warning enough for her to realize that she should not say too much. There was no need to risk the villa's reputation by mentioning that Madam Bouffant was both an actress *and* a courtesan.

"No. She doesn't have a family. Her mother died when she

was nine, and she never knew her father, at least that is what she told me," Bridget said.

Magistrate Hunt raised his bushy eyebrows. "No husband or children?"

"Not that I am aware of." Bridget laced her fingers together, and Nate thought she looked a little nervous. He could tell she wasn't comfortable with omitting the whole truth.

The magistrate scratched his beard. "That is problematic. She will need to be buried, and someone will have to pay."

"That's not a problem." Nate held up his hand. "The burial will be paid for. Madam Bouffant paid us for a month's long stay at Villa De Lacey, and since she won't be able to reap the benefits of her payment, I think the least we can do is pay for her to rest in peace." This was a lie. Neither Frederick nor Madam Bouffant had been paying guests, but the magistrate didn't need to know that.

"Very generous of you." The magistrate nodded at Nate.

Oh, don't worry. It won't be me who pays. It'll be bloody Frederick and Eamont for causing this mess. To the magistrate, he smiled and said, "It's the least we can do."

Magistrate Hunt nodded. "I am curious, Miss De Lacey, as to why you thought someone might have pushed the deceased down the stairs. What do you think she was doing out of bed so early in the morning? And I thought it was especially curious that she was wearing an evening dress rather than her night clothes." He tapped his fingers together. "Something doesn't seem right. Perhaps foul play *was* involved. I think I might need to interview your guests after all. What do you say?"

An alarm registered in Nate's brain. This wouldn't do. He couldn't have the magistrate interrogating the guests. No, it was best to tell the magistrate the truth now. "That won't be necessary, sir," he said.

"Oh?" Magistrate Hunt's forehead creased.

"The truth is, magistrate, that Madam Bouffant came here as a companion with one of the gentlemen—a baron." Nate felt

Bridget's eyes on him. "And, I believe she may have been coming from his chamber. Quite foolishly, she neglected to take a candle with her to light her way. I imagine it's because she wanted to stay completely hidden. I tell you this in confidence, sir, and I do hope this information will go no further than this room."

The magistrate's entire body stiffened. "I see," he said, crumpling up his notes into a ball. "Then it looks like I have my explanation, and my work here is complete."

Nate breathed a sigh of relief. Just as he'd expected, the magistrate had lost all interest once he learned the deceased was a mistress and not a lady of society.

Magistrate Hunt stood up, his posture stiff and disapproving.

"Thank you for coming, magistrate," Bridget said, and she and Nate both stood up. "Do let us accompany you to your carriage."

"That won't be necessary, Miss De Lacey." He put on his top hat and made to go, then hesitated. "I must say, I was delighted when I heard you were turning Villa De Lacey into an inn for wealthy patrons"—he looked from Bridget to Nate—"but I am shocked to learn that you would think to entertain such a woman. Mr. De Lacey would not have approved. And I cannot imagine your aunt does either," he said, and Nate winced, understanding the deep cut Bridget must have felt upon hearing those words. "I do hope you will be more discerning about the guests you invite to our peaceful area in the future."

Bridget's cheeks warmed, and Nate could not let the injustice stand. "She was an unexpected and uninvited guest. The gentleman in question did wrong to bring her. I told him as much. He put us—especially Miss De Lacey and her aunt—in a terribly awkward situation. Miss De Lacey asked them to respect our rules of propriety, but unfortunately, they did not comply. And tragedy resulted."

"Indeed. Well, let that be a lesson to all." Magistrate Hunt bowed and bid them good day.

Once the magistrate had gone, Nate turned to Bridget, who

appeared ashen. "I hope he didn't upset you too much. I thought his comments were uncalled for. None of this is your fault."

"It's not the magistrate I'm concerned about." Bridget squeezed the fingers on her right hand.

"Then what's the matter?"

"I'm afraid we're doing a grave injustice to Madam Bouffant. If Lady Eamont or someone else pushed her, then—"

"Wait!" Nate put his fingers to his lips, hearing voices emerging nearby. The guests were making their way to the breakfast room. "We should go and join our guests. It's best to give the impression that everything is handled and returning to normal."

"But—" Bridget began.

"We'll talk about this later," Nate promised. This was neither the time nor the place for such a discussion. The last thing they needed was someone overhearing Bridget accuse Lady Eamont of murder.

○⃮

BRIDGET EXPECTED THE mood at breakfast to be somber, but she was both surprised and repulsed to discover that the guests filtered into the breakfast room, chatting like it was any other day. They filled their plates with eggs, sausage, and kippers and ate with relish. Lady Eamont seemed especially cheerful, eating with gusto as if she were celebrating Madam Bouffant's untimely demise.

"I wonder where she was going so early in the morning?" Lady Darby cracked her boiled egg with her teaspoon. "Before the sun had even risen, and without a candle. It's no wonder she fell down the stairs—silly woman."

Thankfully, Lady Darby remained oblivious that Madam Bouffant had been Lord Eamont's lover and not a widow from France. But her comment seemed to resonate with a few of the other guests, who glanced at one another, and unsettled Lady

Eamont, who promptly closed her mouth and pushed her plate away as if she'd ingested a spoiled egg.

Lord Eamont's mood was difficult to decipher because he kept a stiff upper lip and ate his food while showing no sign of his earlier distress. But Bridget noticed the sparkle in his eyes that had been evident whenever he'd gazed at Madam Bouffant had disappeared.

She glanced at Jefferson. His face was pale, and he toyed with his food. Like Bridget, he seemed to have been severely affected by the death that morning, and she would have respected him for it if it weren't for his earlier comment about Madam Bouffant having broken her neck. He'd spoken with such authority as though he'd known for certain what had happened. But how could he have known that detail? Could he have been the one to have caused it?

Everyone else at the table, including Lord Frederick, appeared to have a healthy appetite. And why wasn't Frederick upset? At the very least, Madam Bouffant had spent a fortnight with him when they'd journeyed to the Lake District in the same carriage. Yet here he sat, eating his kippers as though nothing had happened.

Bridget put down her fork and eyed the guests, watching each one with suspicion as they ate their breakfast and gossiped amongst themselves. Suddenly, they all seemed like heartless killers—just like the people who'd driven a stake through her papa's heart. *People are capable of immense cruelty. And anyone sitting at this table could be a murderer.*

The smell of bacon and kippers rose to Bridget's nostrils, making her nauseous. She could not stomach staying in the breakfast room a second longer.

Pushing back her chair, Bridget stood up and barely managed to excuse herself before exiting the breakfast room. She retreated to the library, which had long been her sanctuary. Thankful to find it empty, she sat on the window seat and gazed out at the garden, hoping Windermere's calm waters would erase the haunting image of Madam Bouffant's battered body from her mind. The actress had been so animated and vivacious in life that the sight of her broken and bloodied body at the bottom of the stairs was almost impossible to comprehend.

Guilt gnawed at Bridget. She should have told Magistrate Hunt about the ring incident. Lady Eamont had framed and falsely accused Madam Bouffant, and she'd been keenly aware of the courtesan's relationship with her husband. Bridget didn't blame Lady Eamont for her jealousy or anger. Madam Bouffant and Lord Eamont had done her a grave injustice, but that was no excuse for murder.

"I thought I'd find you here."

Bridget looked up to see that Nate had entered the library with Bijou in his arms. "May we join you?"

Bridget's heart warmed on seeing her dog, especially cuddled next to Nate's chest. She smiled and stretched out her arms to receive him. "Of course, you may."

Nate placed the terrier in Bridget's arms and sat down beside her. "I bumped into Eliza as I was coming downstairs. She'd brought him back from the garden. And I told her I'd deliver him to you myself. Although, I must say she didn't seem too pleased about handing him over to me. One would think I'd asked her for her firstborn."

"Never mind Eliza." Bridget kissed Bijou's head and inhaled his scent. He smelled like fresh grass. "She takes her responsibilities quite seriously, and she knows how much I cherish Bijou. How good of her to remember to take him outside, even with all the commotion today."

"And how are you?" Nate asked. "I noticed you left your breakfast untouched."

"I still can't believe it. I can't stop thinking about her—lying there on that cold, hard floor. I can't imagine what she must have been feeling during her final moments as she tumbled down those stairs. Was she frightened? Did she feel pain?" Bridget spoke about Madam Bouffant, but even as she did, she thought of her father—alone, distressed, and friendless in his last moments and beyond. She cradled Bijou, and he tucked his head in the crook of her arm, bringing her instant comfort.

"We've all had a terrible shock this morning. But it will pass," Nate said.

Bridget shook her head. "No, it won't. Not unless we tell Magistrate Hunt what we suspect. He needs to investigate this death. We must tell him what transpired between Madam Bouffant and Lord and Lady Eamont."

"Do you think the magistrate will take your suspicions seriously? One doesn't go about accusing a viscountess of murder without any proof. And even *with* proof, it's not something that can be done lightly. Your magistrate doesn't seem like the type to risk his position for a courtesan's death."

"You're right." Bridget caressed the now-sleeping Bijou. "It grieves me that Magistrate Hunt lost all interest in Madam Bouffant the moment he discovered she was a courtesan and a mistress. And to think he then had the temerity to scold me on the caliber of guests I allowed into my papa's house. I am ashamed that I felt I owed him an explanation as to why that poor woman had been permitted to stay. It's as though her death doesn't matter to anyone at all. But I cannot simply erase her from my mind as though she'd never existed. Courtesan or not— if Lady Eamont or someone else pushed her, then that person must be held accountable, or I will not be able to rest."

Nate ran a hand through his thick, dark hair. "Lady Eamont or someone *else*? You suspect *all* our guests then?"

"I don't know. Maybe. There's some reason to suspect Mr. Jefferson."

"Jefferson! Why?"

"It was something he said. Lady Luxton made a rather cold comment about the big commotion that had been made in the wake of Madam Bouffant's death—quite callous." Bridget saw Nate wince and felt pleased that he seemed to agree with her sentiment. "To which Jefferson replied, 'She broke her neck. Of course, there's a ruckus.' Then later, when Doctor Elias examined the body, he pointed out that Madam Bouffant had, indeed, broken her neck."

Nate frowned. "That doesn't prove anything. Mayhap he deciphered that she broke her neck from the way she was lying and all the blood."

"But that's not everything. I heard him mumble something about Andrew—'It's Andrew all over again,' or something to that effect. What do you think that means? Could 'Andrew' have been another one of his victims? And then there's the implication from Lady Luxton that he might have been one of Madam Bouffant's patrons."

"That seems a bit far-fetched," Nate said.

"I shouldn't doubt it. He seemed extremely anxious at breakfast. He hardly touched his food, and whenever he picked up his fork, his hand trembled."

"Perhaps the other guests are unfeeling. Jefferson is a rather sensitive person, I think."

Recalling Jefferson's blanched face and quivering hand, Bridget nodded. "Perhaps you're right. How long have you known him?"

"About a year. He's a close friend of Dodsworth. That's how I met him. Decent chap."

"Where is he from?"

"I'm not sure. Devon or some such place. Why does that matter?"

Bridget shook her head. "I don't know. It's an inkling I have. In truth, I don't know what to think. Any one of them could have pushed her."

"Or none of them," Nate said. "If you ask me, it is quite plausible that she slipped and fell down the stairs. She was foolish to go creeping around in the dark without a lantern or a candle. But I suppose that is a good thing, too, because she may well have set the house on fire."

"Take Adelia and Lydia Eamont, for instance," Bridget continued, disregarding Nate's comment. Her intuition told her something wasn't quite right, and she couldn't ignore it. "Their father wasn't exactly discreet in his carrying on with his mistress, and they likely resented or even hated Madam Bouffant. And what of Lord Eamont himself? I doubt Madam Bouffant was the faithful sort." Bridget's mind whirled with theories.

"Wait a minute!" Nate said firmly, catching both Bridget and Bijou by surprise. The dog lifted his head and Bridget straightened, looking to Nate for an explanation. "You must be careful. You cannot go about making accusations—not to these people. They have power. The magistrate has already ruled this death was an accident. You'd need a confession from someone to make him change his mind. And that isn't very likely to happen."

"If she were a lady instead of a mistress, the magistrate would not have dismissed her death that easily—and I suspect neither would anyone else," Bridget said accusingly.

Nate blew out his breath. "You're right. But all I'm saying is that we do not know what happened, so we cannot go around making wild accusations."

"Then what do you suggest we do?" A heaviness settled in Bridget's chest. She'd been unable to punish those who'd mistreated her papa, but she would not allow another injustice to go unpunished on her watch. Bridget pressed Bijou closer. Something deep within her soul plagued her. She thought about that morning and the thunder that had woken her. The way she'd heard a scream, but dismissed it, calling it the shriek of the Banshee wind, and gone back to bed. *But what if it hadn't been the wind after all...*

"What is it?" Nate interrupted her reverie. "Why are you frowning so?"

"Two screams," Bridget said, more to herself than Nate. "The first one came in the middle of the night—I thought it was the wind—the storm was such a cacophony of howls and shrieks, I couldn't tell. But now, I believe I was mistaken."

"What do you mean?" Nate asked.

"Later, I awoke to a second scream. That's when I ran out to investigate and saw poor Madam Bouffant at the bottom of the stairs." Bridget blinked, remembering Madam Bouffant's deathly pale face, slack jaw, and glassy eyes staring into the abyss. "She was definitely already dead. I don't know why I didn't realize it before, but I think she'd been lying there for some time. I can't be sure because I didn't touch her, but she looked stiff, and her blood was dark. It didn't look fresh, like the blood that comes out from a cut on one's finger."

"Yes, I noticed that too," Nate said.

"Which means that the first scream I heard was hers and the second one came from someone else."

Nate raised his eyebrows. "So, you think it possible someone else discovered the body, screamed, and then ran away? One of the servants, perhaps?"

"I do." Bridget put a hand on her beating heart. "If only I'd reacted faster and not dismissed the first scream then I could have—"

"What? Saved her? Stopped the killer singlehandedly?"

"I don't know." Bridget massaged her temples. "Maybe she didn't die instantly. Mayhap, I could have gotten her some help. Oh, how awful. I feel terrible."

"You mustn't. There's likely nothing you could have done. She would not have survived such a nasty fall."

Bridget stood and placed Bijou in his bed. The terrier raised his sleepy head, half opening his eyes as if to object before settling back to sleep on the soft pillow inside his woven basket. She knelt to stroke the pup on the bridge of his nose. "At the very least, I could have offered her comfort during her final moments. She must have felt so afraid."

"You heard the doctor, it's likely she died instantly. Besides, you're doing your part now by trying to learn the truth, and if someone is guilty of pushing her, we will bring her justice."

"Do you mean that?" Bridget stood and turned to look at Nate, searching for confirmation in his deep-blue eyes.

Nate nodded. "We can do some investigating ourselves—subtly, of course. We'll start by questioning the servants. And I suppose I can try to root some information from the guests if only to ease your mind. Still, it's a dangerous path to take. We'd best hope that our questions work to prove everyone's innocence, or I may be forced to close Villa De Lacey's doors."

CHAPTER FOURTEEN

RUE TO WINDERMERE'S changeable weather, the sky had cleared by midmorning, and the day showed no signs of the earlier storm. The guests were thrilled and continued to behave as if nothing unusual had taken place—as if a woman hadn't been lying dead on the cold, marble floor mere hours before. They'd eaten heartily and then dispersed happily. Some went for a stroll by the lake, while others went riding on the hillsides or took their carriages to one of the nearby villages. That gave Bridget and Nate the perfect opportunity to interview Abigail and Sarah, whom Nate had summoned to the study.

Bridget glanced around the room. It was still very much her papa's study. His smooth marble globe, goose-feathered quill, and brass inkwell remained in place, as did the paperweight she'd gifted him from her trip to York with Aunt Marianne—a bronze bust of a little terrier resembling Bijou. She hadn't had the heart to pack up her papa's study, and thankfully, Nate hadn't asked her to. He had taken to working in a downstairs room that had a small writing desk, but it wasn't set up for taking private meetings.

Nate invited the two housemaids to sit on one of the buttoned-leather chairs that Bridget knew so well. As a little girl, she used to curl up on one of those chairs while her papa worked, often falling asleep as she waited for him.

Nate gestured that Bridget should sit in her father's high-backed leather armchair behind the desk. She hesitated. *Did he want her to conduct this interview?* She slid into the chair, pleased that Nate was letting her take the lead in their "investigation," but she wasn't ready for the emotions that overwhelmed her as sat on her father's seat, ready to conduct business the way he used to do. She caressed the smooth leather on the arm of the chair, the way she used to do as a little girl when her papa would pull her onto his lap. Delighted to be allowed behind his desk, she would touch everything within her reach, particularly the white-and-brown-spotted feathered quill that tickled her fingers as she ran her hand over it repeatedly. Then Papa would suddenly lean back, pulling her with him, and she'd squeal at the sudden dip in her stomach, which would make Papa roar with laughter. Bridget's eyes stung. She wanted to sink into the leather fabric and allow the chair to embrace her as if it were the embodiment of her dead father.

Nate stood behind Bridget and coughed, pulling her back to the present.

"Are we in trouble, sir?" Abigail widened her green eyes flirtatiously at Nate.

Nate responded in a warm, friendly manner, saying, "Of course not. We only wanted to ask your help that's all."

To Bridget's irritation, she could see that the maidservants immediately warmed to him while still eyeing her with suspicion. *As they should,* Bridget thought. She wasn't here to watch them make eyes at Nate—what sort of maidservants were they to behave openly in such a manner? Unheard of!

"We need you to tell us everything you can about how you found Madam Bouffant this morning," Bridget said, catching the two housemaids off guard. Surprise registered on their faces, and they exchanged a glance.

"I imagine it must have been a terrible ordeal for you," Nate added kindly. "You had a horrible fright, didn't you? I expect that's why you ran away."

The housemaids nodded in unison.

Bridget's irritation faded. Nate seemed to know exactly how to handle them, she conceded. It didn't matter to her how he got the answers out of the two wayward maids, just as long as he got them.

"It were terrible, sir," Abigail said. Her wide green eyes and the smattering of freckles across her nose and cheeks made her look the picture of innocence. "We were off to clean the grates and light the fires in the breakfast and drawing rooms on account of the storm, and that's when we came upon her. She were lying there, all twisted like. Her face were a deathly pale color and there was blood—lots of it."

Sarah, whose plain features were made all the more unremarkable next to Abigail's, covered her face with her hands as if to block out the horrific memory.

"What time did you find her?" Bridget asked.

Abigail and Sarah exchanged another glance. "It were five o'clock, miss. That's the time we are to start readying everything upstairs."

Bridget pursed her lips. They weren't telling the truth. The grandfather clock in the hallway had read half-five when she'd run to the stairs immediately after hearing the scream.

"And what did you do when you saw the body?" Nate asked.

"I saw her first," Abigail said. "Sarah were behind me. I froze. I was so shocked I couldn't speak. Then Sarah came along and almost bumped into me. When she saw the body"—Abigail swallowed—"she near screamed the house down. We didn't want any trouble, so we ran."

"Why would you be in trouble? You hadn't done anything wrong, had you?" Nate said in a soothing tone.

"Wrong, sir?" Both maidservants shook their heads. "Not us, sir. We did nothing."

Their repeated denials and fearful faces made Bridget doubt them.

"Did you touch Madam Bouffant at all?" Bridget leaned her forearms on the desk and clasped her hands together.

"Touch her? Lord no! I almost died of fright when I came upon her. Why would I touch her?"

"To check if she was injured or needed help, maybe?"

"She was beyond help. We could see that much," Abigail said.

"It were so horrible." Sarah shook brown springy curls as if to oust the memory.

"Did you perhaps run to get help then?" Nate asked, providing them with yet another chance to evade blame.

Again, both maidservants shook their heads. "No. We hid away, sir."

"Hid away?" Nate repeated. "Why?"

"We were frightened."

"But why hide?" Bridget pressed, suddenly wondering if she'd seen Madam Bouffant's emerald and diamond brooch pinned to her cherry red dress at dinner the previous night. She did not recall seeing it on the dead woman's body, and it seemed unlikely that the magistrate would have failed to notice something so valuable. Had Madam Bouffant been wearing it? If so, the maids could have stolen it and run away to conceal their crime. "Did you perhaps take something that belonged to Madam Bouffant?" Bridget made eye contact with the servants.

"Take something?" Abigail exclaimed. "Never, miss. I wouldn't touch anything that belonged to a dead woman. It's like asking her to haunt you for the rest of your life."

Bridget nodded. She was inclined to believe them. Many people in these parts were superstitious about spirits and such. And the chilling scream she'd heard suggested that they had been truly scared out of their wits—too scared to approach, let alone touch the body. But if the maids hadn't taken the brooch, then what had happened to it? Bridget made a mental note to search the dead woman's room and cursed herself for not doing so earlier.

"Did you perhaps see someone else there?" Nate asked. "Someone near the body who scared you?"

Both housemaids frowned.

"No, sir," Abigail said. "All the house guests were asleep and the servants down in the kitchen at the early hour."

"We were frightened," Sarah reiterated. "That's why we ran and hid, honest." The maid looked from Bridget to Nate as if appealing for his help. "She were dead. And some folks say that the spirit of the newly dead sometimes lingers behind."

Bridget wasn't impressed by their innocent act. They may not have stolen anything, and she didn't doubt that they'd been genuinely frightened, but they still weren't telling the whole truth. "Is that the only reason you ran, or was it because you were half an hour late starting your work, and you didn't want anyone to notice?" She didn't intend for the housemaids to be reprimanded, but she wanted them to know that she knew they'd lied. Aunt Marianne was in charge of overseeing the servants, but she'd barely ventured out of her room of late. She'd been severely wounded by the way the guests continued to treat her, and their cruel comments had made her lose her spirit. Bridget knew she would need to take charge, and she wanted the housemaids to know that she was paying attention. After all, if they were prepared to lie about one thing to avoid being reprimanded, why not another?

Abigail and Sarah started to protest and reaffirm their innocence, but Bridget stopped them, saying, "You're not in trouble. All I want to know is what kept you up so last night that you weren't able to rise on time this morning."

"I think that's enough questions for today," Nate suddenly interjected.

"Excuse me." Bridget turned and glared up at him. "I'd like to know why they were late," she repeated.

"Is that necessary? They have had a terrible shock." He smiled at the housemaids. "I think the two of you need a rest. Why don't you take the afternoon off?"

The maids' faces lit up.

"Do you mean it, sir?" Abigail looked at him with pure adoration.

"I do. It's been a difficult day for everyone. You may go and get some rest now."

The maids sprang out of their seats, curtsied quickly to Nate, and without giving Bridget so much as a glance, shot out of the room.

Bridget turned to Nate, her chest flaming. What was he trying to hide? What was it that he didn't want her to know about these housemaids or himself for that matter?

$$\rho$$

FOR THE FIRST time since Nate had agreed to revamp Villa De Lacey, Bridget felt disempowered in her own home. His word was the law, not hers. Villa De Lacey belonged to him, not her. And Abigail and Sarah were his servants, not hers. She'd felt that keenly today and suddenly understood how Aunt Marianne must have been feeling of late.

Wanting nothing more than to hold Bijou in her arms, Bridget went directly from the study to the library. The terrier sat up in his basket when Bridget entered the room, greeting her with his wagging tail and a flurry of excited yips. She clapped her hands, indicating that he should come to her, and Bijou sprang from his bed.

"It looks like you've had a good rest." She petted the pup and then scooped him up in her arms. Pressing him close, she wished she could retreat to the privacy of her chamber with him, but she had work to do. So, instead, she made her way downstairs to Madam Bouffant's room. She needed to find that brooch.

Bridget pushed open the door to Madam Bouffant's chamber and gasped. The room was a complete shamble. Clothes were strewn all over, like someone had already searched the place. She put Bijou down and he darted inside and proceeded to sniff the clothing. Could it have been Lady Eamont? Or had Madam Bouffant been searching for something herself? Had she lost the brooch? Perhaps this mess was the reason she'd visited Lord Eamont in his chamber rather than inviting him to hers. Why else would she venture upstairs to see Lord Eamont when his room was next to his wife's chamber? It didn't make any sense. Unless Madam Bouffant wanted Lady Eamont to see her. Perhaps, despite her promise to be discreet, she wanted to get revenge for the disparaging way in which Lady Eamont had spoken to her.

Bridget rubbed her forehead and scanned the mess. She shook her head. All she had was questions and no answers.

Bijou rooted around the room, sniffing every article of clothing and object as Bridget picked up Madam Bouffant's overturned carpet bag and started to fold and pack the strewn clothing inside it. There was no sign of the brooch amongst the chaos. Once she'd finished packing away Madam Bouffant's clothing, she double-checked the drawers and searched every corner of the room. Still, she found no sign of the brooch. It was no longer amongst Madam Bouffant's possessions. Someone had indeed taken the brooch, and the most obvious person was Lady Eamont.

She would need to search Lady Eamont's room—but how? They could arrange a tea party in the garden to get everyone out of the house and gathered in one place, but the viscountess had brought her own lady's maid who was bound to be lurking about her mistress's room. It seems Lady Eamont and her daughters kept the maid very busy, and Bridget doubted they'd let her rest while they were outside enjoying a garden tea. Then there was the matter of Lord Eamont's valet. He too seemed to have a myriad of tasks, so he'd likely be out and about as well. If only she could rely on Nate to help her. But that was out of the question until he stopped hiding things from her. She could no longer trust him. Perhaps, she could arrange something for the servants. *I need something to occupy both the guests and the servants. Something that will enable me to slip away and do a thorough search. But what?*

Bridget arched her back and exhaled. Exhaustion suddenly took hold of her. She needed her own space—if only for a few minutes. She and Bijou returned to her room, the dog cheerfully leading the way as if he knew where she was heading.

Once inside her room, she collapsed onto her bed with Bijou and lay back. How many happy hours had she spent in her beloved room? Never did she think she'd lose what her grandfather had built. She'd even promised herself that she'd only marry a man who'd agree to live at Villa De Lacey for at least half the year. And now, everything was lost. Her plan to keep her home by turning it into an inn had been a fantasy, and it was failing. One of their guests had potentially been murdered. And worse, it seemed that Nate was hiding information from her—no doubt to protect his rich friends. She hadn't told him what her aunt had witnessed from her window at night, reasoning that Aunt Marianne might have been mistaken or was likely making something out of nothing. But when Nate cut her off after she questioned the maids about their late-night activities, effectively ending the interview, her suspicion grew. What did Nate have to hide? Had these moonlight activities her aunt claimed to have witnessed somehow led to Madam Bouffant's death? If so, who was Nate protecting? Is that why he'd been reluctant to ask the magistrate to launch an investigation into Madam Bouffant's death?

She sat up and reached for the miniature portraits beside her bed—one of her handsome papa with his twinkling blue eyes and smart mustache—and one of her beautiful mama, whose blonde hair, blue eyes, and petite features Bridget had inherited.

She gazed at the portraits, an ache filling her heart. *How could I have been so naive to think this plan would work?* Tears pooled in her eyes, and one slid down her cheek just as her the door to her chamber creaked open. Bridget inhaled sharply.

"Who is it?" she called out.

"It's only Eliza, miss." Her lady's maid stood in the doorway in her mourning dress, embodying loyalty and faithfulness. Bridget's heart swelled. She got up and went to embrace the startled servant. "Oh, Eliza, thank you."

Eliza stiffened. She wasn't one for hugs, but she did her best to comfort Bridget by patting her gently on the back.

"There, there, Miss Bridget. Come and sit down. It's been a trying day. How about I go and make you a strong cup of tea?"

"That sounds lovely, but mind you make enough tea for two. You look like you could use a strong cup too."

Eliza nodded and withdrew, and Bridget exhaled, feeling some of the anxiety leaving her body. But the exhaustion remained. She felt as though she'd spent the morning carrying a heavy load on her back.

Eliza returned several minutes later carrying a tray with a pot of hot tea and some lovely biscuits to go with it. "And some scraps for Bijou." The terrier wagged his tail madly as Eliza set the bowl before him.

Bridget poured herself and Eliza a cup of tea, adding a lump of sugar and a dash of milk to her cup and leaving Eliza's black. They sat in silence for a minute, sipping their tea. Bridget ate several biscuits, not realizing how hungry she'd been. She had been too distressed and preoccupied to eat her breakfast. Eliza took tiny sips of her tea and declined to eat a biscuit. She had a small appetite, and as a result, her body was almost childlike in its height and weight.

"Have you noticed any unusual activity in the maids' quarters at night?" Bridget asked after she'd satiated her thirst and hunger.

"There's been all sorts of goings on, miss." Eliza's dark eyes stared unblinking at Bridget. "These young lasses we took on are up to no good."

"What do you mean?"

"They are up until all hours of the night, Abigail and Sarah, whispering and giggling. I hear them scurrying about like mice. I suspect they leave the house after everyone is asleep."

"What makes you say that?"

"I've seen them leaving their rooms well after midnight. My chamber is only two doors down from theirs. And like I said, I heard noises, so I poked my head out my bedroom door. They were fully dressed and wore no bonnets. Disgraceful." She sat back and blinked, her small, pale face the picture of disapproval.

Once again, Bridget thought back to her earlier conversation with Aunt Marianne. *"I've seen strange comings and goings in the garden from my window at night. Men and women cavorting together with no chaperone. One of them was your Mr. Squires."*

"Where do you think they were going?"

"I don't know. But I think they were up to no good, miss. No good at all."

Bridget pondered what both Eliza and Aunt Marianne had told her. Nate had obviously ended the interview to protect someone. She was certain he knew of these late-night comings and goings involving the servants. And why hadn't he said anything about meeting Madam Bouffant in the garden? Could he be the guilty one?

Stop! Bridget felt the churning in her stomach return. She could not start making assumptions about Nate without proof. She had good instincts—or so she thought—and if Nate were a bad apple, she'd know it—feel it somehow. But what if her instincts weren't as good as she'd thought them to be? After all, she'd never have guessed her papa would have acted the way he had—she'd trusted him implicitly—and he'd betrayed her— betrayed himself. Was anyone trustworthy?

CHAPTER FIFTEEN

NATE STOOD BY the window in the study and contemplated all that had gone on that day. He'd seen the change that had come over Bridget's face when he'd stopped her from questioning the maids about their whereabouts the night before. Trust and affection had been replaced with skepticism and anger. It nearly broke his heart, but he had a clear idea of where the housemaids had been going at night, and if he was correct, he did not want Bridget finding out about it. His friend Lord Frederick had caused enough trouble already, and he suspected that his talk of midnight excursions to the lake had come to fruition. He only hoped Frederick's influence on the maids and other guests hadn't led to the disaster of Madam Bouffant's death.

He sighed. Inviting Frederick to Villa De Lacey had seemed like a fantastic idea just after he'd arrived from London. He'd been angry at Edward and missed his old lifestyle, but now he regretted the decision. Frederick was a decent chap, but he was a confirmed rake and wasn't about to change his ways. Nate recalled their years of carousing together—drinking, gambling, women. He'd never really wanted that life. At first, he'd done it to spite his father, who'd been controlling and severe like his brother. He'd resented his father for not trusting him, for thinking that he wasn't capable of handling money, and believing that Edward needed to be left in charge of him. His father had always underestimated him. Nate could still feel the burning resentment in his chest. So, he'd turned to the likes of Frederick, and that had made things worse.

But everything had changed when he met Helen. When she came into his life, he lost interest in the carousing. He wanted to settle down and have a family. Oddly enough, it was Helen who wouldn't let him stop. She loved being seen and insisted on attending every ball and social event in London. He wondered how she did that now with an aging husband confined to a chair. Nate shook his head. What did it matter? He no longer cared what Helen did. But he did care that he'd brought Frederick's chaos to Villa De Lacey and disrupted Bridget's peaceful existence as well as what he had to admit was her clever plan to remain in her ancestral home.

Nate turned from the window. It was time to have a chat with his friend. He needed to find out exactly what had been going on after dark and whether or not it could have resulted in Madam Bouffant's death.

As he walked across the room, the door suddenly opened. He stepped back in surprise when Lady Luxton entered the study. She closed the paneled mahogany door behind her, leaned against it, and gave Nate a sly smile. Her deep-purple dress, complete with a lilac sash, complemented her dark hair and black eyes. Nate swallowed. A mixture of anger, sorrow, and lust coursed through him. Here was the woman who'd abandoned him at the altar, playing games with his heart again.

"What are you doing here, Helen?"

She sauntered toward him. "I thought we could finish the discussion we started last night."

He held up his hand to stop her from advancing. "There was no discussion. I was merely taking a stroll in the garden, trying to clear my head, when you ambushed me out of nowhere. I told you then, and I will tell you now, we have nothing to say to each other."

"I know you don't mean that." She continued to move closer to him. "Don't you think it's time you let go of the past and forgive me?"

Nate ran a hand through his hair. This was painful. Part of him wanted her to go away, but another part wished—*no!* She had no right to keep ambushing him like this.

Helen lowered her gaze and sucked her lower lip as if contemplating her next move. "You know I did what was best for both of us, don't you?"

He chuckled. "How was humiliating me and running away to marry another man—old enough to be my grandfather—best for me?"

The comment seemed to sober her because she straightened her shoulders and abandoned her seductive tone. "When your father died, he left everything to your brother. You had nothing of your own—not even a title. You were at your brother's mercy. And the earl disliked me. He would have turned us into his puppets. But my husband is as rich as Croesus and almost as old. He will die soon, and then he will make me a very rich woman."

Nate sighed. "What of it? That has nothing to do with me."

"My son will need a father. I shall be looking to remarry."

"Your *son?*" Surprise followed by a little stab of pain coursed through him. He'd imagined Helen as a mother many times, but he'd always thought she'd be the mother of his children.

"Henry is a little over two," she said, stepping closer to Nate.

A little over two? Helen had been only married for two years. He backed up once again as the mad thought raced through his mind. "What are you saying?"

She shrugged, a sly smile playing on her lips. "Who knows? Birthing a child is complicated. Sometimes a babe arrives early and sometimes late." She veered away from him and went to lean against Mr. De Lacey's large mahogany desk. "Sometimes they arrive pink and screaming, and other times blue and still. My Henry had a powerful scream. He's a strong and healthy boy."

Nate shook his head. He'd had enough of Helen and her games.

"He was—is—a strong boy like his *father.*"

Nate inhaled, trying to keep calm. She wanted to retain control over him to feed her vanity. That's what all this nonsense was about. She was no different than his brother, and he would not let her manipulate him. "Why did you come here, Lady Luxton?" he said, firmly pushing aside any notions of the child being his and deliberately avoiding using her Christian name this time.

She pushed herself away from the desk and walked toward him once again. "To let you know that I still care—I never stopped caring. And when I heard that you were running an inn—"

"I'm not running an inn," Nate said through gritted teeth. "I merely own the place. Others run it for me."

"Ah yes, that little blond orphan you seem so fond of and the red-haired maidservant, too."

"What are you talking about? Have you been spying on me?"

"Not spying. I'm merely observant, that's all." She crept closer to him—the scent of her intoxicating jasmine perfume invaded his space. He gazed into her large dark eyes and impossibly thick, long lashes and was almost lost to the memory of what had been.

"But you needn't worry. You won't have to settle for servant girls much longer. That's what I wanted to tell you last night when I saw you in the garden before that French whore came along and interrupted me." She pressed her body against his.

"Excuse me?" he said. Clanging bells went off in his brain, alerting him to danger. "You saw Madam Bouffant in the garden?"

"Yes, I saw her creeping about there. She emerged from behind a cluster of trees and gave me an enormous fright. I knew immediately she must have been spying on me. You know how that sort are—always trying to extort money from the rich. And Lord Luxton, bless him, has a temper. Nothing upsets him more than thinking his jewel has been with another man. Don't let that chair of his fool you. So I ran, afraid she'd recognized me."

So *that* had been the reason for Helen's sudden departure. He'd thought it was because he'd turned his back on her. He should have known she wouldn't give up that easily. But what had Madam Bouffant been doing—or rather—where had she been *going*?

"If you ask me, it's a blessing she fell down those stairs. Who knows what she heard or witnessed."

The glint in her eyes as she spoke made the hair stand up on the back of Nate's neck. "If I didn't know better, I'd think you pushed her down those stairs from the way you talk," he said.

"Why would I risk my neck to do such a thing? I got a fright at the time, that's true, but no one would have believed a French whore over the word of a lady."

"Stop calling her that." Nate slid to the side and out of Lady Luxton's reach. "She's dead; show some respect. Madam Bouffant was a guest here—and she was a perfectly respectable French lady."

Lady Luxton laughed, revealing her perfectly straight, pearly white teeth. "Where she came from matters not—but who she was—well, that was plain for all to see. She didn't even try to hide it. There's no place for such a woman at a high-class inn—that's what you are aiming for, isn't it?"

Nate folded his arms. He didn't remember Helen being this callous. Why hadn't he seen it before? Could it be that two years of marriage had changed her this much? Or maybe she'd hidden her true nature from him then. "Do you know what I think?" he said. She cocked her head at him, daring him to say. "I think that you recognized yourself in her. You saw a beautiful young lady who'd manipulated the heart of an older gentleman and latched onto him in the hope of securing his money." He paused. "And deep down, I think you despise that part of yourself."

Her smirk crumbled, and Nate knew he'd struck a nerve. But it only lasted for a second before she regained her smug self-assurance.

"Poor Nate. You still cannot forgive me, can you? But how wrong you are. The French whore and I were nothing alike. I am married, and my husband gave me a title. He will leave my son with a title and both of us with great wealth. I came here to offer you a piece of that, but as always, you are too proud. But no matter, I shan't have to worry about finding someone new when the time comes. No doubt, my butler will have to fend the gentlemen off with a stick." She lifted her chin and turned, striding toward the door.

"Lady Luxton," he said as she gripped the doorknob. She turned.

"Should anything happen to Lord Luxton while you are a guest here, I won't hesitate to relay this conversation to the magistrate."

"Lord Luxton is six-and-eighty years old. He cannot live forever. I doubt the magistrate will disagree with that." She smiled wickedly, blew him a kiss, and exited the room.

────────────

CHAPTER SIXTEEN

THE SERENITY OF the garden seemed surreal in light of what had taken place inside the house that morning. The trail of blood on the stairs, Madam Bouffant's limp body and battered skull—Bridget shuddered and inhaled deeply, trying to shake the image from her mind. But at the same time, she felt guilty for doing so. Here she was enjoying her lovely garden when a woman—a guest at Villa De Lacey—had died a violent death mere hours earlier. Whether or not she'd been pushed, or she had fallen, Madam Bouffant's death had been brutal, and Bridget felt she owed it to her to find out the truth about what had happened.

Bridget glanced ahead and saw Bijou near a cluster of trees, sniffing the ground intently. She smiled and was about to call him when she heard voices. She froze.

"What business do you have following me in here? Go away before someone sees us together!"

Bridget's heart drummed in her chest. The voice belonged to Lord Dodsworth, but to whom was he talking? She crept forward and concealed herself behind a massive oak tree.

Then came the voice of either Adelia or Lydia Eamont. It was impossible to tell which one. "I followed you because I have something of yours."

"What on earth are you talking about? What do you have?"

"Do you recognize this?" She must have taken the object she was referring to and shown it to Dodsworth because he gasped audibly.

"Give me that!" he said.

"No," she snapped back. "But you needn't worry. I don't intend to say anything. Not yet, anyway."

"Where did you get it? Have you been in my room? How dare you!"

"Oh no, there was no need for me to go rummaging around your room. Criminals always confess their sins—or at least, in this case, they drop them when they become so inebriated, they might as well be sleepwalking."

Bridget covered her mouth with both hands to stifle her gasp. *A confession?*

"Please." Lord Dodsworth's voice became beseeching. "You know the consequences. I could hang, for God's sake!"

Bridget bit down on her lip. *Hang? Did Dodsworth just admit that he'd murdered Madam Bouffant?*

Bijou started digging furiously at the spot where he'd been sniffing. Then he pawed at the ground and whined. Bridget put her finger to her lips and looked sternly at him, praying he would refrain from giving them away.

"I am willing to stay silent," Miss Eamont said. "But you must give me something in return."

"Anything. What do you want?"

"A promise of marriage."

Bridget inhaled sharply. One of the Miss Eamonts was trying to coerce Lord Dodsworth into marriage, but which one? Adelia thought herself practically betrothed to Nate, but mayhap she'd realized the futility of that claim and wanted to save face. Yes, that made sense, but was she desperate enough to marry a potential killer? Didn't she realize that if Lord Dodsworth had already killed one woman, he'd readily kill another? What if he attempted to strangle her right here in the garden? She would have to intervene. Bridget scanned the ground for a stick or a rock lest she need to come to the woman's rescue.

"You must be joking," Dodsworth said. "You expect me to marry you? Given what you know about me?"

"That's what I said, isn't it?" And it sounded like Miss Eamont spoke through gritted teeth. Perhaps she was losing her patience with Dodsworth.

"But I will never make you happy." Dodsworth's voice had turned pleading again. "Don't you want to find someone better suited to you?"

A short, shrill laugh emanated from Miss Eamont. "Better suited? We are the perfect match. With this confession locked away in a safe place, I wield all the power. What could be better in a marriage?"

"Love?" Dodsworth said. "Don't you want a chance at happiness?"

Miss Eamont's shrill laughter rang out again, this time louder, causing Bijou to lift his head and tilt it to the side. Once again, Bridget put a finger to her lips, instructing the pup to be silent.

"Are you not familiar with the *Wife of Bath's Tale*, Lord Dodsworth? Chaucer discovered what women most want four hundred years ago, yet men remain ignorant. Women want what every man has—sovereignty in marriage because that equates to freedom—something men take for granted. But I am offering you something better. I'm offering you a marriage that will result in freedom for both of us—each doing as we please. So, tell me, what is your objection to that? Am I so odious?"

"You are not odious. Only a bit—"

"What?"

"Nothing. I didn't mean to—"

"You did. Say it. Only a bit…?"

"Peculiar. You're a little peculiar. The way you and your sister talk in unison and—"

Miss Eamont made an unladylike snorting sound. "*You* are calling me peculiar? *You* of all people? How dare you?"

"Please. I beg you to reconsider. All I want is a chance to live my life as I choose, peacefully and without interference from anyone."

"I would like that too, but as a woman, I may not rest until I marry. If we marry, we shall both be at peace. I shall not stop you from living as you see fit, if you promise me the same."

"What about your mother? Isn't she determined to marry off your sister first?"

So, the voice belongs to Lydia Eamont, not her sister!

"My mother can go to the devil and my sister with her. I'm tired of living by her rules. And with your money, Lord Dodsworth, I won't need to seek my mama's approval. You are a rich man, are you not, my lord?"

"Then you are determined to force my hand, and there is nothing I can do to dissuade you?"

"Nothing. You have until tomorrow afternoon to decide. One way or another, an announcement will be made. Either it will result in a ring on my finger or a noose around your neck."

Bridget scooped up Bijou, whose paws and nose were black from digging and crouched behind the enormous oak with him as Lydia Eamont marched past and back to the villa. Bridget stayed hidden for a few minutes longer, breathing steadily, as she waited for Lord Dodsworth to depart the scene. He did so, walking in the opposite direction of Lydia, toward the lake.

Bijou squirmed in Bridget's arms and let out a shrill bark. She froze. Lord Dodsworth paused, turned around, and scanned the area. Bridget cradled her dog, petting him and praying he'd stay quiet.

NATE FOUND FREDERICK in the smoking room with a brandy in one hand and a cigar in the other.

"Frederick, old boy, I've been looking for you." Nate poured himself a brandy and slid into the chair next to Frederick. "It's been quite a day, hasn't it? Where have you been?"

"Off for a walk by the lake. I took poor old Lord Eamont with me. It's quite healing—the sublimity of nature and all that."

"I quite agree. It's magical. Did Lord Eamont reveal if Madam Bouffant had been in his room? I can't imagine what other reason she'd have had to be roaming around upstairs when everyone was still asleep. I hoped they'd have the sense not to meet at all while his wife was under the same roof as them, but at the very least, I'd expect Lord Eamont to make his way to her room if he were so inclined." Nate shook his head. "The entire thing is so distasteful."

Frederick shrugged. "Who knows? Eamont didn't seem to want to talk about it. The poor fellow is in shock. But I agree. It would have been foolish of them to meet under his wife's nose. It was foolish of him to twist my arm into bringing her here in the first place."

"Yes, so you said. How did he do that exactly?" Nate had learned about the debt Frederick owed Lord Eamont from Bridget, but he wanted to hear the full details from Frederick. It was time his friend was honest with him.

Frederick blew out a breath, pillowing up his cheeks. "I owed him some money—a great deal of money, actually—that I lost in a card game. Foolish of me. I don't usually lose, but I wasn't myself that night, you see. And well, I couldn't pay it."

"What?" Nate leaned forward, genuinely shocked. "You gambled money that you didn't have?" Not paying a gambling debt was an unthinkable disgrace. It could get you excommunicated from society. It was the thing which had caused Mr. De Lacey to commit his own self-murder, after all.

"I was going to pay it, of course, just not all at once. I went to Lord Eamont and asked him for a bit more time. I even offered to marry one of his daughters, but he laughed in my face. I don't know why I thought that would work. I'm merely a baron and one with no real money to speak of. But, I suppose, desperate men take desperate measures and all that."

"Good Lord, Frederick. I had no idea."

"Yes. Don't be fooled by Eamont's soft spot for his mistress. He can be ruthless when it comes to money. I thought he'd ruin me. And then you came along and saved the day with this little venture of yours." He gestured to the area surrounding them. "You see, Lady Eamont had learned from your brother's wife that you had a new estate, and she insisted they come for a family holiday. I suspect she was hoping to snag you into marrying her daughter."

Nate shook his head. "I don't see why Lord and Lady Eamont want me for Adelia's husband. Unlike you, of course, I have no title. Nor do I have money of my own. And I'm essentially a working man now. Aren't they scandalized that I turned my home into an inn?"

"I believe your brother and Lord Eamont have many dealings together—investments and such. They are staunch allies. Your brother has convinced Lord Eamont that you are simply rebelling out of boredom and that once you are married, your little operation will shut down. All you need is a good wife to show you the way. Then, Edward will bring you back into the fold, and this mad little episode in your life will be forgotten. With their families combined, Edward and Eamont can safely keep their fortunes in each other's pockets."

Nate squeezed the bridge of his nose. Would Edward ever stop interfering in his life?

"Anyway, Lady Eamont is so determined to see Adelia married to you that she insisted on coming, and it didn't hurt that all of London is abuzz about the Lake District, what with Wordsworth's *Guide to the Lakes*. The fact that you have turned your villa into an inn is being touted as ingenious by some. They call it a brilliant investment scheme."

Nate smiled. "Edward's words, no doubt." He had to give his brother credit for being a master manipulator.

"Yes. They are all sheep who bend the rules for what suits them. At any rate, I digress. Lady Eamont insisted on coming, as I said, but Lord Eamont didn't seem to like the idea of leaving his mistress behind for such an extended period, so when he found out you'd invited me to the villa, he said he'd forgive a large portion of my debt if I brought his mistress along as my guest. All I had to do was pretend that she was my mistress."

"That sounds like the actions of a man afflicted with insanity," Nate said.

"Well, I think he lost perspective. He despises his wife, you know, and he was quite besotted with Madam Bouffant. But you're right. It did something to his brain. He stopped thinking clearly. Either way, it's over now—for good."

"Do you think Madam Bouffant loved Lord Eamont in the same way?"

"Of course not!" Frederick said. "She loved his money, and she loved the power she wielded over him."

"The power?"

"She was beautiful, and he was besotted—so besotted that he became careless."

Nate thought about how they'd walked along the lake's edge in full view of anyone who cared to look, and he had to agree. "Do you think Lady Eamont might have pushed her?"

Frederick put his cigar to his lips and inhaled. After exhaling a long stream of smoke, he shrugged. "I think that's a tad far-fetched. It's more likely that she fell. The woman enjoyed her drink a little too much. She could have easily tripped."

"And was she inebriated last night?" Nate asked.

"How should I know?"

"Oh, come on Frederick. I know what's been going on with your midnight excursions. My housemaids are barely able to wake up in time to perform their duties in the morning. Madam Bouffant was still wearing her evening dress when she fell. She *was* out, doing something. Are you telling me you didn't see her last night?"

Frederick took a sip of his brandy and then placed the glass on the small table beside him. "You couldn't be more wrong. I've been quite enjoying the tranquility of this place. I couldn't understand what had happened to you at first, but I see it now. This place gets under your skin. It changes you—quiets one somehow."

Nate eyed his friend. Perhaps he was speaking the truth. After all, the Lake District had worked its magic on him, so why not Frederick? Still, knowing Frederick for as many years as he had made that scenario hard to believe.

CHAPTER SEVENTEEN

Although she'd safely escaped Dodsworth's notice, Bridget continued to linger impatiently amongst the trees for a while longer, not wanting to run into Lydia as she returned to the villa. If Lydia suspected that she'd overheard her conversation with Lord Dodsworth, the situation could become dangerous.

Bridget was already acquainted with Lydia's unpleasant nature, but she'd been surprised to witness an aggressive side to the normally mild-mannered Dodsworth. She'd never heard him speak in such a harsh tone before. Then again, Lydia had been blackmailing him at the time, so a little anger could be expected. But what was the hanging offense Lydia had accused him of? If the crime was Madam Bouffant's murder, then Jefferson had to be involved too as she already suspected. He was Dodsworth's closest friend, and it followed that Dodsworth's secret might be Jefferson's as well.

Assessing that it was finally safe to reenter the villa, Bridget put Bijou down and the terrier scampered up the path toward the servants' entrance, no doubt hungry for a bowl of Cook's scraps. Bridget followed, so deep in thought that she didn't even notice Lydia Eamont walking toward her. "Oh, Miss De Lacey there you are. May I have a word?"

Bridget's heart began to pound. What was all this about? Had Lydia spotted her in the garden after all?

But there was no malice in Lydia's expression. She looked flushed with happiness—just like a new bride.

"I want to throw a little party—nothing too grand—only a fancy luncheon or tea." Lydia practically sang her words, and for a moment Bridget was so taken aback by her change in demeanor that she could not answer.

"Miss De Lacey?" Lydia peered at Bridget. "Did you hear what I said?"

"*Uhm.* How…how about tea in the garden?" Bridget stammered. That was exactly what she'd been planning to keep both the guests and the servants occupied while she searched the rooms. "What's the occasion?" she asked, feigning innocence.

Lydia's thin lips curved into a sly smile. "I can't quite say, not yet. It's a celebration of sorts."

"How wonderful!" Bridget clapped her hands to feign enthusiasm. "I do love celebrations."

"Me too! And it will be our secret until tomorrow. I don't want Mama interfering with my plans.

"Very well," Bridget said. "But I shall need to tell Cook in advance so she can prepare, but you're not to worry, she's trustworthy."

"Good, now let's discuss what to serve, shall we?"

Bridget nodded, still stunned by Lydia's change in demeanor—she was rather cheerful and, dare she think it, polite!

🔍

THE NEXT DAY, Nate frowned at the round tables and chairs that had been moved into the garden and arranged in clusters next to each other. Each table was covered with a white linen cloth and housed a bouquet at its center. "Doesn't that seem a bit crass after a woman just died on our floor?"

"I have no choice." Bridget eyed Bijou as he darted between the tables, chasing a squirrel. "Lydia Eamont insisted."

"Lydia Eamont insisted you throw a tea party in the garden?" Nate repeated, stressing Lydia's name as though he couldn't believe what he'd heard.

"Yes, and I think it's a good idea. It has certainly kept everyone busy enough. The servants have been set to work and are too busy to gossip about what happened yesterday. It has also given the guests something else to focus on. Everyone is excited. They are getting dressed for the occasion as we speak."

Nate smoothed his blue waistcoat with both hands. "Will I need to put on a cravat?"

"I should think so," Bridget said.

He massaged his forehead. "Help me understand. Since when does Lydia Eamont order tea parties on demand? Wouldn't Lady Eamont be the one to request such an event? What is it for? It must be costing us a fortune." Nate dropped his hands by his sides and watched as the housemaids arranged white, gold-rimmed plates and silverware on the tables.

"It's not cheap. That's true, but as I said, I think it is good for morale. I've put all the servants to work. Even the guests' staff are helping. As to what it's for, you shall have to wait and see."

She glanced at Nate. He still looked puzzled, but she wasn't about to tell him what she'd overheard in the garden. This tea party was her one chance to keep everyone outside while she slipped indoors to check the rooms, and until Nate started being honest with her, she knew she could not trust him again.

BRIDGET CHOSE A black empire dress, complete with a black sash, and a black, veiled hat for the tea. After dressing, she took Bijou under her arm and went to cajole her aunt into coming downstairs.

"Aunt Marianne, do say you will come to the tea. It's such a lovely day, and we all need some cheering up."

"I don't quite appreciate my status as a dependent on poor Mr. Squires being the topic of conversation at every meal. That's why I prefer to eat in my room," Aunt Marianne said stiffly.

"What if I can guarantee that the guests will be so preoccupied with other news that they won't have time to think about us or our status in this house?"

"Do you mean the death? I'm not quite up for hearing about that woman and her creeping about upstairs either. I'm sorry she fell, but when I think about what she was doing prowling around at that hour…" Aunt Marianne's expression soured, and she declined to finish her statement.

"Not that either, Aunt. Everyone's attention will be turned to something else entirely. They will quite forget about us and poor Madam Bouffant, I promise."

Aunt Marianne frowned. "Why, what do you know? Tell me?"

"It's not my news to tell. If you want to know, you will have to come downstairs." She held out her arm for her aunt to take. "Cook has made the most delicious little jam tarts, baked apples, almond biscuits, and your favorite plum cake."

"Oh, very well." Aunt Marianne pursed her lips but accepted Bridget's arm.

🔍

THE TABLES LOOKED exquisite, and Bridget felt a rush of pride at seeing the pleased look on her guests' faces. Silver tea trays, flowers, fresh fruit, and an array of cakes, biscuits, and puddings filled the length of the table. And it wasn't long before the guests started to indulge in the food as they gazed at the magnificent Lake Windermere. Everyone seemed mesmerized by the blue sky, the stunning mountains, and the crystal-clear lake as they sipped their tea and ate plum cake, lemon biscuits, and trifle. Even little Bijou partook in the feast, lapping milk from a bowl Bridget had placed under the table and enjoying the crumbs and scraps she fed him. The setting was near-perfect.

Until Lydia Eamont, wearing a pastel yellow, empire-waisted gown with a white sash, picked up her silver teaspoon and clanged it against her teacup. Her brown eyes sparkled as she looked proudly around the table, ready to make her big announcement.

Bridget held her breath. Was she going to do it?

"Mama, Papa—everyone—I—we—Lord Dodsworth and I have an announcement to make." She turned to Dodsworth, her face radiant. He went as pale as a white dove and looked as though he might faint.

"What?" he whispered. "Now? You cannot be serious."

"Oh, don't be silly, dear, now is as good a time as any."

"Lydia," Lady Eamont's sharp voice cut across the table, "what is going on?"

Lydia cleared her throat. "Mama, Papa, Lord Dodsworth has asked me to be his wife."

Bridget expected the guests to erupt in surprise. Instead, a deathly silence followed her announcement, but that only lasted for mere seconds.

"Good Lord!" Jefferson said. "What on earth is she talking about? Has she gone completely mad?" He looked at Dodsworth.

"I'm not mad," Lydia said. "Dodsworth asked me to marry him yesterday afternoon when we were alone in the garden." She emphasized the word *alone* and then glared at Dodsworth. "Tell them."

Dodsworth swallowed and his face grew even paler, as though all the blood had been drained from him. "It's true," he said, his voice raspy as though it had been difficult to get the words out. "Lydia and I are to be..." he swallowed, and then choked out, "married."

"Mama!" Adelia Eamont rose from the table and threw down

her napkin. "What is the meaning of this? Why should you keep this a secret from me? You said I would be the one to marry."

To Bridget's surprise, Lady Eamont only blinked and shook her head. Apparently, she was too stunned to speak.

"Mama!" Adelia stamped her foot.

"Heavens, Adelia!" Lydia exclaimed. "Doddy and I are in love!"

"Doddy!" Jefferson exploded at Dodsworth. "She calls you *Doddy*? Since when? When did all this happen? In the last hour?"

Lord Dodsworth hung his head and made no answer.

"Papa!" Adelia shrieked. "What do you have to say about this?"

Lord Eamont blinked as though he'd suddenly become conscious. "I say, Dodsworth, a gentleman should ask the lady's father before proposing," he said, but there was no anger in his voice. It was merely an empty statement.

But Dodsworth grabbed it like a rope thrown in the water to save a drowning man. "You are quite right, my lord. That was rude of me. I quite understand. It's all my fault. We'll call it off. I'm sorry, Lydia, but your father is right."

Lydia looked wildly from Dodsworth to her Papa. She opened her mouth, presumably to shriek her objection when her father said, "No, no, Dodsworth. There'll be none of that. Lydia has already said that the two of you were alone in the garden. She announced it to everyone, so that is it then. She will be Lady Dodsworth."

"Well, this calls for a toast!" Lady Eamont stood and raised her teacup with a forced smile. "My daughter is getting married!" she said, her face flushed and her eyes a little wild so that Bridget couldn't quite make out whether she was pleased or not. But she thought the woman probably wasn't as pleased as a mama desperate to see her daughters married ought to be.

"I think this calls for a real toast, with champagne." Bridget stood up. "I'll go and see to it." She stooped to pick up Bijou and then took the opportunity to slip back indoors before anyone could stop her.

ρ

NATE WAS UTTERLY bewildered. He had known Dodsworth for years. The man was a sworn bachelor. And now, suddenly, to become betrothed to Lydia Eamont, of all people! It was unbelievable. Something was afoot. The poor chap looked quite miserable. And clearly, Jefferson had been kept in the dark because he seemed downright shocked—and not in a good way.

Other than congratulating the couple, Nate did not have a hope of speaking to Dodsworth alone as Lydia had latched onto his arm and looked as if she'd never let go.

"I say, that was a surprise, wasn't it?" Frederick appeared next to Nate. "I had no idea Dodsworth was interested in Lydia Eamont."

"It makes no sense. He's obviously not happy, so what is going on? He can't have done it for the money. At least, and as far as I know, he doesn't have money problems." Nate folded his arms. "I wonder what happened. She must have tricked him into being alone with her—caught him off his guard."

"You don't say." Frederick slipped his hands in his pockets and eyed their mutual friend.

"Do you suppose it could have been the mushrooms that did it?" Nate asked, sensing an opportunity to get some information from Frederick. "The ones that give you Kubla Khan visions? Dodsworth talked about searching for them that first night he was here. I have to say, I was quite surprised—it seemed rather out of character for him. He's never been a wild man."

"They don't make you wild," Frederick said. "They have more of a calming effect."

"So, you've been indulging too?"

"On occasion. They put you in a sort of poetic dreamland. Isn't that the spirit of the lakes?"

"I suppose it is." Nate smiled. He couldn't argue with that.

"Who knows what form Lydia took in poor Doddy's eyes

when he was in his hallucinatory state? She could have been Venus or Helen of Troy herself—whomever he saw, he liked her well enough to propose."

"Good Lord." Nate shuddered. "Well, better Dodsworth than me. I can promise you that I won't be caught alone with Adelia Eamont. There'll be no chance of her tricking me into compromising her."

"*Hmm.*" Frederick ran a hand over the cleft in his chin. "I suppose that's the way to do it—don't ask—just announce in public how you compromised a rich viscount's daughter and are now marrying her. Then all your money problems will be over."

"Don't even think it. If you try that, Lord Eamont will likely challenge you to a duel. Then you'd be up for murder."

"Yes, I do believe you're right. He won't be so friendly to me now that his mistress is dead. I am no longer useful, so I presume it won't be long before he starts demanding repayment of my remaining debt."

"I wish I could help you, but all of my money is tied up in this place. The garden was in perfect shape, but the rest of the house wasn't. I had to spend quite a bit to get it ready, and the upkeep certainly isn't cheap."

"Not to worry. I'll think of something."

Nate followed Frederick's gaze, which, he saw, landed on Helen. She strolled next to her husband and his manservant, who pushed his chair. Helen must have felt Frederick's gaze on her because she turned to him and smiled.

"You're not thinking of—" Nate began.

"Why not? She has plenty of money, and that husband of hers can't be satisfying her. We both have something the other wants."

"She has a son," Nate said, but he was unsure why. It was no business of his what Helen did with her life. She'd offered herself to him, and he'd refused. He no longer loved her; still, the thought of Frederick—was this interest new, or had it existed before—when he and Helen were betrothed? Nate glanced at

Frederick. *How well did he truly know his friend?*

"Don't look at me like that! Every woman you come in contact with can't be off limits to your friends, Squires," Frederick said as if he sensed Nate's thoughts.

"She wasn't just any woman. We were betrothed."

"And now you're not."

"Yes, you have a point." Nate forced nonchalance, even though he didn't feel quite that calm. "Do as you wish, with one caveat."

"And what is that?" Frederick raised his eyebrows in question.

"You'd best hope Lord Luxton remains healthy. One accidental death might be overlooked by the local magistrate, but two certainly will not."

"Good Lord, Squires! How long have you known me? I'm a philanderer, not a murderer."

Nate turned to look at Helen as she walked beside her husband, confined to his chair, and wheeled by his valet. *It's not you that I'm concerned about.*

CHAPTER EIGHTEEN

WHILE THE GUESTS celebrated outside with champagne, the servants and Bijou were permitted to celebrate downstairs with tea and cake. With everyone occupied, Bridget took the opportunity to sneak upstairs and search the rooms. She tried Lydia's chamber first, hoping to find Dodsworth's "confession," but her door was locked. Bridget frowned. Why hadn't she anticipated that? She did not have time to fetch the master keys, so she walked down the hallway to Lady Eamont's room and was relieved to find it open.

She began by looking in the most obvious places—the jewelry box, the drawers, and under the mattress. Not wanting to make a mess but also needing to be quick, Bridget paused, looking around the room and trying to decipher where Lady Eamont could have hidden the brooch. But the room was too clean and neatly organized. She couldn't hope to find it without rummaging through all of Lady Eamont's perfectly wrapped dresses, shoes, hats, bonnets, and gloves.

Feeling deflated, Bridget sank onto a red-velvet-upholstered chair and scanned the room, thinking. She'd searched every inch of Madam Bouffant's room, and the brooch had not been there. She was certain Lady Eamont had it in her possession.

"What are you doing in here?"

Bridget jerked her head up, startled that she was not alone. Adelia stood in the doorway, her eyes red rimmed and her cheeks tear stained. Yet she didn't look sad. She looked furious.

Bridget swallowed. Her mind worked to come up with an excuse for being in the viscountess's room. "I—it's Bijou, my dog. I was looking for him. He sometimes likes to hide in this room," she lied.

"Why? What's so special about this room?" Adelia stepped inside and glanced around.

"Nothing. I mean, I don't know. It's always been one of Bijou's favorite places in the house."

Adelia narrowed her eyes. "You're lying. You left your mutt downstairs with that mad housekeeper. The one who stalks around in all black and speaks barely above a whisper, like some sort of demented specter."

"Her name is Eliza. She's my lady's maid," Bridget said, irritated. "And she wears black because she's in mourning for her master." She stood up, eager to escape Adelia's company. "Now if you'll excuse me, I need to continue my search." Bridget made for the door.

"Do you think me ugly, Miss De Lacey?"

Bridget stopped, startled by the turn in conversation. "I—no, of course not. Why would you ask such a thing?"

"Mama says my eyes are too small. She calls them elephant eyes."

"Pardon?" Bridget said. "Did you say 'elephant eyes'?"

"Yes, haven't you ever seen an elephant?"

"Only in paintings."

"Well, I have seen one up close. There's one in a cage at the Tower of London. It's part of the royal menagerie. The poor thing was far too big to be stuck in a cage. I was shocked by its size. But for such a large animal, they have very small eyes."

"I didn't know that," Bridget said.

"You really should get to London to see them if you can. But I suppose now that you're a pauper it will be out of the question."

Bridget pressed her lips together, stemming her retort. Papa had told her about the king's menagerie, and she hadn't liked the sound of it at all. In her opinion, animals did not belong in cages.

The thought of all those people gawking at the poor beasts made her sad.

"'Elephant eyes and a hawk's nose,' that's what Mama always says."

"There is nothing wrong with your features," Bridget said, trying to soothe Adelia who was becoming increasingly agitated. "I am certain you will make a fine match one day."

Adelia turned back to the mirror and addressed her reflection. "I was supposed to marry Mr. Squires, but I see the way he looks at you." She lifted her eyes to meet Bridget's in the mirror, sending a chill down Bridget's spine.

"I'm sure I don't know what you mean," Bridget said.

"Of course, you do. But it doesn't matter anymore, does it? Lydia has secured herself a husband, and Mama will only let one of us marry. It was supposed to be me. I'm the eldest. She promised."

"What do you mean she will only let one of you marry?"

"If she kept us both for herself, it would look very poorly for her. She'd have failed in society's eyes if she raised two spinsters. But if one makes a good match and the other becomes sickly— too sickly to marry—then no one will criticize her. Pity her, yes, but not criticize. She likes to be in control, you see. And who will she control once her daughters are married? Not Papa. He is out of her reach."

Bridget walked slowly back to her chair and sat down. "Adelia," she said gently, "what do you mean by that?"

Adelia turned abruptly and narrowed her eyes at Bridget. "It's Miss Eamont to you."

"Yes, indeed." Bridget stood. She'd had enough of Adelia's games. "Well, as I said, it's time for me to go and find my dog."

"There's no need for that." Adelia strode toward Bridget. "I think I know what you're really looking for." She swooped down and reached into the back crevice of the chair Bridget had been sitting on. Then, to Bridget's surprise, she pulled out a red-silk pouch.

"What is that?" Bridget eyed the pouch that Adelia dangled before her.

"Look inside and see," Adelia said.

Bridget reached for the pouch and half expected Adelia to pull it back, but she allowed Bridget to snatch hold of it take and it from her. Even before she opened it, Bridget knew what was inside. She could feel the floral shape and weight of the brooch. She pulled open the strings and peeked inside. Sure enough, she'd been correct.

"How did you know it was there?"

"Because as soon as I saw that wretched woman lying at the foot of the stairs, I knew my mother wouldn't let her take that brooch to her grave. So, I asked her about it, and she told me she took it from the whore's room after her accident."

I knew as much!

"Mama said that she had every right to take it. The brooch belongs to her. It's part of a set, and Madam Bouffant had stolen it from her." Adelia snarled rather than spoke her words, and Bridget wondered at whom she was expressing her anger. Was it her mother, her father, or his mistress? Whom did she hate the most?

"So, your mother said she went to Madam Bouffant's room after she fell down the stairs and found the brooch," Bridget reiterated, wanting to be clear about what Adelia was saying.

"That's what she said, but who knows. She may have taken it before."

"Before what?"

Adelia shrugged.

"Adelia," Bridget spoke as gently as she could, "do you think your mama could have—well—pushed Madam Bouffant down the stairs in a fit of anger?" She braced herself for an outburst of scorn and anger from Adelia, but to her surprise, the young woman threw back her head and laughed.

"Do I think she did it? I don't know. Do I think she's capable of doing it? Yes."

"Adelia." As if she were trying to calm an agitated cat, Bridget wanted to proceed carefully. "Why do you think your mama is capable of murder?"

"Murder? Did I say murder?" She tossed her head. "I didn't."

"But, you said you think her capable of pushing Madam Bouffant down the stairs."

The young woman shrugged. "She's capable of great cruelty." *But what did that mean?* "In what way?"

"In the way of feeding her children minute amounts of poison that would make them appear sickly or making them trip and fall in a way that twists an ankle."

"Or by pushing them down a flight of stairs?"

"Oh, yes. That is one of her favorite ways."

"You're saying…" Bridget took a deep breath before proceeding, afraid she already knew the answer but still needing to confirm the truth. "Did she do that to you or Lydia?"

"Countless times."

"But *why?*" It was inconceivable.

"Control. She enjoys having complete control over us. She can be evil sometimes—nay, she *is* evil."

Bridget curled her fist around the small silk sack and felt the weight of the brooch in her hand. Was Adelia telling the truth? Or was she covering up her own crime by pointing a finger at her mama? There was no way to know for sure, Bridget thought as she glanced at the mirror. Adelia stared straight ahead, and then, her brown eyes met Bridget's in the glass—and she saw only malice in them.

As Nate stepped into the villa, he saw Bridget descending the stairs. She had a perturbed look, and Nate could see she was deep in thought.

"You disappeared for a good while," he said, meeting her at

the foot of the stairs.

"Oh." She looked up as if startled to see him. "Yes, I"—she glanced around—"I'd rather not talk about it in here. I don't know who to trust anymore."

Although she was referring to the guests, Nate felt the sting of her comment. He'd sensed her hesitancy to trust him of late, and he decided it was time to find out why. "What do you say we go out on horseback? It's a fine day, and too many guests are out in the garden and by the lake for us to have a private talk down there."

Much to his relief, Bridget nodded her agreement and twenty minutes later, they were cantering up to Orrest Head, the fresh wind blowing in their faces, and the magnificent view of the crystal lake, the mountains, and the green fells enveloping them from all sides.

Both sat on their horses and gazed down at the lake. The view from this height was even more breathtaking than from Villa De Lacey. "It's truly remarkable here," Nate said.

"It was one of Papa's favorite places. We'd ride up here together at least once a week."

They fell silent, enjoying the view, while their horses munched on the lush grass. Finally, Nate said, "So what do you make of Dodsworth's betrothal to Lydia? Were you as shocked as everyone else?"

Bridget looked at him, and he knew she was assessing him—deciding whether she wanted to confide in him. Then she shrugged. "Perhaps he loves her. He may be your friend, but you may not know everything about him. People seem to have many secrets."

Nate scoffed. "I know Dodsworth isn't in love with Lydia Eamont."

Bridget continued to watch him.

"What is it? I feel as though you wish to ask me something."

"I was waiting for you to confess, but it doesn't seem likely."

"Confess? You think I'm guilty of something?"

"I think you're hiding something, either to protect someone else or yourself."

Nate sighed. Had she somehow found out about the maid-servants cavorting with Frederick? He'd hoped to resolve that problem on his own without her finding out about it. "What is it you think I've done?"

Bridget pursed her lips and stared out at the lake. Then she turned to him, seemingly having decided to speak. "Very well. Why did you neglect to tell me that you were out in the garden with Madam Bouffant the night she died?"

Nate gave a short laugh. "Is that what your aunt told you?"

"Yes."

"Well, she's mistaken. I was in the garden that night and, as it happens, so was Madam Bouffant, but she wasn't *with* me." He shifted in his saddle. "I was with Lady Luxton—that is, not *with* her exactly, but…she…well. It's of no matter. But quite frankly I don't know how your aunt could identify anyone in such darkness."

"Didn't you have a lantern?"

"Yes, but it doesn't give off much light."

"Nonetheless, you were in the garden, so she was correct." Bridget lifted her chin. "And if we are to conduct an investigation together then we cannot be keeping secrets from one another."

Nate turned from Bridget and inhaled, drinking in the breath-taking view in front of him as he steeled himself to discuss the ugly truth of his past. "Very well, if you must know, before marrying Lord Luxton, Lady Luxton—or Miss Helen Mortley—as was her name then—was betrothed to me." Nate pressed his lips together before continuing. "She wanted—"

"No, stop!" Bridget held up her gloved hand. "Please don't continue. It's none of my business." She lowered her gaze. "I'm sorry," she said, pink flushing her cheeks. "I thought you were hiding something from me—but I didn't realize it was so personal."

"You didn't trust me," he said.

"I'm sorry." Bridget dropped her gaze. "I see now that I may have jumped to conclusions."

"May have?"

"Did." She glanced at him, her lovely blue eyes wide and sincere. "Do you accept my apology?"

Nate's heart swelled. He'd missed the bond they'd formed over the past few months. "Of course, I do," he said.

"But you say, Madam Bouffant was in the garden?" Bridget asked.

"Yes," Nate said and related what Helen had told him about seeing the actress. "So, your aunt may have seen both Madam Bouffant and me, but we weren't there together for some kind of tryst. I didn't even know she was there."

"Are you saying that Lady Luxton had motivation to push Madam Bouffant down the stairs?"

Nate sighed, deciding to share everything. "I don't believe so. It's more likely that she was—she is—just toying with me. She likes to play games. Madam Bouffant may have startled her, so she ran away, but I don't believe she felt threatened by her. If I know Helen, Lord Luxton isn't the one wielding the power in that marriage."

Bridget nodded. Then she inhaled deeply, and then said, "I have something to confess too."

Nate cocked his head. "I'm listening."

"When you asked me about the tea party this afternoon—whether I knew why Lydia had requested one—I lied. I *did* know."

Nate blinked. She'd lied to his face, and without so much as flinching. Now, she appeared contrite, proving she wasn't able to lie without some sort of attack of conscience. Unlike Helen, he decided, Bridget was a woman with a pure heart as well as a bright mind.

She continued, unaware of his thoughts. "At the time, I wasn't sure if I could trust you because I thought you were keeping secrets from me."

That made even more sense and made her even more upright in his mind. "Never mind that," Nate said, ready to completely tear away the webs of secrecy between them. "I already know about the mushrooms. It's no secret."

"The mushrooms?" Bridget frowned.

"Yes, the ones that give you Kubla Khan type hallucinations. I know Dodsworth has been indulging. Frederick fears that the fungi may have gotten Dodsworth into trouble. He may have found himself in a compromising position with Miss Eamont while in this hallucinatory state, and now he is forced to marry her."

"I had no idea," Bridget said. "But I'm afraid your friend Dodsworth might be involved in something more sinister than eating a few wild mushrooms."

"What do you mean?" A niggling worry tugged at Nate's gut.

"I overheard a conversation between Lydia and Dodsworth in the woodsy part of the garden. I was out with Bijou when I heard their voices. She's holding something over him—a secret. I don't know what Dodsworth is guilty of, but Lydia called it a hanging offense."

Nate's heart stilled. "A hanging offense? Are you certain you heard correctly?"

"Yes, and Lydia has some sort of proof—something that truly scared Dodsworth. That's why I slipped away during tea. I wanted to search Lydia's room."

"And did you find the evidence?" A lump of fear had formed in Nate's throat that he worked to swallow away.

Bridget shook her head. "Lydia's chamber was locked, but I *did* find something in Lady Eamont's room." She took a silk sack from her pocket and handed it to Nate.

He opened it and peeked inside. Was it possible? "Lady Eamont had Madam Bouffant's brooch?"

"It was in her chamber, yes, but that's not everything. It was Adelia Eamont who showed me where her mother had hidden the brooch. And she divulged a lot of information, too, about her mama. Suffice it to say that both sisters despise Lady Eamont. She's been cruel and controlling of them all their lives." Bridget then related all that Adelia Eamont had told her.

"Good Lord!" Nate said. "I always thought of the Eamont twins as strange but harmless. Do you suppose one of the sisters—or both—pushed their father's mistress down the stairs in order to frame their mother for the murder and end her controlling ways?"

"No. Lady Eamont taught her daughters to compete with one another, not work together. Lydia could have done it, but I doubt Adelia did. Until today, Lady Eamont was Adelia's biggest advocate. As her eldest daughter, she was actively trying to see Adelia married to you. But that all changed when Lydia outwitted them."

"So perhaps Adelia pushed Madam Bouffant to protect her mother, and has now decided to try and use the murder against her?"

"That's possible. She never came out and accused her mother, but that would make things a little too obvious. Much better if she accuses her mother of cruelty and stealing and allows people to assume the worst."

"I don't know," Nate said. "It seems a little far-fetched."

"I would have thought so too, but if you'd witnessed what I did today, you'd see that Adelia's behavior pointed toward madness."

"That, at least, puts Dodsworth in the clear."

"Not exactly," Bridget shifted in the saddle. "We have no proof Adelia did anything wrong. She may have found the brooch in her mother's room as she claimed."

"In which case, suspicion would have to fall on Lady Eamont, not Dodsworth," Nate said.

"You're forgetting that Lydia has proof that Dodsworth committed a hanging offense. And when she accused him, he did not deny it."

Nate ran a hand across his jaw. He refused to believe Dodsworth was guilty of murder—or any heinous offense, for that matter. Something else was afoot, and he'd have to tread carefully so as not to expose or endanger his friend while trying to uncover the truth.

CHAPTER NINETEEN

"DO SIT DOWN, Lord and Lady Eamont." Nate invited the viscount and viscountess to sit on one of the buttoned-leather chairs in what had been Mr. De Lacey's study. He'd been reluctant to take it over, not having the heart to ask Bridget to pack away her father's things. He sensed the study meant a lot to her. It was no doubt filled with precious memories.

"What can I get you to drink? Brandy for you, my lord, and a port for her ladyship?" Nate asked.

"Yes," they both answered simultaneously.

Nate poured two brandies and a glass of port, served his guests, and then sat behind his desk.

Lord Eamont took a sip of his brandy. "I imagine you've asked us here because you want to tell us that you've come to your senses and are now ready to commit to our daughter, Adelia."

"It's too late for that," Lady Eamont trilled. "We already have one wedding to plan. I can't possibly think about *two* weddings."

"What are you talking about?" Lord Eamont's thick eyebrows came together in a frown. "They can have a double wedding. That way, I need only pay for one. Lord knows Westerly will be expecting a substantial dowry."

Nate's chest burned at the reference to his brother's demand for a dowry. How dare Edward humiliate him thus?

"Don't they all." Lady Eamont sniffed her port and then placed her glass on the desk.

Nate frowned, wondering if there was something wrong with the drink.

"Well, Squires, I have discussed the matter of a rather large dowry with your brother, but—"

"I'm sorry to disappoint you, my lord, but I have not brought you here to ask for your daughter's hand. My position on marriage hasn't changed. As I told my brother, I plan on remaining a bachelor indefinitely."

"You told Lord Westerly *what?*" Lord Eamont's face reddened.

"He wants to remain a bachelor," Lady Eamont repeated. "That's what I heard him say."

"That's not what Lord Westerly told me." Eamont scowled at Nate. "You have a duty to follow your brother's orders. No wonder your father put him in charge of your well-being."

Nate's jaw tightened. Who was Lord Eamont to judge him? He'd just been cavorting openly with his mistress in front of his family. All sympathy he'd had for the man after Madam Bouffant's death flew out the window. "Insulting me won't change my mind," Nate said.

"Now, look here, sir"—Lord Eamont wagged a finger at Nate—"Lord Westerly and I have an agreement, and you need to adhere to it."

"That's between you and Lord Westerly, not me." Nate extracted the red-silk pouch from his drawer, opened it, and tipped Madam Bouffant's brooch onto the table.

Lord and Lady Eamont fell instantly silent. For a moment, at least. Until Lord Eamont appeared to find his voice once more.

"Where did you get that?" Lord Eamont spluttered as his ears turned beet red.

"Your daughter, Miss Adelia, gave it to Miss De Lacey."

Lady Eamont remained quiet and shifted in her chair.

Her husband didn't appear to notice. "Adelia? Why would she do that? Where did she get it?" he asked weakly.

"She claims that Lady Eamont stole it from Madam Bouffant's chamber after she died. Adelia found it hidden under a chair cushion in her mother's room. And she took it and gave it to Miss De Lacey. I'm not sure why."

"Stole it?" Lady Eamont exploded then, ignoring everything Nate had said about her daughter. "I have no need to steal what is mine, sir!"

Meanwhile, Lord Eamont had gone deathly pale and as silent as he had been in the hours after Madam Bouffant's demise.

"Yours?" Nate placed the brooch back in its silk bag.

"Mine." Lady Eamont's jaw was so tightly Nate wondered how she could speak at all. "Now give it to me." She stretched out her open palm.

Nate hesitated.

"My husband paid for it, so it belongs to me. Now hand it over!"

Nate glanced at Lord Eamont, who sat silently, tightly clutching his brandy.

"Mr. Squires! Do you see this ring?" She turned her hand over and flashed the matching ring she wore over her glove. "It's part of a set, purchased for me by my husband. Now, give me that brooch." She held out her other hand, palm up.

Her husband shifted beside her. "It's true," Lord Eamont said in a low voice. "I purchased that brooch for my wife as part of a set."

Nate had expected such a reaction from Lord Eamont, but he wasn't ready to give up yet. "I'm sorry, my lord. It's just that we all saw Madam Bouffant wearing this brooch on more than one occasion."

"What you saw must have been a cheap copy she picked up in the theater," Lady Eamont snapped. "Actresses always have costume jewelry."

"Well, where do you suppose that brooch is now?"

"How should I know? Perhaps one of your servants stole it. We both know my ring was stolen and then replanted in my room, so you could cover for your servants."

Nate pursed his lips. He couldn't argue with that accusation. Or rather, he decided, he wouldn't.

"Honestly," Lady Eamont continued, "I think Lord Eamont should have a word with your brother about what's been going on in this establishment of yours. If people hear that they are treated like common criminals at your inn and accused of all sorts, then I am certain no one will deign to come here."

Lord Eamont hung his head in apparent resignation.

"I'm waiting!" Lady Eamont said, her hand still outstretched to receive the brooch. She wiggled her fingers.

Nate nodded reluctantly and dropped the silk pouch in Lady Eamont's palm. He had his answer. She'd stolen the brooch just as Adelia had claimed, but that didn't prove she'd pushed Madam Bouffant down the stairs, and even if she had done so, what could he or anyone else do about it? Madam Bouffant was a courtesan.

Lady Eamont was a viscountess.

The magistrate had ruled Madam Bouffant's death an accident. That was the end of it.

Bridget would have to drop her desire to find out the truth lest she wanted to see Villa De Lacey destroyed. One word from Lord Eamont and his brother would slash his allowance. And with Villa De Lacey's reputation in ruins, he wouldn't be able to keep the place afloat. He'd be stuck, living in a crumbling ruin for the next seven years.

Nate sighed. He doubted Bridget would understand. She was adamant that Madam Bouffant had been murdered and was determined to find the killer, something he couldn't help but wonder had to do with her need for justice for her father. The man had died by his own hand, but who was really to blame? Edward, that's who.

In the end, the aristocracy always won, and it would be no different this time.

Lady Eamont extracted the brooch from the pouch and affixed it to her dress, pricking her finger in the process. Blood seeped through the fingertip of her white glove, but she continued to secure the brooch.

"There," she said, "Now it's where it should be." She stood up. "I thank you for bringing it back to me, Mr. Squires."

"Yes, thank you, Squires." Lord Eamont stood as well, albeit more slowly. "Do give some more thought to what we discussed. Your brother and I are quite determined to see our families joined."

Nate stood and gave his departing guests a slight bow, hardly registering anything but the blood stain on Lady Eamont's white glove.

🔍

BRIDGET SLID INTO her seat next to Nate at the dining room table and welcomed the bowl of white soup that the footman set before her. It had been a trying day. She'd hardly eaten a bite at Lydia's tea celebration because she'd had to slip out early and search the chambers. And then her encounter with Adelia Eamont had been harrowing. She hadn't had a chance to speak with Nate again after giving him the brooch during their ride, but what would Lady Eamont do once he gave it to the magistrate? She glanced across the table at the aforesaid lady and almost dropped her spoonful of soup.

Lady Eamont was wearing the brooch, proudly displayed on her chest.

How did she get it? Had Nate given it to her? Or had she somehow managed to steal it again?

But more importantly, why was she wearing it? Was it as some sort of badge of honor? Did she intend to advertise to everyone that she'd murdered Madam Bouffant?

She nudged Nate's arm under the table, and when he turned to look at her, she tried to indicate with her eyes that he should look at Lady Eamont. He must have gotten the message because he turned and looked, but his reaction was not what Bridget expected. Instead of appearing surprised, shocked, and outraged, he simply returned to eating his soup.

Bridget elbowed him a second time, and when he turned, she mouthed the word, "How?"

Nate picked up his glass of port and brought it to his mouth. "Later," he mouthed back, his word hidden behind his glass, before taking a sip of his drink and then turning to say something to Frederick.

She shifted her gaze to Miss Adelia. The young lady seemed subdued—all trace of her earlier outburst and raw display of emotions gone—as if someone had given her a bout of laudanum to mute her. She was focused on her soup as if she had not even noticed the incriminating piece of jewelry on her mother's chest.

Meanwhile, her sister Lydia sat beside her, chatting amiably about her upcoming wedding to all who cared to listen and Dodsworth, now seated beside his intended, looked forlorn. Next to him, Mr. and Mrs. Harley appeared equally miserable though in truth, Bridget had yet to see them smile since they'd arrived.

Apparently she wasn't the only person observing the guests at the table, because suddenly Lady Darby said, "I say, isn't that the dead woman's brooch?"

Her words instantly shut off Lydia's incessant chatter.

Once again, Bridget saved herself from dropping her spoon. She lowered it gently back into the bowl as she gaped at Lady Eamont, wondering what the woman's response would be now that she was trapped.

"What, this?" Lady Eamont pointed to the brooch and spoke in a high tone as if to emphasize her surprise at being asked such a question. "Heavens, no! This brooch is part of a set, see?" She stuck out her hand to show the matching ring. "The one that the dead woman had was similar, as I remember, but not the same. Mine is one of a kind."

"Very similar, I think." Lady Darby dabbed her mouth with her napkin. "Perhaps hers was a counterfeit. It did look rather out of place with the rest of her outfit, as I remember."

"Oh, yes, I wager it was most definitely a cheap copy." Lady Eamont went back to taking tiny sips of her soup.

Bridget glanced at Nate again, but it seemed he was taking great pains to focus on his own bowl and not make eye contact with her. What on earth was going on?

ρ

"THE INVESTIGATION MUST end, I'm afraid. We are going to have to accept that Madam Bouffant's death was a tragic accident," Nate said when they finally convened in the study once the after-dinner activities were over and most of the guests had retired to bed. Even so, they stood by the bookshelves, pretending to peruse the books as they conversed, lest anyone should stray into the library.

"I disagree. I think that is yet to be proven," Bridget shot back. "Isn't that what we agreed?"

"But we cannot prove anything. It's all speculation." Nate glanced down at the open book in his hand as though they were discussing its contents. "Besides, there's no point. The magistrate is satisfied that Madam Bouffant fell down the stairs, and Frederick believes she may have been inebriated, so if we keep this up, it will only end up costing us dearly."

"Magistrate Hunt lost interest in the whole affair the moment he heard Madam Bouffant was a courtesan. Is that why you are giving up too?"

Nate sighed. "Of course not. But it does make things more difficult, especially when you think her killer is a peer, and that is conjecture at best."

"What about justice? Isn't it our duty to find out for certain?" Bridget couldn't believe how callous Nate was being. A person had died, and no one seemed to care. Even Lord Eamont had recovered from his grief rather quickly.

Well, they might have all dismissed Madam Bouffant's tragic

end, but she wasn't going to. Bridget gave Nate a hard stare. "She was a guest at Villa De Lacey, and we owe it to her to find out the truth."

"Bridget, I'm going to say something you may not like to hear, but I think it important you hear it all the same." He snapped the book shut in his hand.

Bridget stiffened. "Go on then."

He put the book back on the shelf and fingered the spine of the next as if deciding whether or not to select it. "I think your preoccupation with Madam Bouffant's death might have something to do with your papa," he said kindly. "It can feel unjust when someone takes their own life. It feels unfair, and there's no one to blame. You want justice, but there is none to be had. So perhaps you wish to seek it elsewhere."

Bridget's chest flamed. She straightened her shoulders and looked directly at Nate, but she no longer saw him. Instead, she saw the Earl of Westerly sitting across from her papa at the gambling tables, raking in a pile of money with the keys to Villa De Lacey on top.

"I know who is to blame for my father's death," she said. "There was no justice for him, just as there will be no justice for Madam Bouffant. They're mere commoners to you lot, after all." Tears pricked her eyes, and she turned quickly from Nate.

"That's not fair," Nate spoke gently. "I never—"

"I'd like to be alone, please," she said.

Nate remained silent for a few seconds before he said, "Of course," and moved past her.

Bridget wiped her eyes and waited until she heard Nate leave the library before taking shelter in a nook between two massive mahogany bookcases. It was a place she'd liked to sit as a child whenever she felt alone or afraid. The enclosed nook shielded her from the world and gave her complete privacy whenever she needed it. There, she crouched in the dark and let her tears flow freely—the heartache she'd been trying so hard to push aside was now exposed and raw like an open wound.

She wasn't sure how long she'd been sitting in the concealed space before she'd finally exhausted her tears and lifted her head from her knees. Her first thought was of Bijou. It was time for her to dry her eyes and collect the terrier from Cook. She smiled as she imagined her little dog, snuggled next to the fire with his tummy full of scraps. Perhaps she should leave him in Cook's care tonight. He hated to see her sad, and she hated to see him distressed.

Bridget started to get up when she heard voices and stopped to listen. A man and a woman had entered the library.

"I tell you, I can't do it anymore." A woman spoke in a hushed voice, and Bridget strained to hear. "She's put me in confinement. I'm hardly allowed out of my room. And it's all for nothing. If there truly was a babe then I could bear it, but—"

"There will be a babe," a man's voice interjected. "Just give it more time."

"We've given it five years!"

The speakers, Bridget realized, were Mr. and Mrs. Harley. Good Lord, she was inadvertently eavesdropping on a private conversation between a husband and wife. How awful! Bridget pressed herself against the wall, wishing it would open up and swallow her so she could disappear.

"Things are different now. I have a plan. One that will guarantee us a child."

"Do you mean the maidservant?" Mrs. Harley's tone grew bitter.

Bridget stifled her gasp with her hand.

There was a heavy silence.

"Did you think I didn't know?"

"I'm doing it for us. She doesn't mean anything to me," he said defensively.

"Which one is it? The pretty redhead or the plain brunette?"

Abigail and Sarah! Bridget's eyes widened in the darkness. She could not believe what she was hearing. Did Nate know about this? If so, it was far worse than he'd let on.

"It doesn't matter which one. The only thing that matters is that we get what we need. If we don't, my aunt will cut us out of her will. Is that what you want?"

"How do you know this plan will work? What if *you* are the one who can't sire children?"

"What a thing to say to your husband!" Mr. Harley said. "The responsibility to bear a child lies with the woman."

"I realize as much. Believe me, I am keenly aware of my failure to give you a son." Her voice faltered. "I'm sorry. I spoke out of malice."

"No, you didn't. The truth is that the same has been suggested to me. Apparently, there are such occurrences in men, and I have taken that possibility, and the one that the housemaid herself could be barren, into consideration."

"How so?"

"Lord Frederick has agreed to help—for a fee."

"I beg your pardon?"

"There are *two* willing maidservants," Mr. Harley said slowly. "If you understand my meaning. So, we have twice the chance of ending up with a babe, or if both women bear children, then we shall call them twins."

"Do you mean to say Frederick would be willing to give up his child?"

"More than willing. He says he has several already."

"Good Lord! By whom? No, don't answer that. But tell me, how will we fool your aunt? Don't you think she'll eventually notice I'm not with child?"

"We'll go to the continent—all of us—until after the birth."

"How can you be sure the maidservants will give up their babes?"

"Because they are shallow young women with few scruples, and we can make them rich—at least richer than either could ever hope to be."

Bridget inhaled sharply. She could not believe what she was hearing.

"Shh," his wife said. "I heard something. Is there someone else in this room?"

Bridget held her breath as she heard them moving about the library.

"I don't see anybody," Mr. Harley said.

"Listen," Mrs. Harley said.

A short silence followed. Bridget held her breath and held still. Suddenly, she heard footsteps. A single pair of booted feet. A man! But leaving, or entering the room? Or moving toward her? Had she been discovered? *Oh no!*

Then she heard Frederick's voice. "Mr. and Mrs. Harley, what a pleasant surprise."

She let out her breath and sank against the shelf as he continued, "Are you planning on a little reading before bed, madam?"

"Yes, I have found what I want and was just going upstairs. Good evening, gentlemen." Bridget heard the swish of skirts and the soft pad of kid slippers as Mrs. Harley exited the library.

"Well, we'd best get to the lake. One of us needs to get a maid with child, so your aunt doesn't leave you to fend for yourself. Which one will you take tonight? The redhead or her dark-haired friend?" Frederick said.

Bridget stood trembling and covered her face with her hands. What was going on in her home? Her papa would turn in his grave if he knew. And what about Nate? Did he know about this scheme? Is that why he'd cut short her interview with Abigail and Sarah?

Well, she would not let it continue. It was time for Nate to dismiss Abigail and Sarah and get his awful friends out of Villa De Lacey! This was not the plan she had in mind for her ancestral home. She wanted all of these evil, plotting people gone.

✄━━━━━━━━━━━✄

CHAPTER TWENTY

BRIDGET STEPPED OUT of her dark hiding place into the warm glow of the firelit room and felt an immediate sense of calm. The library, with its wall of books and smell of leather, always soothed her spirit. She turned to the fireplace and thrust out her hands, embracing the heat, while she stared into the dancing, orange flames, and thought about all that had gone on in the past few days.

There was no point talking to Nate. He'd only been humoring her and wasn't actually on her side. It infuriated her to think that he'd gone along with her "investigation" because he felt sorry for her. She supposed in his mind, she was fragile because of the way her papa had died. He claimed that what she really wanted was justice for her papa, and not Madam Bouffant.

But she knew the truth. Nate was making excuses because he didn't have the courage to go against anyone in the ton. He refused to acknowledge that Madam Bouffant had been murdered because the suspects were too important—too rich and powerful—to ever accuse them of murder. In the meantime, the servants at Villa De Lacey were running wild, and she knew that Nate didn't care to do a thing about it, so she would have to take matters into her own hands.

She reached for a lantern that stood above the fireplace, extracted the candle, and gently thrust the wick into the fire. Once the wick caught light, she secured the candle back inside the lantern and set off for the lake. Abigail and Sarah may have thought they were too clever to get caught, but she'd prove them wrong.

It was a chilly evening, and Bridget regretted stepping out *sans* coat as she weaved through the outer thicket of the garden. To avoid being seen, she'd chosen to steer clear of the garden proper, which provided a direct path to the gates of Villa De Lacey. She wanted to take Abigail and Sarah by surprise, catching them at the lake with Mr. Harley and Lord Frederick and then Nate would have no choice but to dismiss them. Perhaps, his friends would then grow bored and depart as well. *So be it.*

But as Bridget continued her determined trek, weaving through the trees in the darkness, an eerie feeling came over her. The night was filled with familiar noises—the rustle of leaves as owls took flight from the trees and the light, quick steps made by rabbits and other small animals going about their nocturnal business. These were the comforting sounds of her childhood. But as she approached the edge of the garden, Bridget thought she heard a heavier step behind her. She turned abruptly, her heart drumming in her chest as she held up the lantern. Its faint light proved to be useless for seeing anything more than a step in front of her.

"Is anyone there?" She shuddered, trying to keep her voice steady. "Nate?" she called, hoping more than anything to hear his voice. As angry as she'd been with him, she now longed for his presence by her side. But she was only met with silence.

Bridget narrowed her eyes, peering into the darkness, desperate to see who was out there. But she heard and saw nothing. Yet she felt the unwanted presence—the life and breath of another person nearby. She knew in her bones that someone else was there. Oh, why had she marched out of the house alone like a petulant child when a murderer was on the loose?

"Hello," Bridget called again, her voice shaky now.

Silence.

"I'm going down to the lake. Whose coming with me?" she sang the words, trying to sound light and cheerful. But inside her stomach rolled with fear. She swallowed. Her throat felt as dry as a dusty well.

She took a deep, calming breath. *It's only my imagination. No one is here. All I need to do is turn around and keep walking.*

Just then a cold wind hit her from behind, extinguishing her candle. Darkness engulfed her. She turned on her heel and fled, her chest heavy with fear. Suddenly she flew forward, gasping the cold into her lungs as she grappled with the air. But gravity won. Then everything went black.

$$\rho$$

THE SIGHT OF Bridget's limp, muddied, and bloodied body almost brought Nate to his knees. His valet had woken him only minutes before with the news that the gardener, Thomas, had found Miss Bridget outside, bleeding from the head and half frozen. Upon hearing this, Nate had shoved on his robe and raced out of his room, just in time to see Thomas coming up the stairs with Bridget in his arms, followed by her weeping aunt, and faithful lady's maid.

"Is she alive?" He looked frantically from the gardener to Aunt Marianne and back to Bridget's listless body.

"Aye, luckily," Thomas said. "But she's chilled to the bone an' dead weak. I'm afraid this nasty gash on her forehead cost her a lot of blood, sir."

Aunt Marianne pressed a handkerchief to her face and whimpered. And Eliza stared at Nate with accusing black eyes.

"Let me take her." Nate stretched out his arms to relieve the gardener's burden. "I'll see to it that you are rewarded for this act."

"No, please! I want no reward. My act has nothing to do with kindness. I've known Miss Bridget since she were a wee girl, an' I'd do anything to protect her. My reward will be laying her safely onto her bed if you please, sir."

"Of course." Nate stepped back and let the man pass. Despite Thomas's advanced years, muscles bulged on the man's arms and legs. He was still fit and strong enough to carry Bridget with ease.

Nate followed them into the room and as the gardener carefully lowered Bridget onto her bed he asked, "Has the doctor been called?"

"Aye," Thomas said, turning to face Nate once Bridget was safely being tended to by her aunt and lady's maid.

Nate tore his gaze from her still form and pale face. He swallowed, feeling helpless and somehow, at fault. "Good. I'll go downstairs and wait for him."

"Good idea, sir. We should leave the ladies to care for Miss Bridget," Thomas said.

Nate nodded in agreement, though he had no desire to leave. He tried desperately to catch another glimpse of Bridget but Aunt Marianne bodily ushered the men out of the room and closed the door behind them.

"Tell me everything that happened," Nate said as he walked downstairs with Thomas. "How did you find her?"

"I was making me way about the grounds as always this morning, seeing what needed tending to, and there she were, lying face down in the dirt. I got the fright of me life, I did, seeing her there. Almost thought my heart would give way. It looked to me like she tripped over a tree root. We have so many of them in the thicket." Thomas shook his head. "I can't think why Miss Bridget were in the outer thicket of the garden at night. She knows better. And she were without her pup. Curious that. She always keeps her dog with her."

"Does anyone know where Bijou is?"

"Aye, Cook has him. She says Miss Bridget left the little beast with her overnight. She weren't worried because Miss Bridget had done so before on occasion."

"What about a lantern? Was she carrying one?"

"Aye, I found it beside her, the candle extinguished, of course. Poor lass."

Nate nodded. It was obvious to him what had happened. He'd abandoned the investigation into Madam Bouffant's death and made light of Bridget's concerns. And then she'd decided to continue alone, taking it upon herself to play sleuth in the middle of the night. He really was at fault. If anything happened to her, he'd never forgive himself.

🔍

IT WAS NOT long before Doctor Elias arrived, but it seemed like an eternity to Nate. He paced the carriageway outside Villa De Lacey, not caring that he still wore his nightshirt and robe. He was consumed by a concoction of worry, guilt, and anger. He worried that Bridget wouldn't recover, felt guilt over his role in first encouraging and then dismissing her ideas about Madam Bouffant's death, and he was furious with her for risking her safety. How could she have wandered out into the garden alone like that?

If she died…*No.* He shook the thought from his mind.

Doctor Elias's coach finally passed through the gates of Villa De Lacey and made its way up the driveway.

"She's upstairs," Nate said as the doctor stepped out of his carriage, clutching his black medicine bag. "Let me take you."

"No need. I was present at Miss Bridget's birth. I know in which room she resides." The doctor swept past Nate, who followed him.

Eliza, who must have heard the doctor make his way up the stairs, opened the door to Bridget's chamber before they had time to knock.

"It's best you wait out here." Dr. Elias turned to Nate as he attempted to cross the threshold into Bridget's chamber. "The young lady may not be conscious, but she'll want her privacy."

Nate took a step back. "Of course," he said. "I'll be right outside."

The doctor disappeared into the room. Eliza gave Nate a cold look as she curtseyed and then shut the door in his face.

Nate shuddered. Did Eliza blame him for what had happened to Bridget?

He couldn't blame her, he admitted. The fact was, he'd let her down by dismissing her concerns…

The image of her still form, with her blond ringlets spread over her pillow like a halo around her beautiful pale face rose in his mind. If he had only been more reactive! He would not let her down again, he vowed.

CHAPTER TWENTY-ONE

B RIDGET HAD REGAINED consciousness, but she was weak and in a lot of pain. She'd tripped over a tree root and hit her head on another, which had left her with a nasty gash and bruises. The doctor had given stringent orders that she rest, and Aunt Marianne was taking them seriously. She had barred Nate from Bridget's room, though he promised not to do anything more than sit quietly by her bedside. He just wanted her to know that he cared—that he was there if she needed him. But Aunt Marianne wouldn't budge. She and Eliza kept guard of their patient like a two-headed Cerebus, and while he longed to be the third head, they rejected his offers outright. There was nothing he could do but wait.

In the meantime, he did what he could for Bridget. First, he summoned Abigail and Sarah to his study and gave them a stern warning. There'd be no more disgracing Bridget's ancestral home. Villa De Lacey was going to be the exclusive and respectable inn Bridget hoped for, and the housemaids were ordered to play their part or look for employment elsewhere. Next, he resolved to revive the investigation into Madam Bouffant's death. If justice for the courtesan would make Bridget happy, then he'd get it for her.

"THERE YOU ARE, Nathaniel." Nate heard Helen's voice behind him.

He turned. "My lady," he said stiffly. It irked him that she continued to call him by his Christian name after she'd lost that privilege. "What can I do for you?"

"Oh, Nate," she said, slinking toward him. "You don't have to be so formal."

He said nothing and waited for her to answer his question.

She pursed her always-tempting cherry lips. Although, he realized, he no longer felt the desire they'd always inspired, especially as he now recognized she used her beauty to manipulate men. Why hadn't he realized this before?

"I require an extra room, but it seems as if all your staff have disappeared. I can't find that little blond housekeeper of yours." She tossed her head.

"If you mean Miss De Lacey, she's the hostess, not my housekeeper. And she's been taken ill. Why do you need another room? Is yours not satisfactory?"

"It's not for me. It's for my son and his governess. They're arriving today."

Nate's stomach dropped. *Her son.* A little over two years old, she'd said. The child was older than her marriage. Nausea rose in his throat. He'd tried not to think about it, but that was easier said than done when the child was going to be under the same roof as him.

"Nathaniel?" she said. "Did you hear what I said? My son, Henry, and his governess will be arriving any minute now."

Henry. "Yes, I heard you. It's fine. We have extra rooms. It won't be a problem. Is that all, Lady Luxton?" Nausea rose in Nate's throat. He needed air. He started down the stairs.

"I should like you to meet him," she said. "He has my eyes but your lovely hair."

It was as if a boulder had landed on his chest, but he did his best not to let Helen see his distress. Instead, he ignored her comment and continued moving away from her, working hard to maintain a sedate pace when all he wanted to do was run.

"It was your brother's doing, you know," she said, following him.

He gripped the banister. Helen knew all his weak spots and had no qualms about digging her nails into them.

"Edward didn't think me good enough for you. He threatened to cut you off without a penny if you married me. And I couldn't stand the thought of us being poor. I just couldn't!"

Do not engage with her, he told himself. As he reached the bottom of the stairs, he noticed Eliza approaching with Bijou under her arm.

Nate's heart lifted. "Eliza," he said when she reached him. "How is Bridget?"

"Still weak," Eliza said stiffly. The maid was a woman of few words, so she did not elaborate.

"Can I see her soon?"

Eliza shook her head. "Her aunt will not permit it."

"Will you ask her?"

"I must take Bijou for his walk."

"Of course," Nate said. "You can ask her when you return."

Eliza narrowed her dark eyes and put Bijou down. The little white terrier wagged his tail and shot across the hallway toward the front door.

"Bijou, heel!" the maid ordered, scurrying to catch up with him. Then she picked him up and turned, heading toward the servants' exit. As she passed Nate again, he could have sworn he heard her mumble, "Curse you!"

"Goodness, it seems to me your housemaids have the run of the inn," Helen said, sweeping across the foyer. She stopped next to the front door and gave him an imperious look. "Am I to open the door myself?"

The gentleman in Nate would not allow him to ignore the lady, so he followed, despite knowing that he should turn and walk the other way.

Helen waited for him to open the front door. As soon as he

did, a stately black coach came to a halt in front of the house. Her haughty attitude disappeared as she rushed outside.

"It's him. My Henry is here." She lifted her skirts to hurry across the portico and down the steps.

Nate stood by the door, watching as a middle-aged woman stepped out of the carriage carrying a young boy. The child clutched his nanny's dress with both fists and wailed as his mother attempted to take him from the woman.

"Do put him down, Miss Eagleton. You baby him too much."

The nanny put the child down, but he clung to her skirt and cried. "I think he's tired, my lady. It's been a long journey for him."

"Oh, Henry!" Helen said. "I've spent too much time away from you, haven't I?" She picked up the child and murmured something in his ear while gently swaying two and fro. The little lad was soon placated. He stuck his thumb in his mouth and laid his head on his mother's shoulder.

Nate's heart wrenched. He'd harbored so much anger toward Helen for so long that the warm sensation he felt upon seeing her hold her child unnerved him. Despite wanting to let go, he could not turn away. If this child—Henry—belonged to him, he would not be able to walk away from Helen.

He held his breath as Helen ascended the steps leading to the house with Henry in her arms. Nate wavered, torn between wanting a closer look at the child and needing to keep his distance from Helen. Before he could think to move, Helen was upon him with the child. She stepped inside and said, "Henry is tired. He'll need to get settled in his room as soon as possible."

"Of course." He pulled the bell cord to summon one of the maids. "Someone will be here shortly to see to the room." He glanced at the child—a sweet-faced little boy with large, dark eyes like his mother's, thick dark curls, and plump, rosy lips.

Nate's chest contracted. *Could he be mine?*

His thoughts were interrupted when Abigail appeared at his side.

"You rang, sir." She curtsied.

"Lady Luxton's son and his nanny have arrived. Show them to one of the empty rooms upstairs. Then fetch the footman to see to their luggage."

"Yes, sir," Abigail said, and Nate was pleased to see that his earlier lecture had not fallen on deaf ears.

"Nathaniel, darling, do be a friend and carry Henry upstairs for me. He's getting awfully heavy." Before Nate could object, she thrust the child into his arms. Surprisingly, the exhausted little lad didn't resist. He simply snuggled in the crook of Nate's neck and stuck his thumb back into his mouth. An odd mixture of tenderness and fear consumed him. He both wanted to embrace the child and give him back to his mother at the same time.

"I think he likes you," Lady Luxton said.

"Where is Lord Luxton? Shall I take to boy to him?"

"Oh, dear, no. Lord Luxton is having a nap. He has little patience for children and needs his rest. Henry's quite comfortable in your arms, don't you think?"

The child shifted and made a soft sucking sound, which tore at Nate's heart. He placed a gentle hand on the child's back and carried him upstairs to a room that housed two single beds.

"Will this do, my lady?" Abigail asked. And Nate was impressed with her polite demeanor, again pleased that she'd taken his warning seriously.

"Put Henry on the bed," Helen instructed Nate. "Gently, now. You don't want to wake him."

As Nate lay Henry on the bed, the child's eyelids fluttered open briefly before closing again. His beautiful, long, dark lashes were so like his mother's that watching him took Nate back to the days when he used to gaze lovingly at Helen as she slept. And the memory brought another wrenching twist to his heart.

"MAY I JOIN you for a stroll in the garden?" Helen asked as they exited Henry's room.

Nate's voice caught in his throat. He'd spent two years building a wall between himself and Helen to keep her out of his thoughts and heart, and now it all appeared to be crumbling. Despite everything—all the anger, pain, and humiliation she'd caused him—he still cared for her. And more than that, he needed to find out if that little boy was his. He wasn't like Frederick. He could never leave a trail of children in his wake. If he'd sired a child, then he wanted to be there for the boy—somehow. Still, he hesitated.

"What I told you earlier about Edward is the truth," Helen said.

Nate stopped. He didn't believe her. Edward was cold, but even he wouldn't stoop that low.

"He threatened to cut you off without a penny if I married you. He said he had bigger plans for you. Plans that would enrich the family, and he didn't need a merchant's daughter interfering with them."

Fury grabbed hold of Nate's throat and choked him. She was lying. She had to be lying. He strode forward and marched down the stairs. He didn't want to hear what she was saying.

Helen followed him, out the door to the garden. When she caught up to him, she said, "Edward arranged my marriage. He knew Lord Luxton was looking for a wife and would settle for a woman without a dowry or title as long as she was young, fertile, and beautiful. He wanted an heir, and he thought he could sire one."

"Did he?" Nate asked.

"I made sure that he thought as much." She looked at him, her large dark eyes so lovely and familiar that he had to look away. "I was already with child. He knew no differently."

"Why didn't you tell me?" Nate said, not turning to look at her.

"You know why. You would have insisted that we elope to

Gretna Green, and then your brother would have spent the rest of our lives controlling us, forcing us to beg for his scraps."

"My brother is too proud to let a member of his family live in poverty. He would have given me my fair share."

"We would have had a house, yes, but he would have controlled where we lived and how much money we had. He would have dictated where Henry went to school and how he was to be raised."

"But we would have been together!" Nate said through gritted teeth. "And I would have had my son!"

"You would have hated being controlled by Edward. We all would have been miserable, including Henry."

"I'll never forgive you for taking my son away from me."

"Lord Luxton is in poor health, and he will leave Henry with a title and a large inheritance—enough money to free you of your brother forever. You *can* be a father to your son."

She was right. He couldn't change the past, but Henry was only a baby. He could be a father to him. He could have Helen back. But he no longer wanted her.

Yet, he could not have his child without her.

"Nate." She reached for his arm. He pulled it away from her.

"I can't talk about this now. It's all too much—too soon. You talk of your husband as if you were a widow, but Lord Luxton is alive. He is your husband and Henry's father."

"I'm only asking you to spend some time with your son and to think of his future."

He turned to her. "Is that all you're asking?"

"For now, yes."

"This feels like manipulation," Nate said. "First, you try to seduce me, and when that doesn't work, you send for Henry and use him to toy with my emotions. It's all about control for you, isn't it? It's all just a game."

Her face soured. "You always think the worst of me. Why can't you believe I did what I thought was best for all three of us?"

Nate shook his head. He didn't know what to think anymore.

"Is it the orphan?" she asked.

"What?"

"Miss De Lacey. I've seen the way you look at her."

Nate's chest tightened. He didn't know how he felt about Bridget, except that the thought of losing her made him physically ill. "I don't owe you any explanations," he said, turning to leave. He'd had enough of this conversation.

"I just want Henry to get to know you, and you to know him," she said, and he stopped. "You're right. You don't owe me anything. But he deserves to get to know his father. If you want to be part of his life, I'll not deny you. There need be nothing between us if that's what you wish."

Nate had no idea if she would ever be true to her word. Helen said and did whatever was needed to get what she wanted. But he'd also seen and loved the good in her, and this gesture warmed his heart to her. He turned to her and said, "Thank you."

Then he walked off in the opposite direction, his mind reeling with all he'd just been told.

❧ ❧

CHAPTER TWENTY-TWO

NATE GRAVITATED TOWARD the outer edges of Villa De Lacey's grounds, where thick, burly trees surrounded the property. This was the area Bridget had ventured alone at night. But why? Was it because he'd refused to tell her about what had been going on at the lake? Had she wanted to see what the housemaids were doing at night?

It was all his fault. He'd dismissed her questions and interrupted her interview with Abigail and Sarah. And he'd done it all for selfish reasons. He'd kept the information from her because he hadn't wanted her to know what a rotten rake he'd been in London and what rotten rakes his friends still were. Because of his cowardice, she'd ventured into the dark thicket by herself, and now she lay abed in a grave condition.

"Are ye searching for this, sir?"

Nate looked up to see Thomas coming toward him and holding up a lantern. "It's the one Miss De Lacey dropped. I was on me way to bring it inside."

"Thank you, Thomas. Would you show me where you found it? I'd like to see where she fell."

"Aye," the gardener said. "It's just down here. Follow me."

They walked several feet deeper into the thicket until Thomas stopped in front of an enormous tree with bulging roots that erupted from the ground.

"I found the lantern next to this one. She left behind some blood behind, poor lass."

Nate kneeled down to see a dried blood smear on the gnarled bark. He turned and looked back at the path she'd walked from the house. "I wonder what she was running from," he said, more to himself than Thomas.

"Running, sir?" Thomas said.

"Yes, the blood and the severity of her injury suggest that she fell with some force. She likely tripped over the first root, flew forward, and hit her head on this one." He pointed to the blood-stained root.

"I can't think who'd be chasing her." Thomas frowned at the spot.

"Maybe something frightened her. An animal?"

"I dunna think so. All we have around here are squirrels, rabbits, birds, an' maybe a snake or two. But Miss De Lacey has lived here all her life. She's not easily spooked by the wildlife."

Nate chewed the inside of his lip, pondering. What if it weren't an animal that had scared Bridget? What if it were a person? And what if that person pushed her and meant to kill her—just as he or she had pushed Madam Bouffant down the stairs?

Nate scoured the surrounding area, looking for clues—something that would tell him whether or not another person had been present at the scene.

"Did you see any footprints when you found Miss De Lacey this morning?"

"Footprints? No, I weren't looking for any footprints. But I suppose some of hers were in the mud"—he glanced down—"and some of mine and yours now too."

Nate peered at the muddle of footprints and nodded. Then something caught his eye. A bit of gold sticking out of the earth. He stepped forward and bent to retrieve it. "A button!" he said, pulling the round bit of metal out of the ground and wiping the dirt from it with his gloved hand. It didn't belong to Bridget. She'd been wearing all black as usual when she'd been found, and she'd worn no coat, which had contributed to her body half freezing. "Were you wearing a coat this morning when you happened upon Miss De Lacey? Is this by chance your button?"

"I was wearing the same coat I am now," he pointed to his brown overcoat. "And I don't see no buttons missing from it. An' that button's too posh to be mine."

Nate looked from the gardener's plain brass buttons to the metal one in his hand, which sported an intricate floral design. True, the button may have been lying there for some time. Perhaps, it had been there for months, before Bridget started to wear black. Although, it did not look tarnished enough for that.

Nate slipped the button into his pocket. There could be a perfectly innocent explanation for the button's presence at the crime scene. Or, it could belong to someone who had cause to push or frighten Bridget. Either way, he intended to find out if any of the guests were missing a coat button.

🔎

SEVERAL DAYS LATER, Bridget felt well enough to get out of bed, but she was met with fierce resistance from Aunt Marianne. "You're not yet strong enough! The doctor said you should not overexert yourself."

"I'm fine, Aunt. I promise. If I stay in this bed one minute longer, I shall go mad." Bridget inspected the damage to her head in her handheld-looking glass. A nasty purple and yellow bruise surrounded the red gash in the center of her forehead.

"It looks horrible," she groaned.

"That's why you need to stay in bed," Aunt Marianne said.

"I need fresh air," Bridget insisted. She wanted to return to where she fell to see if it would trigger any memories. She couldn't recollect a thing about that night or what had happened. All she remembered was talking to Nate in the library; everything following that was blank. "And I need to speak with Mr. Squires. How has he been coping while I've been in bed and you and Eliza have been spending all your time hovering over me?"

"He's managed quite well, I think. He seems to have tamed Abigail and Sarah into compliance."

Abigail and Sarah. The names resonated in her mind. *I recall hearing something about them—something important—but what was it?* She tried to remember but her brain refused to cooperate.

"Has Mr. Squires asked to see me?" Bridget said.

Aunt Marianne hesitated.

"Aunt?"

"Several times a day. He's not stopped badgering me with questions," Aunt Marianne said with a measure of irritation, and Bridget could not help but smile. She was pleased to hear that Nate cared. "But I told him you're not ready to resume your duties as hostess yet. And he agreed with me. He thinks you need your rest."

"Oh, Aunt!"

"These people don't deserve you, Bridget. Look what they've done to you." Aunt Marianne's eyes had gone from stern to watery, and Bridget saw what her aunt had suffered the past few days. She got out of bed and embraced her. "Don't worry," she whispered. "All will be well. I promise."

BRIDGET FELT A rush of energy flood through her when she saw Nate standing at the foot of the garden, waiting for her. He smiled as she approached him with Bijou at her heels, and her heart skipped. Something about Nate made her feel alive.

"How are you feeling?" Nate's dark-blue eyes reflected his worry as he looked at her bandaged head.

"Foolish." She laughed and gently touched her wrapped wound. "I'm embarrassed to have caused so much trouble for everyone. I should not have ventured out in the dark by myself. I cannot think why I did it."

Nate ran a hand over his square jaw, which Bridget noticed had grown stubble. "I'm afraid it might have been my fault. I'm sorry if I upset you in the library."

"Upset me? What did you say? I recall being in the library with you, but I don't remember our conversation."

Nate looked relieved. "Never mind then," he said. "It doesn't matter anymore. All that matters is that you get well."

"But it does matter. I can't remember a thing, and I'd like to know what prompted me to venture into the thicket alone at night and without my coat."

Nate blew out his breath. "I imagine you were doing some sleuthing."

"Mayhap. That memory remains out of my reach—I fear it has something to do with Abigail and Sarah. They're both well, I take it?"

He nodded. "Yes, I chatted with them, and their attitude has greatly improved."

"All is right, then," Bridget said, although she felt there was something more. Her brow creased in thought, and she immediately felt the tight pain in her forehead.

"What is it?" Nate reached for her. "Do you need to go inside and lie down?"

"No, I'm fine." Bridget raised her hand. "I was just trying to recall the events of that night."

"What do you remember about your fall?" Nate asked. "Were you running from something or someone?"

Bridget shrugged. "I don't remember anything."

"Do you think someone could have been following you? And that's why you ran?"

A cold chill traveled down Bridget's spine. "I don't know. Why? Do you think someone was following me?"

Nate fished the button out of his pocket and gave it to Bridget. "I found this on the ground near to where you fell. Do you recognize it?"

Bridget turned the button between her fingers. "No, it's not mine. At least I don't think belongs to me." She frowned. "I suppose whom it belongs to depends on how long it was laying out there."

"It looks shiny and new, so I don't believe it's been lying in the dirt for months. If someone was following you that night, then I believe it may belong to that person. And it may be the same person who pushed Madam Bouffant down the stairs."

"Are you saying that someone wanted me dead?"

"It's just a theory. Is there anyone you can think of who might want to harm you?"

"Me? What threat could I pose to anyone?"

"Perhaps someone believes you know something. Maybe you saw or heard something you should not have."

"Dodsworth," Bridget said. "I told you what I overheard between him and Lydia."

"I thought you weren't seen."

"I didn't think I was, but perhaps I was wrong."

Nate dropped his gaze, and Bridget knew he couldn't accept the idea that his friend was guilty of anything.

"I'll speak with him and see what I can find out. Anyone else?" he asked looking up at her.

"There's always Adelia Eamont and her mother."

"True. Those two have had some very strange behavior of late. I suppose we'll have to spend the next few days staring at their buttons."

Bridget laughed. "I can't think of a better way to spend my time."

Nate took her hand in his and lightly traced his thumb over her bandaged forehead with his other. "I meant it," he said. "I couldn't bear it if something were to—"

Just then, Bridget spotted Lady Luxton, accompanied by another woman and a child, walking toward them. She watched the little boy toddle between the two women. To whom did he belong?

"Mr. Squires," Lady Luxton called as she approached them.

"You remember Henry, don't you?"

Nate's posture stiffened. "Yes, of course," he said, looking uncomfortable, yet he did not take his eyes off the boy.

"Wonderful. Perhaps you will indulge us by helping him sail this paper boat on the lake? Unfortunately, his papa is not feeling well today, and he could not accompany us. Show him your boat, Henry."

The child held up a paper boat, and Nate's entire face seemed to smile. It was as though he knew and loved the child, Bridget thought.

Bijou, who'd been investigating a patch of grass, trotted toward them wagging his tail. When he reached the child, he jumped up, trying to snatch the boat. The little boy let out a frightened wail, and Nate scooped him up in his arms.

"Don't worry, Henry. Bijou is a friendly pup. He only wants to play. Should we all go to the lake together and put your boat in the water?"

The child nodded repeatedly, and Nate beamed.

Bridget could not help but smile. It was obvious that Nate had affection for the child. But why was he so attached to the child of his former betrothed and the man she'd discarded him for?

"Miss De Lacey," Lady Luxton said, acknowledging Bridget for the first time. "I heard about your accident. I do hope you are feeling better."

"Yes, I am. Thank you for asking," Bridget replied, genuinely surprised by the woman's kind gesture.

"Good." She gave Bridget a tight smile. "I was beginning to think there were no servants left at Villa De Lacey."

Bridget's smile faded. She glanced at Nate, but he was focused on the child and apparently hadn't heard Lady Luxton's slight.

Bijou raced a circle around Nate and Henry, yapping and jumping up. The child squealed and Lady Luxton pursed her lips in disapproval.

Bridget scooped the terrier up in her arms. "If you'll excuse me," she said.

Nate gave her a brief look as if to say, *we'll resume our conversation later*, before turning his attention back to the boy in his arms.

"Boat!" Henry cried.

Nate laughed. "Shall we go put it on the water and see if it will sail?"

Bridget watched as Nate turned and headed to the lake with Henry in his arms and Lady Luxton by his side. She would think they were a happy family if she didn't know better. Just then, Lady Luxton turned and gave her a look that could freeze Lake Windermere.

CHAPTER TWENTY-THREE

Aunt Marianne was waiting for Bridget as she entered the villa. "Really, my dear, I must insist that you come back to bed. You will exhaust yourself. You are not yet healed."

Bridget's head had indeed started to ache again, and she longed to rest it on her soft pillow, but she was not ready to go back to bed. "Allow me to check on the servants first, Aunt. I want to see how everyone has been getting along without me."

"Absolutely not! You get yourself upstairs, and I'll check on the servants," Aunt Marianne ordered.

Bridget opened her mouth to object, but Aunt Marianne had already stalked off in the direction of the servants' stairs.

"Miss De Lacey!"

Bridget looked up to see Mrs. Harley coming down the stairs. "I'm so pleased to see you up and about. I heard that you had a nasty fall in the woods. What an ordeal."

"Thank you," Bridget said, surprised that yet another guest was inquiring about her well-being. She hadn't thought any of them cared. "How kind of you to ask after me."

"Well, I know what it's like to be stuck in confinement." She caressed her exceedingly slim belly. "It can get lonely sometimes."

Bridget nodded. "How have you been feeling? I hope you have been comfortable here."

"Everything has been delightful," Mrs. Harley said. "I only wish Mr. Harley's aunt would allow me to enjoy all Windermere has to offer." She sighed. "I know the babe's health is the most important thing, but as I said, it does get lonely."

"I'm sorry," Bridget said.

Mrs. Harley shrugged, and said casually, "I'd be happy to sit with you while you recover if your aunt will permit it. I could use the company myself."

"Oh," Bridget said, a little uncomfortable with the woman's strange request. "Thank you, but I don't plan on spending any more days in my room. I have work to do. This inn isn't going to manage itself."

"Is Mr. Squires so demanding that he's going to force you back to your duties already?"

"No, of course not. He wishes me to rest. I prefer to keep busy."

Mrs. Harley nodded. "Well, if you're not going to stay abed, perhaps you'll permit me to walk out with you in the garden every now and then. Lady Darby won't let me out on my own in my condition, and I should like someone else's company besides my lady's maid. It will be refreshing. I understand you know everything about the garden plants and trees."

"Of course," Bridget said. "I would love to accompany you sometime. Perhaps, not today." She gestured to her forehead. "I am feeling rather tired today."

"You poor dear. Do you remember how it all happened? What made you go out on your own in the middle of the night like that?"

Bridget's cheeks warmed. "I don't remember anything at all from that night. One bump on the head and the entire evening has been erased from my memory."

"Is that so?" Mrs. Harley's small eyes widened an inch. "That must be a relief to forget the whole frightening ordeal."

"Not entirely. I wish I could remember. Believe me, I am trying very hard."

"It's best you don't, dear." Mrs. Harley gave her a faint smile. "The mind can play such awful tricks."

Bridget frowned and then immediately winced as she felt the pain in her forehead. She had to remember to stop doing that.

"Well, I must get back to my room now. The babe's health is most important you know. But we shall walk soon. I promise."

What a strange encounter, she thought as she watched Mrs. Harley make her way back upstairs.

$$\rho$$

"THAT'S IT! GENTLY now." Nate crouched by the lake holding Henry over the water as the little boy poked his makeshift boat with a stick, sending it out into the lake.

The paper vessel floated a few feet from the shore and the child clapped. Nate clasped the boy close to him as they both watched the little boat. He marveled at the child's rosy cheeks and sweet smile. How was it possible that two days ago he knew nothing about this boy? This sweet child who he instinctively knew belonged to him.

"Oh, look, Henry, your papa is here." Henry's nanny appeared at Nate's side. "Let me take you to see him." She stretched out her arms.

The smile faded from Nate's face as Henry left his hold.

"Papa!" Henry pointed to Lord Luxton, who had been wheeled down to the lake by his valet. Lady Luxton remained beside Nate as he watched Henry's nanny place him on Lord Luxton's lap. The little boy rested his head against Lord Luxton's chest as the manservant pushed them away on a walk.

"He's the image of you," Lady Luxton purred.

"That matters not. His father is Lord Luxton."

"For now," she said.

"Forever." Nate watched as Lord Luxton and Henry moved farther in the distance.

Lady Luxton sighed. "When Lord Luxton dies, Henry will need his true father. I know you won't abandon him." Then she left him, walking in the direction of her husband and son.

Nate swallowed the bitter lump in his throat, as he watched the group, feeling the pain of what might have been.

⚲

WANTING TO CLEAR his head, Nate walked for some time down the shore, embracing the glacial lake and its surrounding greenery. He did his best to push Helen out of his mind, slipping his right hand into his trouser pocket, and feeling for the button. There was no question in his mind that someone had been following Bridget and had intended to do her harm. But who?

Remembering the blood seeping through Lady Eamont's white glove after she'd pricked herself with Madam Bouffant's brooch, her name was the first that came to his mind. There was something deranged about that woman. She had a cruel, bloodthirsty streak and he did not doubt that, given the chance, she would have gladly pushed Madam Bouffant down the stairs. She also had a solid motive to hurt Bridget. Adelia had given Bridget the brooch, informing her that her mother had stolen it. Although that did not seem to threaten Lady Eamont, she may have been concerned that Adelia had revealed other secrets to Bridget as well.

And what about Adelia herself? If she were half as mad as Bridget had said she'd been on the day of her sister's big announcement, then they were all in trouble. Finally, there was—

"Dodsworth?" Nate said as he spotted his friend emerging from the lake, stark naked, with Jefferson following behind him. Nate grinned. They'd braved the cold and gone for a swim. There was nothing better than stripping off one's clothes and plunging into the refreshing waters of Lake Windermere. Perhaps, he'd join them.

He walked toward his friends as they dressed, ready to surprise them. He was glad to see Dodsworth as he still wanted to ask him about his sudden betrothal to Lydia. Maybe it wasn't too late to warn him about the Eamonts. He deserved to know the madness that was about to become his family.

But as Nate got closer, he saw that the atmosphere between his friends had changed. Dodsworth and Jefferson weren't smiling anymore. They appeared to be involved in a heated discussion. Jefferson was shaking his head and gesturing with his hands, and Dodsworth looked to be pleading.

Nate stopped, uncertain what to do. Then Dodsworth put one hand on Jefferson's shoulder and another on his face. The way they looked at each other spoke volumes, and Nate suddenly understood what Lydia had meant by a "hanging offense." They were lovers. She'd discovered their secret—and she'd used that information to coerce Dodsworth into marrying her.

Nate felt the fool. How had he not known? Dodsworth had been his friend for years. Granted, proclivities such as his weren't information one bandied about. But he'd always thought of Dodsworth as a rake. Now he understood that his friend must have been living in fear that someone would discover the truth, so he'd played along, telling everyone he wanted to remain a bachelor and enjoy his freedom.

Not wanting to intrude, Nate backed away and turned onto a path leading away from the lake. The shock of the discovery was soon replaced by another thought. Dodsworth wasn't a murderer, but could Jefferson have killed to protect their secret?

CHAPTER TWENTY-FOUR

"LORD, NO! NOT again!" Bridget stumbled back in fright upon seeing the body floating face down in the shallow rectangular fountain lorded over by Venus. Abigail's unmistakable red hair fanned out in the water beneath the statue of Venus like *Hamlet*'s tragic, drowned Ophelia.

"I found her just like this," Thomas said, his voice shaky. "She's drowned. Poor lass."

Nausea rose in Bridget's throat as she surveyed the scene—a dead woman, cloaked in black, floating in a fountain, her lantern flung to the side—just as hers had been. Suddenly, an immense terror swept over her as fragments of that night returned to her mind. She recalled the cold darkness and the sense of a malevolent presence behind her. She hadn't tripped. Someone had *pushed* her. And she felt certain that the same thing had happened to Abigail. Someone had wanted them both dead and this time, the killer had made sure the job was properly done. "Abigail didn't just drown," Bridget said out loud. "She was murdered. I'm certain of it."

"I think you're right." Nate gripped the back of his neck as he stared at the drowned housemaid. The sheer horror on his face assured Bridget that he could no longer pretend all was well at Villa De Lacey. There was no mistaking it now—a killer lurked amongst them.

"Who could have done this?" Nate's jaw tightened and Bridget could see the fury in his expression. "It's utterly heinous!"

"Poor Abigail! She must have been so frightened." A cold fear passed through Bridget, and she wrapped her arms around herself. *It could have been me lying in that fountain.*

"We must act quickly to keep the guests from this scene." Nate paced. "Thomas, help me pull her out. Bridget, go inside and get a sheet to cover the body, then send the footman to fetch the magistrate. But tell him to be discreet." Nate glanced at the sky. Dawn was breaking through the clouds. "We still have a few hours before the guests start filtering outside for their morning activities."

Bridget had been rooted to the spot, but the idea of the guests enduring the sight of Abigail's bloated dead body propelled her forward, and she raced to the house with Bijou following at her heels.

🔍

LESS THAN AN hour later, Magistrate Hunt stood over Abigail's lifeless body. He peeled back the sheet, exposing the young woman's blue lips and dull green eyes that stared into the abyss. She looked as cold and lifeless as a neglected porcelain doll.

The magistrate kneeled and smoothed his hand over her eyes, closing them, and she instantly looked more peaceful. "So, you think someone killed her, do you?" Magistrate Hunt turned to Nate. "There doesn't seem to be any injuries to her body—no blows to the head or marks around her neck. Could your housemaid swim?"

"I doubt it, but it's a long shallow fountain. All she had to do was stand up," Nate pointed out.

"Not if she was inebriated or otherwise impaired." The magistrate stood up and surveyed the area. His eyes landed on Bijou, who sniffed something on the ground, whimpered, and retreated.

"I say, what's the mutt found?" Magistrate Hunt asked.

"What is it, boy?" Bridget bent to stroke the pup's fur as he cowered next to her. "What scared you?"

Magistrate Hunt stepped forward and inspected the area where Bijou had been sniffing. Then he bent and picked something off the ground. "It's a small pouch of mushrooms," he said, emptying the little bag and holding the contents in his palm for the others to see.

Bridget, Nate, and Thomas peered at the fungi in the magistrate's leather-gloved hand.

Bridget glanced at Nate, who said, "It think it's—"

"Deadly," Thomas said decisively.

All three turned to the gardener.

"Deadly?" Bridget asked. "Do you mean these wild mushrooms? The ones that give people Kubla Khan visions? Why should they be deadly?"

"No." Thomas's gray eyes danced with fear. "These might look the same as the harmless ones, but they're not. These here will kill you."

"Good Lord!" Nate said. "I warned them about this! I specifically told them to check with you, Thomas."

"Aye, so they did. I begged them not to go hunting for wild mushrooms by their selves." Thomas's lined face took on a pained expression. "That's why I picked the mushrooms for them myself—I know which ones are right. I gave them the right ones, I swear it."

"Of course, you did, Thomas," Bridget said. There was no doubt in her mind that Thomas had picked the correct mushrooms. He'd lived in the Lake District all his life and was an expert on its plants. Even with her knowledge, she always left the mushroom foraging to Cook or Thomas, and she never let Bijou near any wild fungi.

"This poor lass must have gone out looking for some on her own." Thomas's entire face seemed to crumble as he stared at the mushroom.

"Just which gentlemen are you referring to, Mr. Thomas?" Magistrate Hunt asked.

The gardener glanced at Nate, clearly afraid to articulate the truth aloud.

"I believe he is referring to our guests Lord Frederick, Lord Dodsworth, and Mr. Jefferson," Nate said. "They read about vision-inducing fungi in some ancient text and wanted to use them for relaxation purposes—as the poets do with laudanum."

"Why didn't they use laudanum then?" the magistrate barked. "It's much safer than foraging for wild mushrooms."

Nate shrugged. "I don't know. I suppose they thought this would be more interesting."

"I don't see what that has to do with your housemaid. Why would she go in search of vision-inducing mushrooms? It seems like very odd behavior for a maidservant." The magistrate raised his eyebrows at Bridget as if silently admonishing her. She shrank back, remembering his painful rebuke when Madam Bouffant died—"*Mr. De Lacey would not have approved.*"

"You're correct, magistrate." Nate interrupted the cold silence that followed. "It certainly is odd behavior for a servant, and we do not condone it. I warned Abigail a few days ago about her inappropriate conduct and threatened her with prompt dismissal if it continued."

"Is that so?" Magistrate Hunt's creased brows cleared, and he nodded his approval. "Well, then, it seems clear that your wayward servant ate a poisonous mushroom after mistaking it for harmless fungi and suffered the deadly consequences. It's a case of bad judgment all around."

"Aye, but death wouldn't be immediate," Thomas said. "There'd be a good deal of stomach pain, nausea, and the like that could last for some time."

"Yes, well, that makes sense. I conclude that she ate the fungi at some point before leaving the servants' quarters and then became weak and sick as she ventured into the garden where she stumbled toward the fountain, no doubt wanting a sip of water or to cool her face. She must have been carrying this purse of mushrooms on her person and dropped it at some point before she fell into the water. With the poison eating away at her insides, she didn't have the strength to save herself."

"What if she didn't pick them herself? What if someone gave them to her, letting her think they were the harmless fungi," Bridget said.

"And who would have done that? Do you have reason to believe that one of those fine gentlemen Mr. Squires mentioned wanted her dead?"

"No." Nate held up his hands. "I believe Miss De Lacey is merely expressing her concern because this is the second death at Villa De Lacey."

"The second accidental death," Magistrate Hunt said. "Both of which resulted from poor judgment and bad behavior. I do not doubt that this wayward housemaid of yours had no one but herself to blame for her death. You say she was behaving in a manner unbecoming to a servant of a respectable household and had received a warning along with the threat of dismissal. That does not bode well for her character. I hesitate to malign the characters of your reputable gentlemen guests by insinuating that they might have had something to do with the death of this servant." Magistrate Hunt turned to give Bridget a stern look that seemed to say, *Do better next time, Miss De Lacey.*

Bridget hung her head, her chest flaming from the burn of the magistrate's condemnation. Nate was right to discourage him from investigating this murder. Clearly, he thought Abigail deserved her fate just like Madam Bouffant. The investigation would fare better in her and Nate's hands.

NATE WAS RELIEVED once the magistrate departed with Abigail's body, but he knew it would be a long time before he could erase the disturbing image of the young housemaid floating in the water beneath the statue of Venus, whose flowing tresses, voluptuous physique, and youthful glory were an ironic reminder of what the nubile Abigail had been like in life.

"What are we to do?" Bridget asked, settling Bijou on her lap once they were safely ensconced in the study. "How are we to break this news to the servants? And what about the guests? They are all sure to leave once they learn there has been yet another death on the grounds of Villa De Lacey."

"We don't tell them," Nate said. "Not just yet anyway."

"How is that going to work?"

"We'll say that Abigail has left our service and returned home to Yorkshire for a family matter. Then, all we need to do is observe everyone's reactions and behaviors. The guilty party is bound to reveal him or herself." The very notion made Nate sick to his stomach. He hated having to spy on his friends, but what choice did he have? Abigail's death was not an accident, despite what the magistrate had concluded.

"Can it be that simple?" Bridget stroked Bijou's white fur as he snuggled into the crook of her arm.

"No," Nate said, "but it will allow us to continue our sleuthing in secret—without anyone feeling threatened. One thing is clear to me though—whoever killed Madam Bouffant also killed Abigail, and I believe the same person tried to harm you. I don't believe all three of you tripped. That's too much of a coincidence. I think all of you were pushed from behind."

"We were—at least I was. I've remembered something from that night—the presence of someone behind me." She shivered. "I felt it when I saw Abigail in that fountain."

Nate himself shuddered. He scared him to think how close Bridget had come to death.

"Perhaps whoever killed Abigail did so to keep her quiet," Bridget said. "Maybe she saw or heard something that exposed Madam Bouffant's killer." Bridget bit her lower lip before she said, "It follows, then, that I must have seen or overheard something that propelled me to venture outside. Although, I can't think what for." She rubbed her temples. "I wish I could remember what happened that night."

Nate turned and gazed out the window where Lake Windermere's blue water sparkled on the horizon. He needed to tell Bridget what he'd witnessed between Dodsworth and Jefferson at the shorefront. But he was loath to think how she would react to his discussing such a delicate topic with her.

"What is it?" Bridget urged. "If I am to find out who attempted to kill me in my own home—your home—then I need to know everything, even if it involves your friends. I know how you wish to protect them."

"It's not that." Nate pressed his fingertips together. "It's rather a delicate subject."

Bridget frowned and Nate saw her wince and then deflect the pain. "Don't keep things from me because you think me too delicate. Nothing can shake me after everything I have suffered. My father's death…the way he died…the way he was buried with a stake in his heart…nothing you tell me could shock or grieve me more. I am no longer the innocent young lady I was a few months ago."

"Very well." Nate inhaled, readying himself for the uncomfortable conversation, before relating everything he'd recently learned about Dodsworth and Jefferson.

Heat spread up Bridget's neck and across her cheeks as he spoke, but every time he stopped, she instructed him to keep talking. "So, Dodsworth has agreed to marry Lydia Eamont to keep her quiet," Bridget said when Nate finally finished speaking. "And you think Madam Bouffant and Abigail somehow discovered their secret, so he murdered them?"

"I don't believe Dodsworth is capable of murder," Nate said firmly. He'd known Dodsworth for years and in spite of his friend's dire secret, in truth he couldn't shake the notion that the man was as decent as they come.

"Jefferson, then?" Bridget offered. "He knew Madam Bouffant had broken her neck before the doctor checked her. And it is he and Dodsworth who've been taking the fungi, correct?"

"Yes. In fact, it was Jefferson who first raised the idea of taking them. He found it in the ancient text and carried a sketch of the mushroom with him here. It's possible that both Madam Bouffant and Abigail discovered Dodsworth and Jefferson's affair and then tried to blackmail Dodsworth. He has a lot of money, so he is a good target for blackmailers. Furthermore, they were always at the lake and could easily have seen something they should not have. Dodsworth would have had no choice but to keep paying them for eternity. It would have been that, or pay with his life. And although I don't believe Dodsworth is capable of murder, I don't know Jefferson well enough to say that he isn't."

"Do you suppose I discovered Dodsworth and Jefferson's secret the night of my accident?"

"It's possible you overheard them talking in the library," Nate said. "You lost your memory of that night after the fall, so that would explain why no one has tried to hurt you since."

"But why would I have ventured through the thicket alone at night?" Her cheeks flushed scarlet. "You don't think I hoped to catch them together, do you?" She shook her head. "No, I would never. Nor would I reveal such a secret to anyone. I wouldn't want someone to hang for the crime of love. Never! Their secret would have—will always be—safe with me."

"Well, *you* know that, but Jefferson may not. But I agree, it doesn't explain your presence in the thicket after dark." Nate sighed. "The truth is it's likely my fault you were out there. You may have heard something about the servants and their cavorting at the lake. I suspected that was happening, but I didn't tell you because I wanted to be certain. And after you were hurt, I gave Abigail and Sarah a stern warning about their behavior. But clearly, they didn't heed it because now Abigail is dead."

Suddenly, Adelia's name rang throughout the villa, bouncing off the walls and floors, as Lady Eamont howled it repeatedly. Nate and Bridget looked at each other and jumped out of their seats. There couldn't possibly be another dead body at Villa De Lacey, could there?

CHAPTER TWENTY-FIVE

"**C**ALL THE MAGISTRATE!" Lady Eamont shouted as Nate and Bridget entered the main landing on the first floor, where a crowd of guests had gathered. "Adelia has been abducted!"

Nate blinked, trying to make sense of the frantic woman's statement. "Abducted? What makes you think that?"

"She's not in her room! Clara readied Lydia and me for breakfast as usual, and then she went to dress Adelia, only to find her bed empty. She's vanished."

"Perhaps she went out for a morning stroll," Lydia said, her tone perfectly calm and lacking her mother's hysteria.

"Yes, that sounds right. Early morning is the most beautiful time of day." Bridget forced a cheerful tone but glanced worriedly at Nate as she spoke, and it was clear to him what she was thinking. Why had Adelia disappeared the same morning that Abigail had been found floating in the fountain? Either Adelia was a killer, or she was another yet-to-be-discovered victim. The thought made his blood run cold.

"Since when does Adelia take walks on her own?" Lady Eamont wailed to no one in particular. "She's not permitted to go out unaccompanied! She's been abducted, I tell you!" She whirled around and glared at her husband. "Why haven't they sent for the magistrate yet?"

"Because you're suffering from hysteria," Lord Eamont barked. "Adelia went for a walk, and you are screaming the house down."

"She is not permitted to go out on her own!" Lady Eamont repeated in a thunderous voice. Her face turned red as a beet, and Nate feared the woman might faint.

He held up his hands in a calming gesture. "Before anyone panics, we should go out and search for her. If we don't find her, we will call the magistrate." He locked eyes with Bridget and saw the same fear in them as he felt weighing on his chest.

"You expect me to go traipsing all around Windermere when my daughter has been abducted?" Lady Eamont shrieked.

"Miss De Lacey and I will go, and we'll enlist the gardener's help. The three of us know the grounds best, so the search will be more efficient. I am certain Adelia is enjoying a stroll in the rose gard—" He stopped, the image of Abigail's floating body rising in his mind. "I'm certain we will find her and escort her safely back to the villa."

"When you do, tell her I'm going to lock her in her room and throw away the key." Lord Eamont huffed audibly, turned, and marched back to his chamber.

Nate raised his eyebrows. He was starting to feel sorry for the Eamont sisters.

🔍

"I SHAN'T BE able to stomach it if we find another body," Bridget said as she stepped into the garden with Nate and Bijou. How did Villa De Lacey go from being her safe and peaceful home to being a killer's haven?

Nate shook his head. "I hope that isn't the case. This is starting to feel like a nightmare."

They located Thomas near his cottage and explained what needed to be done. Then the three of them set out, combing the grounds. Nate and Bridget traipsed through the thicket that surrounded the garden. The deeper she ventured, the more rapid her heartbeat became. She stopped at the spot where she'd fallen, still marked with her dried blood. Her mind flashed back to the night of her accident, restoring flickers of her memory.

"Hello? Is anyone there?"

A cold wind snuffed out her candle, but not before she glimpsed a flash of red. Fear gripped her throat. She turned and ran. Then everything went black...

"Bridget?" She felt a hand on her shoulder and jumped.

"What is it?" Nate asked. "Have you remembered something?"

"I—I'm not sure. I think I saw a flash of red before the wind blew my candle out."

"The person was wearing a red coat?"

"I don't think so. It might have been a red dress or vest. It was just a flash. It could have been my imagination. I don't know." She trembled. "I'm sorry, I can't be certain."

"Don't be sorry." Nate inched closer to her. "You've done well. This could be important. But perhaps we should turn around and go back now. Thomas and I can finish the search on our own."

"No, I'm just being silly. I've walked this path a thousand times, and I won't stop now."

Nate nodded and took a polite step back. "All right, then, I think we should go down to the lake. Let's hope we find Adelia enjoying the serenity of the water and mountains there."

"Yes, let's hope," Bridget said, exhaling to release the tension that had nested in her chest.

🔎

BUT ADELIA WAS not at the lake. They trekked up and down the shore for an hour to no avail.

"What are we going to do?" Bridget rubbed her forehead. "What if she has been murdered too? Do we have a crazed killer on the loose at Villa De Lacey?"

"Let's not panic," Nate said. "We don't have another body, so we can't declare her murdered."

"What if the killer dumped her body in the lake instead of the fountain?" Bridget turned toward the calm waters of Lake Windermere.

"If I hadn't witnessed what we both did this morning, I'd say you were going mad." Nate walked to the edge of the water. "Unfortunately, it's now looking like a plausible scenario."

"Good Lord." Bridget attempted to rub the exhaustion from her face.

"But we must ask ourselves, why would someone want to kill Adelia Eamont and dump her body in Lake Windermere? Surely, we have to rule out Lady Eamont now," Nate said. "She might be a selfish and cruel mother, but would she murder her own daughter? And if not her, that brings us back to Jefferson. Although I don't know why he'd want to murder Adelia when Lydia is the one blackmailing Dodsworth."

"We shouldn't dismiss Lady Eamont yet," Bridget said, thinking back to Adelia's comments regarding her mother. "When we were alone upstairs, Adelia said her mama would feed her and Lydia minute amounts of poison to make them sick or make them trip and fall in a way that twists an ankle by pushing them down the stairs."

"That's right." Nate's face turned white. "I recall you telling me. But it seemed so contrived that we didn't take her seriously."

"I know." Bridget dropped her gaze. "She said so many outrageous and awful things that I doubted her. And now…" She couldn't finish her sentence. If Lady Eamont had hurt Adelia, she'd be to blame.

"Don't blame yourself. Adelia was unhinged that day," Nate said, as if reading her thoughts. "You couldn't be expected to believe everything she said."

Bridget gazed out at the lake and imagined Adelia's lifeless body under the water. She shook her head, trying to cast off the image.

"Don't upset yourself. We don't know what happened yet. It's still feasible that all of you met with some type of accident, and Adelia is sitting under a tree somewhere."

"You can't possibly believe that."

Nate sighed. "You're right. I don't. There's definitely a killer amongst us, and all we can do is pray that Adelia is not the latest victim."

$$\wp$$

BY THE TIME they returned to the house, breakfast was over, and the guests had gathered in the drawing room. An agitated Aunt Marianne stopped them just as they were about to enter and address the guests.

"I do hope you found Abigail while you were out searching for that wayward Miss Adelia. She has conveniently disappeared and left Sarah and Eliza to do everything on their own. And you know Eliza does not like to interact with the guests. They upset her." Aunt Marianne spoke in a low voice so the guests in the living room couldn't hear.

"Abigail hasn't disappeared, Aunt," Bridget whispered. "She's—"

"What are you doing, standing there and whispering to each other?" Lady Eamont shot out of her seat and strode toward the door. "Have you found my daughter? Where is she? I demand you tell me at once!"

Nate entered the drawing room and Bridget followed. Her heart hammering. She now believed that Lady Eamont was a very dangerous person.

"I'm afraid we couldn't find her." Nate clasped his hands together, likely to stem his nerves. "It might be time to call the magistrate."

"So, it's as I said!" In contrast, Lady Eamont threw up her hands. "She's been taken! And all you've done is waste time. Her abductor could have taken her to Scotland by now."

"Adelia hasn't been abducted, Mama." Lydia stood up and glanced at the mahogany clock above the fireplace. "But you're correct about one thing—she is in Scotland."

"What are you talking about?" Lady Eamont's entire face narrowed into an expression of tight anger.

"Adelia and Mr. Jefferson have eloped," Lydia said calmly.

"Oh, thank heavens!" Bridget exclaimed.

"Eloped?" Lady Eamont spewed the word out of her mouth as if it were poison.

"That's correct." Lydia smiled.

"My word," Lady Darby said. "This is a scandal."

Lady Eamont took a threatening step toward her daughter. "Your sister would not have gone willingly with that blaggard!" She turned her glare on Nate. "Get the magistrate to fetch my daughter home. She does not have permission to marry that merchant or whatever he is. We don't even know where he comes from. He doesn't have a title or—" She looked from her husband to Nate—"He's a nobody. She'll be ruined!"

"You're too late," Lydia said. "Scotland isn't that far from here, so by the time, you find her, she'll be married."

"This was *your* doing!" Lady Eamont pointed a finger at Lydia.

Bridget was surprised and touched to see Dodsworth put a supportive hand on Lydia's shoulder.

"No, Mama," Lydia said in a strong voice Bridget had never heard her use before. "It was *your* doing. You have been tormenting us for years, controlling our every movement and thoughts, and now we are both free of you."

"What did you do?" Lady Eamont narrowed her eyes. "How did you manage to convince Lord Dodsworth—a confirmed bachelor—to take you as his bride?" She looked from Lydia to Dodsworth. "Something is afoot, and I am going to find out what it is."

"It's no wonder you're surprised, Mama. You spent your

turning us into pariahs, training us to talk in unison like parrots and dressing us alike so you could parade us about like dolls. And at the same time, you pit us against each other, trying to marry Adelia off to Mr. Squires and forcing me to remain at home as your companion for life all because Papa despises you."

"Now that's going too far!" Lord Eamont said.

Lady Eamont slapped her daughter across the face. "How dare you speak to me thus?"

"Stop these theatrics immediately!" Lord Eamont thundered. "Adelia is lost to us. That's the end of it," he said. "The girl has made her choice, and she will live with it."

"This is entirely your fault!" Now Lady Eamont turned her fury on Nate. "If you had stuck to the agreement your brother made with us then Adelia would be married, and both our families would be enormously enriched. But you have always been a wastrel. Your father knew as much, but your brother refused to believe you could not be reformed. So, what did he do? He gave you this beautiful villa, and how did you thank him? By setting your sights on a bankrupt *felo de se*'s daughter who is no better than your servant." She turned her furious glare on Bridget and there was no mistaking the murderous intent in her eyes.

Bridget took a step back, expecting the woman to lunge at her.

"I *said* that's enough!" Lord Eamont thundered. "It's time for you to sit down, my lady."

Lady Eamont straightened her shoulders and turned back to Nate. "We will be leaving this place tomorrow and reporting back to Lord Westerly. I wouldn't be surprised if he cuts you off without a penny."

"I'm afraid you won't be going anywhere," Nate said.

She stopped and stared at him. "Excuse me?" she said haughtily.

"There's been another death at Villa De Lacey, and this time the magistrate suspects foul play." Nate was lying, but for good reason. "No one may leave until we find out who is responsible."

"I don't think that will be possible, old chap," Dodsworth

said. "The king has summoned all peers back to London for Queen Caroline's adultery trial. It begins on August 17th. That's in three weeks. And it takes two weeks to journey back to London."

"Exactly," Lord Eamont said. "He is quite right. There'll be no defying the king, even for the magistrate."

"Oh, I should like to be back in London for the trial too," Lady Darby said. "It's an event not to be missed."

"You won't be allowed to attend the trial," Lady Eamont said frostily. "It's only for the lords."

"I'm well aware"—Lady Darby turned her nose in the air—"but I shall attend the tea parties and enjoy the gossip and speculation."

Bridget gaped at the woman, somewhat repulsed by the fact that she seemed to be looking forward to the spectacle of another woman's predicament.

"I shan't be going. I think the entire trial is shameful." Lady Luxton tucked a stray curl behind her ear. "The queen has done nothing wrong."

"Is anyone here interested in the fact that someone else has *died*?" Nate folded his arms and scanned the room.

Everyone stopped talking and turned to look at him. He finally had their attention.

Bridget held her breath, waiting for Nate to break the news.

"For heaven's sake!" Lady Luxton snapped. "Who has died? Is it that little white mutt that's always running around?"

Bridget scowled. Bijou, exhausted from the morning's chaos had crept upstairs and was likely curled up on his blanket at the foot of her bed.

"It's one of the housemaids," Nate said, and Bridget watched the faces of the guests as he spoke. "Her name was Abigail."

Everyone fell into a stunned silence.

"Is this a joke?" Frederick asked.

"No joke, I'm afraid. Abigail is dead."

A short, high-pitched shriek pierced the air, and everyone turned to see Mrs. Harley collapse to the floor.

═══════════

CHAPTER TWENTY-SIX

"**M**AKE WAY!" LADY Darby swung her walking stick at the people gathered around Mrs. Harley. "Crowding her won't help. She needs to breathe."

The crowd, threatened by the lady's stick, stepped back, and Mr. Harley took the opportunity to step forward and scoop his wife up in his arms.

"Be careful! She's with child!" Lady Darby barked.

"Put her on the settee," Nate instructed. "And someone fetch the smelling salts and call for a doctor."

Just then, Mrs. Harley's eyelids fluttered open, and she attempted to sit up. "There's no need for the salts or a doctor," Mr. Harley said. "She's fine. It was only a fainting spell."

Bridget stopped, confused. Surely, they needed a doctor.

"What are you saying?" Lady Darby thumped her walking stick on the floor. "The woman is with child." She lifted her stick and thrust it in Bridget's direction. "Send for the doctor—immediately!"

"PLEASE, YOU HAVE to help me." Harley cornered Nate. "Cancel the doctor—turn him away at the gate—anything, but he cannot examine my wife."

"She's not with child," Nate said, recalling what Harley had told him the first night he'd arrived.

Harley shook his head.

"In here." Nate ushered Harley into the study and poured the man a brandy. "I don't think we can stop the doctor from carrying out his examination, but you needn't worry. You are the husband. He's not obligated to share information about your wife with Lady Darby." Nate leaned against his desk and folded his arms. "But tell me, what do you plan to do? Tell Lady Darby that she lost the child?"

Harley lifted his glass and swallowed some brandy. "No, we had another plan." He bounced his leg as he spoke.

And suddenly Nate knew what had happened. He remembered Frederick suggesting that Harley impregnate a housemaid—that also explained Mrs. Harley's fainting spell. She had lost a child after all.

"Abigail was pregnant!" Nate said through gritted teeth. "With your child."

"Not necessarily mine." Harley continued to bounce his leg. "The child might have been Frederick's."

"I don't understand."

"I wanted a guarantee that at least one of the housemaids would get with child, and Frederick already has a string of them, so I paid him to—"

"*One* of the housemaids!" Nate curled his hands into fists but restrained himself from hitting Harley. So *that* was Frederick's secret.

"I'm sorry," Harley said. "I was desperate! Don't you understand? We can't have a child of our own. And my aunt will cut me off." He dropped his head in his hands. "What am I to do? When Lady Darby discovers that Mrs. Harley is not with child—indeed never has been with child—then all is lost."

"I think you have bigger problems at hand!" Nate said. "You seem to forget that Abigail has been murdered!"

"It wasn't me. I wanted her to have my baby—Mrs. Harley wanted it too. Why would I kill her?"

"I never suggested you did. But you created a situation that could have led to murder."

"How? All I did was offer her a better life. I was going to pay her a large sum. She's a—she was—a servant, for goodness' sake!"

"Shut up!" Nate said. He could not believe Harley's level of selfishness. "Is Sarah also with child?"

Harley shook his head.

"Then there is a possibility that she was jealous that her friend had been successful where she had not. Abigail was going to get a large payoff and a new life to go with it. Whereas Sarah would be stuck in service for the rest of her life."

"Good Lord! Are you suggesting that Sarah killed Abigail?" Harley gaped at Nate.

"It's certainly possible." Nate pushed back his hair with both hands, and Harley hung his head in shame. "Did you give my maidservants fungi?"

"What?" Harley jerked his head up.

"Did you give the housekeepers vision-inducing fungi?" Nate repeated, his jaw aching with tension.

"Not me. But Frederick may have done—did. He said it made them more"—Harley licked his lips—"compliant."

"Good God!" Nate massaged his aching jaw. He must have been clenching his teeth for ten minutes straight.

"Why is that important?" Harley asked.

"Who else knew about this?" Nate said, ignoring Harley's question.

"Just the four of us and…"

"And?" Nate said.

"Mrs. Harley. She knew. I couldn't keep it from her. I wanted—needed—her consent for obvious reasons."

"Did she consent? Or did you leave her no choice?"

"My aunt left us no choice." Harley drained the rest of his glass and set it down.

Nate shook his head. He could barely contain his fury. "Well, it looks like your plan has come to naught."

Harley stood up and gave Nate a pleading look. "They were both willing. It would have benefited us all—"

"Get out!" Nate growled.

Harley hesitated. "Please, try to understand."

"Go!" Nate said.

After Harley rushed out of the room and closed the door behind him, Bridget stood up. She'd been sitting next to the window, listening silently to all that had been said. Nate was not even sure that Harley had been aware of her presence in the room.

"I'm sorry you had to hear that," Nate said. "It was quite distasteful and not at all meant for a lady's ears."

Bridget gave him a hard stare. "I told you not to worry about that. I need to hear the facts—all of them—no matter how distasteful. That aside, it wasn't the first time I heard that conversation."

"You knew about this?" Nate frowned. "How?"

"I didn't know that I knew until I heard Harley talk about it again." She sat on the chair Harley had vacated.

"Again?" Nate put both hands on the desk and leaned slightly back.

"That was the information erased from my memory after my fall. I heard Mr. Harley and his wife talking in the library after you left."

"And they didn't see you in the library?"

She shook her head. "I was concealed in a nook. I must have decided to go down to the lake to stop what was happening to the housemaids."

"But why didn't you speak to me? Why go by yourself—" Nate stopped, remembering with fresh shame his conversation with Bridget that night and the comments he'd made about her papa. "Never mind. I'm sorry," he said. "I was insensitive to you that night. It's no wonder you avoided me."

"My memory of that night is still unclear," she said, brushing off his apology, "but I do recall my utter shock at overhearing the conversation between Mr. and Mrs. Harley. I don't know what possessed me to venture out on my own—I don't know what I thought I would do if I caught the housemaids with the Harley and Frederick, but I do know that someone must have followed me. And whoever it was wanted to stop me from going to the lake."

"Someone must have been watching you and waiting for an opportunity to catch you alone."

Bridget shuddered visibly, and Nate imagined the idea of someone watching and waiting for an opportunity to kill her.

"Thus far, we've assumed that the same person who killed Madam Bouffant and Abigail also wanted to silence you—do you still think that way?"

"I don't know. Lady Eamont had reason to kill Madam Bouffant, and she clearly blames me for your refusal to marry Adelia, but what reason could she have to kill Abigail?"

"Abigail may have discovered something. Perhaps, she witnessed more than she revealed when she found Madam Bouffant's body. Maybe she saw Lady Eamont and used that information to blackmail her."

"But Sarah was with her. Wouldn't her life be in danger too?"

"Abigail said that Sarah was a few seconds behind her. She's the one who screamed and alerted you. Abigail may have caught a glimpse of Lady Eamont before Sarah arrived." Nate drummed his fingers on the desk. "Unfortunately, we have no proof whatsoever and barely time to find any."

Suddenly, Lady Darby's shrill voice sounded outside, along with Harley's muffled voice.

"It seems that Lady Darby has been given the news after all," Nate said.

Bridget exhaled. "Yes, it does. I imagine it must be awful for Mrs. Harley. She cannot help it if she is barren, and then to be made to feel like a failure and to have her husband punished and humiliated for something that cannot be helped."

"I agree. She's lucky that Lady Darby doesn't have the authority to chop her head off. I have the feeling that's exactly what she would do if she had the power."

Bridget bit her lip. "I've just thought of something."

"Are you going to share it with me?" Nate asked.

"We've been going off the assumption that there's only one offender, but perhaps there are two."

Nate tilted his head, interested to hear more.

Bridget stood up. "I think I need to spend a bit of quality time with Mrs. Harley."

"You what?" Nathan asked, but Bridget was already out the door.

$$\mathcal{Q}$$

BRIDGET KNOCKED ON Mrs. Harley's chamber door and was greeted by her lady's maid.

"I've come to check on Mrs. Harley." She smiled. "How is she feeling?"

"She's still poorly." The lady's maid held the door ajar. "I'll let her know you came—"

"Oh, the poor dear." Bridget pushed past the maid and stepped into the darkened room.

"Is that Miss De Lacey?" Bridget heard Mrs. Harley's faint voice.

"Yes, ma'am. I tried to tell her you were indisposed but—"

"Wait outside," Bridget instructed the servant before she could finish her sentence.

The maid hesitated.

"How kind of you to come, but I'm afraid you've caught me in an awful state." Mrs. Harley lay on her settee with a damp cloth stretched across her forehead.

"Mrs. Harley requires a strong cup of tea," Bridget instructed the maid.

"Lady Darby said—" the maid began.

"Tea would be lovely." Mrs. Harley's faint voice sounded from within the darkened room.

"Do as your mistress asks," Bridget said. "She requires tea." And, seeing the uncertainty on the maid's face, she added, "You're not to worry. I am here to cheer her spirits."

This seemed to placate the servant, who nodded and exited the room.

Mrs. Harley sat up. Her eyes were swollen, and her face was red from crying.

"Oh, my dear," Bridget said, sitting next to her on the settee. "I'm so sorry."

The woman nodded and fresh tears spilled down her cheeks.

"As you know, I recently experienced a devastating loss of my own, so I understand your pain. But there is still hope. You must stay positive. I am certain you will soon find yourself with child again."

Mrs. Harley shook her head. "I shan't. I can't..." The rest of her sentence seemed to have been strangled in her throat, and she was unable to continue.

A stab of guilt almost made Bridget abandon her task, but self-preservation propelled her forward. "What do you mean you can't?" she asked as gently as possible.

"I was never with child." Mrs. Harley placed a hand on her stomach. "Although, I started to believe I was. The mind can play such wonderful tricks, can it not?" She smiled through her tears as though the memory of her delusion brought her pleasure.

"But Abigail was with child, wasn't she?" Bridget asked, maintaining the same gentle tone.

Mrs. Harley nodded. "She claimed to have been. She told Mr. Harley that she'd missed her courses—although it did seem rather soon—only a matter of days. Still, the hope she gave us..." Mrs. Harley shook her head and dabbed her tears.

"So, her child was Mr. Harley's?"

Mrs. Harley jerked her head up as though she'd just woken from a trance. "No—I—what are you implying?" She feigned ignorance.

"Don't be alarmed, Mrs. Harley. Such practices are not un-common and quite understandable," Bridget lied. She had no idea if such practices were common, but they were certainly unknown to her.

"Yes, of course. I forget that you were once—well, before your father's..." She frowned. "It seems all is lost for both of us. Lady Darby knows I am barren. She will disinherit my husband." Mrs. Harley twisted her hands. "Oh, she's a wickedly cruel woman. I think it's her constant monitoring and harsh criticism of me that has made me sick and unable to keep a babe in my womb."

"I think you might be right. And that's why you must begin to heal yourself." Bridget patted the woman's hand. "Sitting on this settee all day won't do you any good. Why don't you wash your face and come outside? Bijou is due for his walk, and the fresh air will do you good."

"You're too kind, but I'm afraid to leave my room. Lady Darby is furious with me. I cannot face her."

"Then it might please you to know that Lady Darby has shut herself away in her chamber, so you needn't worry about her. And if we do happen to encounter her, then you will not be forced to face her alone. I shall be by your side."

"You're too kind, Miss De Lacey. I don't deserve it."

"Nonsense!" Bridget stood up to open the curtains and light flooded the room. Then she walked to Mrs. Harley's clothing chest. "Why don't we find you something cheerful to wear?" She opened the chest and pretended to scan the piles of neatly folded dresses, but her eye was fixed upon a red dress that sat amongst a separate pile of clothing. Her heartbeat accelerated as she reached for the garment.

"This one will do nicely," she said, snatching the dress from the pile. "It's such a lovely red. You'll feel much better once you put on something pretty."

"Oh, not that one," Mrs. Harley objected. "That one's missing a button on the sleeve. You took it off the mending pile."

"Missing a button?" Bridget said, her heart now pounding in earnest. She peered down at the small gold button on the left sleeve. It was identical to the one Nate had shown her.

"Do you know, Mr. Squires found a button lying in the grass that looks just like the one on this dress? He picked it up near the spot where I had my fall and thought it might belong to me. Shall I fetch it?"

Mrs. Harley paled.

"Are you quite well?" Bridget feigned concern.

"I feel rather dizzy all of a sudden. Perhaps it's better if I rest."

"If you wish. I'll just take this dress with me and—"

"No!" Mrs. Harley said.

"But how will your lady's maid mend your dress without the button?"

Mrs. Harley frowned. "Well, I suppose you're right. She will need the button, but it's not urgent. You needn't rush. I'll send her to collect it from you tomorrow."

Bridget sauntered back to the settee, still holding the red dress. "What do you suppose your button was doing in the outer edge of the garden? You've been confined to your bed since you got here, and when you do venture outside, it's only for a short stroll with your lady's maid."

"Some days, when I am feeling strong, we go for a longer walk. I must have lost it then."

Bridget shook her head. "I don't think Lady Darby would have permitted your lady's maid to take you to the thicket where treacherous tree roots abound, and squirrels run underfoot. She would have been far too fearful that you would fall. But I'll be happy to ask her for clarification."

"Mayhap, a bird picked it up from the garden and dropped it in the thicket." Mrs. Harley smoothed her dress and avoided looking at Bridget.

"That's an idea," Bridget said. "Or mayhap you followed me into the thicket, pushed me, and left me for dead."

"Never!" Mrs. Harley half rose from her seat but then seemed to lose the energy she needed to stand up.

"How did you know I'd overheard your conversation with Mr. Harley in the library that night?"

"I don't know what you're talking about!"

"You were worried that I was going to prevent Mr. Harley from carrying out his plan, weren't you?"

"I'm tired. I'd like you to leave." Mrs. Harley dropped her head in her hand.

Bridget stood up. "Perhaps, I should put my theory to the magistrate then. We'll let him decide. Now that he has a murder to investigate—"

"Stop!" Mrs. Harley held up her hand. "It was me. I had a feeling someone else was in the library that night. So I pretended to retire to bed and then waited in the shadows to see if anyone followed Mr. Harley and Lord Frederick after they left. That's when I saw you, emerging out of your hiding place. I knew that you would tell Mr. Squires, and he'd put an end to the plan."

"So you followed me and tried to murder me?" Bridget asked.

"Of course not. I only wanted to frighten you—to divert your attention—and make you return home. But I didn't push you. You tripped over a tree root just as you were told."

"And you left me there, injured and alone, all night. I could have died. But, mayhap, that's what you hoped would happen."

Mrs. Harley dropped her gaze to her lap. "I was frightened and desperate. You have no idea what it is like to be a barren woman who is desperate for a child. Month after month I disappoint my husband, his aunt, and most of all myself. Why? I've been good all my life. I went to church like a good Christian woman, I was an obedient daughter, I married the man my father chose for me—yet I have failed as a woman."

"Abandoning an injured person who might very well bleed to death is neither good nor Christian," Bridget said.

"Perhaps I have given up trying to be good."

"Is it possible, then, that you grew jealous of Abigail? I'm certain it seemed like an injustice that she managed what you could not in such a short time."

Mrs. Harley shook her head. "You're wrong. Abigail and Sarah were our only hope. Losing Abigail and her babe has cost us everything. Lady Darby has learned about our scheme and will never believe Mr. Harley has a true heir unless she sees it growing in my belly daily and witnesses the midwife deliver it from my womb into her arms. When Abigail died, she took our future with her." She wiped her eyes with the back of her hand. "I am sorry to disappoint you Miss De Lacey, but I am not your killer."

Bridget sighed. The woman was right. Mrs. Harley might have behaved reprehensibly, but she wasn't guilty of murdering Abigail or Madam Bouffant. Her time was wasted here. The killer needed to be rooted out, and she had to work fast, or he or she'd escape with the rest of the ton back to London for Queen Caroline's impending trial.

CHAPTER TWENTY-SEVEN

"**S**HE LEFT YOU to die?" Nate said aghast after Bridget relayed her conversation with Mrs. Harley. "Then she has shown that she is capable of murder. We cannot rule her out."

"I am starting to think everyone is capable of murder," Bridget said. "How blissfully naive I was just a few months ago to the evils of mankind. I've lived in a sheltered world, surrounded by beauty and serenity for one-and-twenty years, like a little fool."

"Your papa did his best to protect you. That was his job."

"You're right. Poor Papa. And I couldn't even give him a proper burial. All I have left of him is a lock of his hair."

"I'm sorry. I blame my brother for that. The least he could have done was use his influence to arrange for your father's return. He's an insensitive beast."

"It's not your fault." Bridget blinked back her impending tears and took a deep breath. If she started crying now, she'd never be able to stop. She straightened her shoulders. "I believe Mr. and Mrs. Harley are innocent of the murder. They are both devastated that their plan failed. However, we do need to consider Sarah. As you told Mr. Harley, she may have been angered to discover that Abigail won the prize, so to speak."

"That's right. Whoever gave the Harleys a baby would have profited generously. I am certain that set the housemaids in fierce competition with one another."

"True, but then again, Sarah had no reason to kill Madam Bouffant."

"She may have—they may have—if Madam Bouffant discovered what Abigail and Sarah were doing. She might have wanted a piece of their prize, and they may have seen cause to push her down the stairs. Perhaps they weren't late to start upstairs that day. Mayhap they were there on time and saw an opportunity to push Madam Bouffant down the stairs after they caught her creeping out of her lover's room when everyone else was still asleep. Maybe they pushed her and then ran away, only to return later to 'discover' the body."

"Good heavens! That's diabolical. But if it's true, how will we obtain proof? Perhaps I'll put Eliza on that task. She sees and hears all."

"You shouldn't do that. We have to consider everyone."

Bridget blinked, taken aback by his comment. "What are you saying?"

"I'm saying everyone is a suspect."

"Eliza has been in our service since before I was born. She nursed my mother when she was dying." Bridget gave a short, angry laugh. "And may I remind you that these deaths started after your guests arrived from London."

"Fair point," Nate acknowledged. "All I'm asking is that we keep this investigation between us. We don't need a myriad of amateur sleuths in the house. It would mean putting people in danger."

Bridget nodded stiffly, still hurt by Nate's comment about Eliza. "You're right. That's the last thing I want."

"Good. We'll interview Sarah together."

"And what of Frederick?" Bridget said. "He had motive to kill both women. When I inquired about her brooch, Madam Bouffant implied she had more than one patron. When I asked her if Frederick had given it to her, she replied that the young ones were too cheap. But she never denied that Frederick was one of her patrons."

"Oh, I am certain he was. Frederick fancies himself to be a *Don Juan*. He did not spend a fortnight journeying to Westmorland with a beautiful courtesan and act the polite gentleman the entire time—not Frederick!"

"Then he may have fallen in love with her and been overcome with jealousy when she refused to leave Lord Eamont. And the same scenario applies to Abigail."

Nate shook his head. "No, it's a good theory, but it doesn't work in Frederick's case. The man has no real heart. He doesn't become attached to anybody except perhaps himself."

"He's your friend, so he must be attached to you."

"Not at all. He and I indulged in the same vices for a time, and that's the extent of our friendship. He's quite bored of me already."

"Very well, what of Jefferson and Adelia? We can't ignore the fact that they disappeared the same morning Abigail died. Not to mention Jefferson's strange behavior and his mumblings about 'Andrew' and 'broken necks.'"

"Right. As it turns out, I have an explanation."

"Oh?" Bridget said.

"While you were with Mrs. Harley, I interviewed Dodsworth. It was a difficult conversation because I had to tell him what I overheard on the shores of Windermere yesterday. He seemed surprisingly relieved that I knew his secret. He has even come to terms with his pending marriage to Lydia. After realizing that a marriage of convenience was the safest and best way for both of them to gain their freedom, the two of them helped to arrange Jefferson and Adelia's elopement. The Eamont sisters are finally free of their mother, and Jefferson and Dodsworth will be free to continue as they were, undetected."

"Then how do you explain Jefferson's odd behavior the day Madam Bouffant died?"

"He assumed she broke her neck because that's how his younger brother, Andrew, died. He fell down the stairs when they were boys and broke his neck. It was a tragedy that left deep scars on Jefferson's heart. That is why he was so shaken by Madam Bouffant's death."

"Dear Lord, how awful." Bridget covered her face with her hands. "The poor man. How horrible it must have been having that memory dredged up. And to think I wanted to accuse him of murder."

"Yes, well, you couldn't have known," Nate said. "That said, it seems Sarah is our prime suspect with Lady Eamont a close second."

"What about Lady Luxton? Are you certain she isn't capable of—"

"I'm certain." Nate said.

"You have to consider that she did have a motive after Madam Bouffant disturbed the two of you in the garden. Is it a coincidence that Madam Bouffant was found dead the very next day? Also, she made a rather callous remark after Madam Bouffant was killed. It appears she held a grudge against the woman. And who knows, she may have had a grudge against Abigail too. She seems to dislike other women." She knew for sure that Lady Luxton held her in no high esteem.

"She can be harsh, that's true. But I know her, and believe me, she is no killer."

"Very well, then," Bridget said, her heart sinking. The way Nate had jumped to Lady Luxton's defense told her that he still harbored feelings for his former betrothed. And then, there was her son, whom he seemed to love. There was no doubt about it— their attachment was far from severed.

♀

SARAH'S BLUE EYES were red rimmed and swollen from crying. But it was the fear in them that unnerved Bridget.

"I didn't mean for her to die." The maidservant shrank into the oversized leather chair in the study.

"What are you saying?" Nate leaned on the desk with his forearms and peered at Sarah. "That you killed Abigail by accident?"

"Killed her!" Sarah's voice reached a high pitch. "No! I mean—I don't know." She looked from Nate to Bridget. "Can you wish someone dead?" she asked, her face scrunched and her eyes pleading.

Nate's thick brows came together in a frown.

Bridget, who sat beside Sarah on one of the two oversized leather chairs in her papa's study, leaned over and touched the housemaid on the arm. "What do you mean, Sarah?" she asked kindly. "Are you saying that you wished Abigail harm?"

Sarah's features contorted as if she were in physical pain. "I wished her dead."

"Yes, but did you—" Nate started, and then stopped when he caught Bridget's eyes on him. She shook her head ever so slightly to indicate that he needed to be quiet.

Bridget turned back to Sarah and gently squeezed her hand. "*Why* did you wish her harm?" she asked, keeping the urgency out of her voice. "Did you feel threatened by her?"

Sarah shrugged.

"Perhaps you were jealous?" Nate suggested.

Sarah grimaced and fresh tears rolled down her cheeks. Bridget gave Nate a hard stare. He didn't seem to realize that patience and kindness were imperative now. If Sarah felt threatened or blamed, she'd shut down and all would be lost.

"Don't be ashamed," Bridget said in a soothing tone. "We all feel jealous sometimes."

Nate seemed to finally understand as he retrieved a handkerchief from his pocket and handed it to the housemaid. "Why don't you tell us what happened."

Sarah pressed the silk cloth to her eyes and took a shaky breath before speaking. "Mr. Harley offered us a good deal of money to—well—his missus is barren, you see, so—" She let out a sob.

"Don't worry, we know that part already." Bridget patted the servant's hand. "You needn't go into detail about it."

"I know it sounds horrible, but I ain't ever had a lot of money, and he promised us—whichever one of us gave him a child—a grand life. At first, I didn't want to do it because it were obvious that Mr. Harley preferred Abigail to me. She was so pretty an' Mr. Harley were always talking about how they both had copper hair. I knew he wanted her to be the one to bear his child, and then I'd be left with naught." She stared at the handkerchief in her hands and shook her head.

"But Abigail convinced you to do it, didn't she?" Bridget coaxed.

Sarah nodded. "Abigail swore we'd stick together, whichever one of us got with child first, it didn't matter, we'd share the fortune. We'd give the Harleys the child, take the money, and set up someplace together—take care of each other." Sarah made a strangled sound as another sob escaped her throat.

"Go on," Bridget said gently, although she was having a difficult time sympathizing with the woman.

Sarah dabbed her eyes with the handkerchief again and sniffed before continuing. "At first, it were just Mr. Harley. He'd have both of us—one after the other."

Bridget's face flushed at the maid's frank talk, and she forced herself not to look at Nate. "But then Lord Frederick started 'helping.' He always wanted Abigail. So, I'd go with Mr. Harley." She twisted the handkerchief. "It didn't seem to matter to Mr. Harley whose babe he got so long as he got one."

"And it angered you that Mr. Harley and Lord Frederick preferred Abigail?" Nate said. "Because they thought her prettier?"

"Or because she was more likely to get with child than you?" Bridget said, glaring at Nate. He'd said the wrong thing again.

"No," Sarah said. "Truly I didn't care. Because Abigail said we'd share the money no matter who got with child. We'd run off together, get a home, and have servants of our own."

Bridget frowned. *Just how much money did Mr. Harley offer them?*

"But that's not what happened is it?" Nate interjected again. "Abigail wanted it all for herself, didn't she?"

Sarah nodded. Her gaze was fixed on her boots. "When Abigail learned she were with child, everything changed." She looked up. "She talked of how she was to escape service and live a grand life as Mr. Harley's mistress. She said that Mrs. Harley was dowdy and barren, and that Mr. Harley wanted her instead. She'd have her own quarters in London, new dresses every week, and money to buy sweet treats, perfume, and whatever else she wanted."

"Abigail broke her promise to you, so you killed her," Nate said.

"No!" Sarah looked from Nate to Bridget, her eyes wild. "I don't know. I wished it—I prayed for her to die!"

"You did more than wish, didn't you, Sarah?" Nate said. "You gave her the wrong type of mushrooms, then you followed her and pushed her into the fountain."

"No," Sarah said. "I never did. The mushrooms always came from Mr. Harley or Lord Frederick. We kept them in a little sack in our room. Mr. Harley warned us not to pick our own. He said we might get the wrong ones and then we could die."

"You knew exactly what to do then," Nate said. "You knew what would kill her and then you did it."

Sarah's body trembled. "It's true. I wished her dead and the devil made it happen."

"You made it happen. You switched the mushrooms in the bag, didn't you?"

"It weren't fair!" Sarah cried. "When Lord Frederick started taking up with Lady Luxton, he stopped helping Mr. Harley. Abigail went with Mr. Harley every night. He seemed to forget all about me. That's why Abigail got with child and not me. That's why I wished her dead. I didn't mean for her to die. But I prayed for it!"

Bridget swallowed. She could see that Nate was no longer listening. His face had turned as pale as the mist that hovered over the lake, and his lovely, dark-blue eyes had turned black.

"Did you say Lady Luxton?" he asked in a hoarse whisper.

NATE'S HEART RACED as he made his way to the smoking room. He'd let Helen manipulate him once again. And she'd used Henry to do it—their son! A thought struck him. *Was* Henry his son? Or had Helen been sleeping with Frederick or another man while they were betrothed? *What a fool I've been!* He pushed open the door to the smoking room and burst inside.

"Good Lord, Squires! You almost handed me my death. What on earth is the matter?"

Nate went straight for the cigar box without taking off his jacket or slipping on a smoking robe. He picked out a cigar and held it between his trembling fingers—unable to bring it to his lips and light it.

"I say, are you unwell?" Frederick asked.

"No." Nate wetted his lips, which had suddenly turned as dry as his throat. "I was just wondering. Have you made any strides in your plan with Lady Luxton?"

"My plans?" Frederick gave Nate a lopsided smile.

"Yes, you mentioned the other day that—" Nate coughed. His throat had dried again.

Frederick cocked his head. "What is it, Squires? Don't tell me you still care for her. If I thought there was still something between you two, I would not have—"

"Don't apologize. It's nothing like that."

"That's a relief." Frederick leaned back in his chair and inhaled his cigar.

Nate dropped his own cigar back in the box and went to pour himself a brandy. He felt sick to his stomach, but he couldn't blame Frederick. After all, that man had only done what he'd said he was going to do, and he'd not protested at the time. It wasn't Frederick's fault that Helen had fooled him once again.

But he didn't care about her so much as he did the child.

"She doesn't love me, you know," Frederick said as Nate sat down beside him with a brandy in hand. "She'll never marry me. No, I'm only a diversion because she's bored with her husband. But, she is beautiful so—"

Nate's chest tightened. "I don't think Helen is capable of loving anyone," he said.

"You might be right." Frederick nodded. He put his cigar to his lips and inhaled.

Nate waited until his friend had exhaled a thick stream of smoke before speaking again. "What about the child?"

"Are you asking who I think fathered the boy?"

Nate nodded, his heart drumming in his chest.

"I don't think it's Lord Luxton's, I can tell you that much." Frederick eyed Nate. "He could be yours. He's the right age, and he has your coloring."

"She swears he is mine." Nate sipped his brandy.

"Or…he could be your brother's." Frederick locked his dark eyes on Nate's.

Nate almost choked on his brandy. He extracted his handkerchief from his pocket and coughed into it.

"I'm sorry," Frederick said. "I thought you knew."

"Knew *what*?" Nate said through gritted teeth.

"I thought Helen was the reason for your acrimonious relationship with Edward."

"No. Our relationship is acrimonious because Edward is a pompous prig. Helen would never—not Edward—what would be the point? He was already married. She wanted a title and the money and power that comes with it."

"You've always been blind when it comes to Helen." Frederick put his cigar to his lips and inhaled. "She puts Narcissus to shame. The woman wants power over every man she encounters, and she thought that your brother would become as besotted with her as you. That meant he'd ply her with money and whatever else she wanted. And she wouldn't have stopped at him either. Had you married her, you would have been a cuckold more times than you could count."

"Stop," Nate warned. "I don't want to hear about it. I know that I have always been a fool when it concerns Helen. Still, I never imagined Edward would stoop that low. My own brother! Do you imagine that if I knew"—Nate shook his head—"that he'd still be alive? I'd have challenged him to a duel—brother or no brother."

"I think in his mind, he believed he was saving you," Frederick said. "She knew he held the purse strings, and he knew she could be bought. It's not that he wanted her for himself. It was more that he didn't want her for you, so he set a trap for her, and once she fell into it, he had complete control of her reputation."

"Don't you dare defend him," Nate snarled.

"Edward could have ruined her chances of marrying anyone. Instead, he arranged for her to marry Lord Luxton. Perhaps, because he knew she was with child and cared enough to secure the lad a good future."

"I said, don't defend him." Nate clenched his fists. "Whatever Edward thinks, that child cannot belong to my pale-as-a-lily brother," Nate spat.

"I tend to agree. He is the image of you."

"But I will never know for certain." Nate gulped his brandy. Perhaps Edward had done him a favor. He'd been blind to Helen's duplicity, and life with her would have been miserable. Still, it had been unintentional. Edward didn't care about his happiness. He'd interfered in his marriage to control him. He was the despot of his own little kingdom.

Nate swallowed more brandy. He hated that Edward controlled his inheritance, dolling it out to him as an allowance each month, and withholding the money at his will. It was time to sever his dependence on that bastard. He had to make Villa De Lacey work for him, and that meant discovering who the killer was before anyone else ended up dead.

$$\approx\!\!\approx\!\!\approx$$

CHAPTER TWENTY-EIGHT

BRIDGET APPROACHED THE rose garden cautiously, causing an impatient Bijou to scamper ahead of her. The horror of seeing Abigail's body floating in the fountain that morning replayed in her mind with each step. She stopped at the fountain's edge and inhaled, shaking away the image, before straightening her shoulders and forcing herself to look at the water.

She searched for missed clues, but there was nothing except a few floating leaves on the surface of the fountain. She circled the area slowly, her eyes scanning the ground, but again she found nothing. The rose garden was the most-cared-for part of the garden, and Thomas kept it flourishing and manicured. And it seemed that he'd already cleaned any mess that would have evidenced Abigail's suffering and murder.

Bridget sat on the fountain's rim and listened to the soft trickling of the water. It had always been the most tranquil area of the garden. She glanced up and studied Venus's perfectly sculptured face. Her stone eyes were serene and all-knowing. *What did you see? If only you could speak.*

Whoever killed Abigail had shown her no mercy. But what drove a person to act in such a way? High emotions had to be at play. She thought of the pain and fear that had engulfed her upon learning of her father's death. Though it was self-inflicted, she'd wanted to blame someone else. Had she come face to face with Nate's brother in those early, agonizing weeks, or the ignorant men who'd probably desecrated her father's body before they'd buried it at a crossroads, she might have wanted to lash out at them. Even now, she could feel the anger rise in her chest. The truth was, one could love so strongly that it turned into hatred. Had that been the case for Madam Eamont? If so, it followed that jealousy—or, rather, humiliation—fit as motivation in her case. And if Abigail had witnessed her push Madam Bouffant, she'd need to silence her. As to the vicious nature of the crime, her own two daughters had testified to the woman's propensity for cruelty. But how to prove such a thing short of a confession from the woman? If only there was something…

Bridget stood and turned to the carefully tended bushes of red, pink, and white roses. They were arranged in clusters of color next to the fountain. The little rose garden had been her mother's favorite area and because of that, it became a sanctuary for her father. He often tended to the flowers himself, getting on his knees beside Thomas to prune them.

A stab of guilt almost took Bridget's breath away. She had not been to visit her father's memorial for several weeks, not because she didn't think about her papa constantly, but because visiting his grave had become too painful since Madam Bouffant's murder. The horror of seeing the woman's battered corpse had killed her fantasy of her papa resting peacefully in his grave. She had been forced to face the truth: her papa's mangled body, destroyed by his own hand, lay at some unknown crossroads amongst thieves and murderers.

All she could do was pray that his soul had found its way home, to her and Aunt Marianne. She had to believe that, or she'd go mad with grief.

Bridget leaned forward to smell a bush of white roses. Her father had loved the white ones the most. They were pure and innocent like her mama—that's what he'd always said. She evaluated the flowers, looking for the most beautiful white rose on the bush to pluck for her father's makeshift grave. It was time she swallowed her pain and paid her respects again. The grave might only contain a lock of his hair, but it was all she had left.

🔍

GRIEF'S HEAVY WEIGHT bore down on Bridget as she drew near her papa's gravestone.

Then she saw something that made her freeze: an arrangement of red roses lay on her papa's grave. Her heart shattered in her chest.

"Oh, Aunt Marianne," she cried and strode forward. Bijou picked up his pace and followed, staying close to her side. "Oh, my poor dear aunt!" She sank onto the ground beside the grave and Bijou settled by her side, wagging his tail. "You've been coming to pay your respects all alone."

Aunt Marianne had suffered terribly upon learning that her brother's body would not be returning to Villa De Lacey, and Bridget had hoped the little grave would give them both comfort. Instead, it had proved to be a painful reminder that he'd been denied a Christian burial and that his family had been denied his remains. For this reason, Aunt Marianne had started avoiding the site, but now it seemed that she had taken some comfort in the little spot, just as Bridget had hoped she would.

She lay the white rose next to the arrangement of red roses. The flowers, she saw, were fresh. When had Aunt Marianne come? Surely, she had not picked these roses today. Mayhap yesterday?

Just then, Bijou pounced onto the mound and started digging furiously, sending the arrangement of roses scattering.

"Bijou, no!" Bridget scolded.

But the enthusiastic terrier just buried his face in the dirt; when he lifted his head he shook it as if he'd caught something. He growled fiercely and wagged his tail with excitement.

"What is it? What do you have?"

Bijou gave the object another shake, freeing it from the ground. Then he proudly revealed his prize to Bridget—a black lace handkerchief.

"Where did that come from?" Bridget took the handkerchief out of Bijou's mouth. *It must belong to Aunt Marianne, but how did it come to be buried in the ground?* She peered at the hole Bijou had dug, took off her gloves, and started to push the earth he'd removed back over it. But something inside her made her stop.

She had a sudden urge to retrieve the little box in which her father's lock of hair was secured. She wanted to gaze upon the lock of hair once more, to touch it, smell it. She reached down for the box, but it was no longer there.

Bridget started digging furiously. Watching her, Bijou yapped and pounced on the grave to help, digging by his mistress's side. The hole they made grew, but the box never materialized. Bridget stared at the gaping space in the earth and creased her brows. *Someone has taken it.*

🔎

BRIDGET GOT TO her feet and wiped the dirt from her dress. Then she retrieved her gloves and started toward the villa, followed by Bijou. Had Aunt Marianne taken the box containing Papa's hair? She couldn't think why her aunt would do such a thing. But if not her, then who? The only other people who knew about Papa's little grave were the gardener and the servants.

Just then, Bridget heard Nate's voice—he was angry. She looked up to see him standing with Lady Luxton a few feet away and froze. Sensing the anger emanating from the two people, Bijou cowered at her feet.

"Was it because of Frederick? Is that why you did it?"

"Did what, Nathaniel? You sound like a lunatic raving about nonsense."

"You know what I'm talking about. You killed those two women! First, you pushed Madam Bouffant down the stairs after you caught her coming out of Frederick's bedroom and then you murdered the housemaid because he was sleeping with her too."

"Now I see that you really *are* a raving lunatic. Why should I care if Frederick whores himself out to an actress and a housemaid?"

"Because you like to be the center of every man's world—mine, Frederick's, my brother's!"

Lady Luxton's mouth clamped shut.

"So, it's true," Nate said, his voice clipped.

"He forced me. He was determined that we should not be married."

"Are you saying my brother forced himself on you?" Nate growled.

"Not in that way. He...well, *convinced* me. He's a powerful man."

Nate threw back his head and laughed. "You're ridiculous, trying to convince me that my brother seduced you. Edward is a block of ice; he couldn't seduce a harpy." He shook his head. "To think I let you manipulate me using that child. Your *son*, for God's sake!"

"He's your son too!"

"I'll never know, will I? His mother is so untrustworthy that he could be anyone's child—Lord, he might belong to the butler or the gardener!"

Lady Luxton's face flushed red. "How dare you!" she said, swiping her nails across Nate's cheek.

Bridget gasped, but the pair didn't notice her. They were too absorbed in their anger and pain.

"I'll make sure you never see Henry again!" Lady Luxton spat the words. "Never!"

Bridget could see Nate's body sag, and her heart ached for him.

"You truly are evil, Helen," he said. "I don't know how I could have stayed blind for so long. I think you are capable of hurting anyone who gets in your way, and that includes Madam Bouffant and Abigail."

Lady Luxton laughed. "A whore and a maidservant are no

threat to me. Now, why don't you go back to playing magistrate with the orphan you are so fond of? I am going to gather my husband and *my* son and leave this place. And I dare you to try and stop me!" Lady Luxton strode back toward the villa.

Nate put his hands on his hips and cursed out loud.

Bridget remained paralyzed, uncertain about what to do. Why hadn't she walked away earlier?

Nate turned then, and she saw the shock on his face as he registered her presence. "Bridget, what are you doing here?"

"I'm sorry," she said, going toward him. "I was about to start walking back to the villa and"—she shook her head—"I'm sorry. I didn't mean to listen."

Nate ran a hand through his hair. He looked positively miserable, and for a moment, they both remained silent. Bijou, still sensing the tension in the air, remained close to her side. Finally, Bridget said, "I'm sorry about what she said—about Henry."

"I don't know why I accused her—I should have left well enough alone. But I was so angry after finding out about..." He squeezed the bridge of his nose. "Now, Henry will be lost to me forever." He dropped his hand and looked at her with grief in his eyes.

"Then you didn't mean what you said. You don't think she's a killer?"

"I doubt it. Helen is too vain to be threatened by the likes of Madam Bouffant and Abigail. She'd take greater pleasure in stealing their lovers than killing them. No, Helen wants her victims alive. That way, she can enjoy torturing them."

Bridget swallowed. She wished there was something she could do to help ease his pain, but she knew better than anyone that there was no magic potion that could erase the agony of loss.

Nate glanced at Bridget's soiled gloves and dress. Then his gaze fell on Bijou's earth-smudged face and paws. The little terrier, frightened by the acrimony in the air, had been extraordinarily quiet.

"Have you two been doing some digging?" he asked, coming

forward to pet Bijou. Seeing Nate's friendly smile back on his face, Bijou wagged his tail and moved to greet him. "My, you are a mess." Nate ruffled Bijou's fur.

"I'm afraid something awful has happened," Bridget said. "My father's grave has been raided. Someone stole the box containing his lock of hair and my mama's letters," Bridget choked on the last word.

"What? Why? Who would do such a thing? Did your father have enemies in the town—people he owed money perhaps?"

Bridget shrugged. Had someone asked her that question six months ago, she would have replied, *Of course, not!* But she wasn't certain of anything anymore. "The box and the lock of hair aren't worth money, so I don't know why someone would want it. Someone must have acted out of malice." She bit her lip, unable to imagine anyone hating her father. He'd had his faults, but he'd been a good person.

"Malice or love," Nate said. "Both of those emotions are strong motivators. And malice often follows love."

"What are you saying?" Bridget asked.

Nate ran a hand over his jaw and frowned in thought. "Your father spent a lot of time in London, didn't he?"

"Yes, gambling, so I've learned."

"But what if he went for another reason also? What if he had a lover there?"

Bridget recoiled with surprise. She'd never thought about another woman in her father's life, but of course, it was possible. But who? "And you think his lover came here to dig up his lock of hair?" The idea was absurd.

"Perhaps she's already here. Mayhap she's one of the guests. And if her love has turned to malice, for whatever reason, she might have come here to wreak havoc and spend her anger."

Bridget took a step back. "You think…whoever took my papa's lock of hair also murdered Madam Bouffant and Abigail?"

"I think it's possible," Nate said.

"But who?" Bridget said. "Lady Eamont?" She laughed. "Or

Lady Luxton?" She shook her head. "No. It's impossible."

"What are you saying? That it's impossible someone loved your papa?"

Bridget stiffened. "Of course not. But your theory is too far-fetched. Those two women are only capable of self-love. You know that as well as I do. And who else is there? Mrs. Harley and Lady Darby?" She gave another nervous laugh. "It's utterly preposterous."

"We have to consider every possibility, no matter how unlikely it seems."

Bridget frowned. *Love or malice.* She repeated the words over in her mind, letting them marinate. Could someone at Villa De Lacey have been in love with her papa? And if so…who?

Suddenly, with a sinking in her stomach, it dawned on her.

＊ ━━━━━━━━━━━━ ＊

CHAPTER TWENTY-NINE

I T WASN'T DIFFICULT to find her papa's box in Eliza's room. She'd hidden it in the most obvious place—under her bed. Bridget recovered the box and opened it to find the lock of hair still secured inside. She stroked the golden lock and smiled. Nate had been wrong. The thief and the killer weren't the same. Eliza had no malice in her. All she'd wanted was to have Papa close to her. She'd acted out of love.

Bridget lifted the false bottom inside the box and checked to see if her mother's letters were still safely tucked within. Her eyes burned with tears of joy and sadness when she saw the letters folded in place and tied together with a faded red ribbon. It had been difficult for her to bury these precious remnants of her parents in the ground, but it was the only way to keep them together in death and give her papa the burial he deserved.

Bridget closed the box and sighed. She knew that she'd need to have a difficult discussion with Eliza, and she wasn't looking forward to it. She didn't have the energy to do it right away. It had been a trying day, and Bijou was in need of a bath. She'd put the box in her room and decide how to broach this sensitive topic with Eliza tomorrow.

Just then, she heard her aunt shout. Bridget hurried out into the hall.

🔍

"Good heavens!" Aunt Marianne threw her hands in the air. "What are we to do without a proper set of servants?"

Nate and her aunt stood in front of Sarah's chamber door, which she had seemingly barred shut. Despite their knocking and pleading for her to come out, they'd received no reply from the housemaid.

"I'm going to have to break down the door," Nate said. He peered at Bridget. "She won't come out," he explained.

"Is that really necessary?" Aunt Marianne bristled.

"I'm afraid so. After what happened to Abigail, I don't think we can take any chances."

"Oh, I pray that she is unharmed," Bridget said as Nate stepped back, inhaled, and readied his body to meet the force of the door.

He lunged forward and slammed into the door with all his weight. The door shuddered, and a scream sounded from within. At least they knew Sarah was alive. Nate lunged for the door again, and this time it flew open, the chair wedged under the doorknob toppling over from the force. They entered to see Sarah crouched in the corner of her bed, clutching her covers and trembling with fear.

$$\rho$$

Thirty minutes later, once Bridget had managed to calm the housemaid down, Nate sat across from the two women in the study. Sarah clutched her cup of tea in both hands like a child, and looked at them with terror-filled eyes.

"Now, Sarah. Why don't you tell us what has frightened you so?" Bridget asked in a quiet voice.

"It's her. Abigail."

Nate leaned forward on his desk. "Abigail? Did she say something to you before she died?"

Sarah shook her head. "Not before. Last night. She visited me in the middle of the night. I awoke and saw her standing over my bed. She were dressed in her black cape an' holding a candle, her face all white and ghastly looking."

Nate frowned. "It sounds like you were having a nightmare, Sarah."

"It weren't a dream!" Sarah insisted. "She were real! She were so close to me that I could touch her coat. She were real—come back from the dead."

"Did she say anything to you?" Bridget asked.

"She told me to get out of this house. To go home to my family or end up dead like her. She said she were cold in that water all night. Cold and lonely." Sarah squeezed her teacup. "I don't want to be drowned and spend eternity in freezing water."

Bridget glanced at Nate, who shook his head. "Sarah, either you were having a dream, or someone was playing a trick on you."

"This weren't no trick." A tear slid down Sarah's cheek. "I'll not spend another night in that room. I want to go home to my family."

Bridget worried her lower lip. Nate was right. If Sarah hadn't been dreaming then someone wanted to frighten her into leaving Villa De Lacey, and Bridget was certain she knew the identity of the culprit.

BRIDGET SAT ON her bed, trying to muster the courage to do what she knew she must, although the terrible twist and churning in her stomach grew worse by the second. She'd excused herself from Nate's company soon after the interview with Sarah, not wanting to discuss her thoughts. They were too frightening—too terrible to comprehend.

She was quite certain that Eliza had been the one who had frightened Sarah. Eliza disliked the young maid and had easy access to her room, which was next to her own. The question that now tormented Bridget was *why*? Was Eliza trying to save Sarah's life by terrifying her into leaving, or was she the killer?

Another gut-wrenching attack of nausea assailed Bridget. How could such a thought enter her mind? Eliza had been the most loyal and faithful servant at Villa De Lacey.

Yet, it was possible—no, probable—that she'd ransacked Papa's makeshift grave, stealing the last piece of him that Bridget had left. At the same time, she'd acted out of love—Bridget was certain of that. Grief made people do strange things.

Now, she picked up her wooden box and cradled it. How she wished she had her parents by her side to give her the advice and comfort she so desperately craved. Opening the box, she removed her papa's lock of hair and lifted the false bottom where her mother's letters to her father lay. She'd read them countless times and always took great comfort in seeing her mama's neat script. Sometimes, she'd trace the script with her fingers and feel her mother's soul seep inside her. Her mama had poured her thoughts and love into those words, and Bridget needed some of that now.

Oh, mama. How I wish we'd had more time together. She fingered the letters and then frowned. The paper felt different—stiffer and thicker than the delicate, worn paper her mama had used to write to her papa.

Why? How? She extracted the bundle and carefully untied the red ribbon that secured the letters. When she unfolded one of the letters, her heart dropped.

These were not her mama's letters.

Instead, those had been replaced by ones written in a crude scrawl. Hardly able to believe her eyes, Bridget read:

My Dearest Master,

Another wun is dead an' gon. I did it all for you my luv, an' I shall keep doin' it until all the filth an' sin is washed away.

Yur faithful servant,
Miss Elizabeth Moon (Eliza)

Bridget dropped the letter and covered her mouth with her hand, which trembled violently. Her suspicions about Eliza *were* true—but they couldn't be. She hadn't truly believed her maid guilty of murder. Not Eliza! Anyone but her faithful lady's maid!

Just then, the door to Bridget's chamber creaked open and Eliza stepped inside. "You sent for me, miss."

Bridget looked at her lady's maid, her body shaking, and her eyes brimming with tears.

"I see you found the box," Eliza said as though she were talking about a lost slipper. "And you read my letters to your papa." The maid closed the door and walked to where Bridget sat on her bed. She stooped to pick up the letters. "You shouldn't have done that. Those were private."

Bridget nodded because she could not speak.

"Then you understand why I had to do it? Why I had to get rid of those women? They were bad women—disgraceful. They brought shame on your papa's house." Eliza's dark eyes seemed larger and blacker than usual as she fixed her gaze on Bridget, but they were devoid of emotion. How had she not noticed their coldness before? Now she noticed how her face and thin lips were tight and how her brown fringe peeked out from under her bonnet along with a few stringy hairs. She was exceedingly pale— even more so than usual—and looked rather ghoulish in her black mourning dress. "You mustn't blame yourself." Eliza secured the letters with the red ribbon and slipped them into her pocket. "It's your mama's bad blood that makes you act so impulsively. But I will protect you as I always have."

"What do mean?" Bridget asked, her heart pounding and her body trembling. "What have you done with Mama's letters?"

"They're gone, just like her. It's my job."

"What is?" Bridget asked, confused. *Gone?*

"To keep the evil out. To keep the house pure and respectable for my master."

Bridget's breath caught in her throat, but she forced herself to speak. "Is that why you killed Madam Bouffant and Abigail?"

"They deserved to die. They were sinners—adulterers under the master's roof. You lost your way inviting them here. You brought evil into this house, but it's not your fault. Your mama, she were low born. Half your blood is tainted."

Bridget brushed the insult away. She didn't know why Eliza would malign her mama, but there was a more urgent matter at hand. She wanted—needed to hear a confession from Eliza's own lips. "Did you push Madam Bouffant down the stairs?" she asked, praying inside that Eliza's answer would be *no*. "Tell me."

"She had no respect, creeping out late at night with Lord Frederick and then parting ways with him upstairs only to enter Lord Eamont's chamber. A married man, he is. Sinner, she was. I watched her, saw it all."

"So, you waited for her to come out of Lord Eamont's room?"

"Those silly housemaids were late to prepare the breakfast room as always, so I went in their stead. That's when I saw her, wearing the very same dress she'd worn the night before. I watched her start down the stairs. She were unsteady on her legs from the long night. She were going to fall. I could see as much. But I couldn't wait for her to do it on her own, so I gave her a little push, and down she tumbled. She screamed, but the wind was howling something fierce, so no one heard her cries."

I did, Bridget thought.

"I went to the breakfast room to do me duties and then I waited for those silly maids to find her."

"So that's why you were already upstairs when Abigail found Madam Bouffant's body," Bridget said, more to herself than Eliza. "I remember you came down the stairs and handed me a sheet to cover her body. I was so distraught I didn't think anything of it at the time."

Bridget could barely breathe. Her own Eliza, a killer! She wanted to shut her ears and pretend she had not heard the confession, but she knew she had to press Eliza for more, or she might never know the truth.

"And Abigail? You switched the bag of mushrooms Mr. Harley had given her, didn't you? Then you followed her and pushed her into the fountain."

"Not pushed. There were no need for that. The poison made her sick. She tried to drink from the fountain, but I pushed her head under the water. She beat her fists and kicked something fierce, but she were too weak. When she stopped, I put her in the fountain."

Bridget's pulse raced. She eyed the chamber door. Would Eliza let her go? Or would she try to harm her too? She grabbed her father's lock of hair, threw it into the wooden box and closed the lid. Then, tucking her treasure safely under her arm, she forced herself to stand. "You'll need to wait here for a bit, understand?" She clutched the box and backed away from Eliza. "The magistrate will want to speak with you. But you're not to worry. He'll understand," Bridget lied as she slid toward the door.

Eliza made no move toward her. She simply stood, a small but frightening figure in black mourning attire, following Bridget with her dark gaze.

"I were a good servant to my master. He'd lost his way. He couldn't see your mama for what she truly was. I did what was needed to protect him and you."

Bridget's heart contracted with fear. She froze. "What do you mean? Protect him from whom?"

"She were with child when the master brought her home. With child before they'd wed. That child were lost. The Lord knew it were a sin and would not let it enter this world."

"Are you talking about Mama?" Bridget's voice came out in a whisper.

Eliza walked toward Bridget, who backed herself into the wall. Eliza stopped in front of her, reached out, and stroked Bridget's hair. "You were different. And so like your papa from the very first. That's why I always took care to protect you."

"I don't understand. What are you saying? You took care of Mama during her illness, didn't you? You nursed her—"

"It were you and my master I cared for—protected. I saved him and you from her by feeding her the poison that made her ill."

Bridget's breathing shallowed and her head began to spin. "You poisoned Mama?"

With that, her calm and her reason fled; she turned and lunged for the exit, dropping the box in her bid to escape. It crashed to the floor just as the door flew open. Bridget swallowed her scream and fell into her aunt's arms.

"What is going on here?" Aunt Marianne stumbled back from the force of Bridget's embrace.

"She killed them—all of them. Including Mama." Bridget looked into her aunt's alarmed face. "Eliza killed *Mama*."

"Don't be ridiculous! Calm yourself. What is this all about?" Aunt Marianne looked from Bridget to Eliza.

"Check her pocket. The letters. They explain everything. We must send for the magistrate."

"There'll be no need for that." Eliza walked to Bridget's bed and sank onto her mattress. "I'm not long for this world."

Bridget's heart drummed wildly in her chest as the meaning of the maid's words—and her strangely tight face and ashen appearance—occurred to her. "What did you do?"

Eliza put a hand on her stomach. "Self-murder," she said. "Just like my master." Her eyelids fluttered as though she struggled to keep them open. "Bury me at the crossroads beside him, so our restless souls can be together for all eternity." Her thin, pale lips stretched into a ghostly smile. Then she clutched her abdomen with both hands before she fell to the floor.

"What is happening?" Aunt Marianne screeched.

"She's eaten poison." Bridget ran to Eliza, reaching to feel for a pulse. "Call the magistrate and the doctor. Hurry!" she cried out, even though she knew it was too late. Her lady's maid was dead.

※—⟡—※

CHAPTER THIRTY

WITH A HEAVY heart, Nate watched from the study window as Lady Luxton stepped into her regal carriage. The nanny entered after her, carrying little Henry. Seeing the child disappear into the coach produced a crushing sensation in his chest.

Helen did not take kindly to rejection. She would use the boy to punish him. And he'd likely never see his child again.

He knew in his heart the child was his. He'd felt the connection as soon as they'd met. The carriage rolled down the path to the gates of Villa De Lacey, passing through them for the last time.

Exhaling, he turned to Bridget, who had just finished sticking the last of her mother's letters, which she'd found torn to pieces in Eliza's dresser drawer, together.

She glanced up at Nate, her lovely blue eyes filled with pain. "How is it possible to know someone your whole life—to live in the same household together—and yet know *nothing* about them?"

"Oh, it's possible," Nate said, coming to sit opposite her. "When I was betrothed to Helen, I knew nothing about her true personality. In my eyes, she was an angel with a good and loyal heart. If any man had tried to tell me differently, I would have challenged him to a duel. Yet, I could not have been more wrong. And as for my brother—well, I always knew what he was, but I never imagined he'd sink so low as to…" He shook his head, not wanting to offend the lady by finishing his sentence.

"But I was living with a killer, and I *trusted* her. I knew the way she insisted on wearing full mourning for Papa as though she were his widow was strange, but I never saw the evil inside her. I thought she was acting out of devotion and maybe love."

Nate let out a short laugh. "Do you know, that's what Frederick said about my brother. He betrayed me because he thought he was trying to save me—that too was an act of love of sorts. But that's not love. It's only the way an evil person tries to justify their actions."

Bridget nodded, and Nate's heart wrenched for her. Betrayal from someone close to your heart was a cruelty no one needed to endure.

"The other guests will be leaving," Nate said. "Why don't you stay up here while I see them off?"

Bridget squared her shoulders and stood up. "No," she said. "Let's do this together."

🔍

"WELL, THIS PLACE is simply marvelous." Madam Bouffant's sapphire and diamond floral brooch sparkled on Lady Eamont's bosom as she sashayed toward her awaiting coach with her husband and daughter in tow. "It's exactly as Wordsworth described it. Isn't it, darling?" She flashed a smile at Lord Eamont as though they were the happiest couple in the world, one who'd just been on a lovely holiday together.

Lord Eamont nodded, but his face and voice remained impassive. "Yes, my dear. Wonderful."

"It's a pity we must leave so soon," she addressed Nate. "But as you know, Lord Eamont and Lord Dodsworth are summoned by the king to Lady Caroline's trial, and I have a wedding to plan." She grabbed Lydia's arm and pulled her close, while making no mention of Adelia. "It is going to be the wedding of the century. Only the best for the future Lady Dodsworth."

Lydia gave her a tight smile and nodded in agreement. "That's right, Mama."

Bridget marveled at the woman's ability to live in a fantastical bubble of her making. If life was not what she wanted it to be then she simply made it so, and sadly for them, her family appeared to play the same game.

She watched Nate as he bowed to his guests, and they climbed into their carriage. Together, it seemed, they breathed a sigh of relief when it pulled away. Then they turned to the next guests.

Mrs. Harley hung her head as she approached her carriage, still ashamed of her actions. She'd followed Bridget and left her injured and bleeding in the thicket overnight. Still, Bridget held no animosity toward the woman. The poor creature had been treated abominably by Lady Darby. Besides, Eliza's anger and venom toward those she viewed as the enemy made Bridget want to steer clear of vengeance and grudges. So, she reached for Mrs. Harley's gloved hands and said, "I do hope you will come see us again."

The woman raised her head and gazed at Bridget. "You are too kind, but you can't mean that—not after what I did to you."

"I do mean it." Bridget squeezed the woman's hands. "What you did was wrong, but I believe you acted under a great deal of stress."

Mrs. Harley swallowed. "Thank you. I don't know what will happen to us now. Lady Darby is sure to disown us."

"You mustn't let her bully you. I am no expert, but I am certain that if someone were making such demands of me, not to mention berating me on a daily basis, my womb would shut down altogether. What you need is time away from Lady Darby. I do wish you'd consider staying a bit longer."

Mrs. Harley's face lit up and she turned to her husband who, in turn, glanced at Nate.

"I think she's right," Nate said. "You *should* stay."

Bridget smiled, pleased to see that after all the death and darkness, Nate had chosen to forgive his friend.

Mr. Harley straightened his back like a man who'd just had a heavy load taken off his shoulders. Then he turned to his wife and said, "There's no need for us to return. Indeed, it would be oppressive to do so. This is not London. We have enough to survive on out here, at least for the meantime."

"How wonderful!" Bridget embraced Mrs. Harley.

"What's going on here?" Frederick said as he and Lord Dodsworth approached in their traveling clothes.

"Harley and his wife are staying," Nate said. He looked up at the driver. "Turn the coach around and unpack their trunks," he instructed.

"Staying?" Frederick said. "Do you mean—is the housemaid Sarah…"

"No," Mr. Harley snapped.

"Sarah has been sent home to her family," Nate said. "The ordeal was too much for her. Not to mention her behavior—she is gone. We intend to hire more experienced and reliable servants going forward."

"Well, I'd like to say you've become boring, old boy. But our stay at Villa De Lacey was anything but tedious. I daresay, all of London will soon be abuzz about Windermere's infamous 'murder inn.' Half the ton will beseech you with requests to come and stay once the king is finished with his trial."

"Well, we don't intend to have a repeat performance." Nate embraced Frederick and turned to Dodsworth.

"I do hope Lord Westerly will allow you back in London to attend my wedding," Dodsworth said.

"Then you intend to go through with it?"

"Of course. I promised Lydia her freedom and shall give it to her, just as she has given me mine. She and her sister will live as Lady Dodsworth and Mrs. Jefferson under my roof, and they shall want for nothing, including children if they so please. They no longer need to fear their mother, and Jefferson and I will no longer need to fear persecution."

"I'm pleased for you," Nate said.

"I'm pleased for me, too." Dodsworth smiled and slapped Nate's shoulder with obvious appreciation and affection. Bridget realized it had to be a relief not to have to hide his true self anymore, especially with an old friend. He stepped back. "Well, then. I must be off now, or I shall have to answer to the king," Dodsworth said.

Nick grinned and nodded.

The two men climbed in their respective carriages, and Bridget stood beside Nate and watched as they rolled down the pathway toward the gates.

"I think we should take a stroll in the garden," Harley said, taking his wife's arm in his. And the woman who'd looked so frail and meek when she'd first arrived gave her husband a radiant smile.

Bridget understood her sudden transformation. She knew what it meant to feel hopeful again.

Just then, Aunt Marianne exited the villa and walked toward them. "That's everyone gone, then," she said when she reached them. "And you'll be pleased to know, Mr. Squires, that all the guests settled their accounts with us before departure."

"Everyone?" Nate raised his eyebrows.

"Everyone," Aunt Marianne repeated. "I presented each with a detailed invoice this morning."

"Even Lord Frederick?" Nate inquired.

"Yes, even Lord Frederick," she replied.

"Well, I'm amazed," Nate said. "Perhaps Frederick is changing his old ways."

"I hardly think so," Aunt Marianne said. "It was Lord Dodsworth who took care of his expenses."

"Of course, it was," Nate said. Love him or hate him, Frederick was who he was, and he would likely never change.

"Now if you'll excuse me," Aunt Marianne said, "there are servants that want hiring and need training."

"Thank you, Mrs. Brixton," Nate said. "Villa De Lacey wouldn't have a chance without you."

Aunt Marianne kept a straight face, but Bridget knew she was pleased. It was as if she'd renewed her faith in the inn after learning the problem lay within her own household.

When they were alone again, Nate offered Bridget his arm and said, "Shall we?"

She looked up at her beloved ancestral home with its Lutetian stone walls and pale-blue shutters and smiled. "Please," she said.

Author's Note

William Wordsworth was the most famous poet to emerge from the Lake District, where he was born in 1770. Wordsworth and his fellow poets, Samuel Taylor Coleridge, and Robert Southey, who also lived in the Lake District, became known as the Lake Poets. Other Romantic poets like Shelley and Keats were also inspired by the Lake District's stunning landscapes. The Lake District became a tourist hotspot for the wealthy (who had the means to travel there) in 1820 after Wordsworth published *A Guide through the District of the Lakes in the North of England* (Guide to the Lakes). It is this popular travel guide that Bridget relies on to save her beloved ancestral home, Villa De Lacey.

ABOUT THE AUTHOR

Aviva holds a master's degree in English and has a keen interest in British literature. She is an anglophile and Brontë enthusiast who is happiest when traveling to or writing about England. Inspiration for her first book, The Mist on Brontë Moor, came after she visited the Brontë Parsonage in Haworth.

Born and raised in Cape Town, South Africa, Aviva now lives in Southern California with her husband, two daughters, and rambunctious Yorkshire terrier—named for the oft-forgotten Brontë brother Branwell.

Website: www.avivaorrauthor.com
Twitter: twitter.com/aviva_orr
Facebook: facebook.com/AuthorAvivaOrr
Goodreads: goodreads.com/author/show/6464067.Aviva_Orr
Bookbub: bookbub.com/profile/aviva-orr